The Dark End of the Street

New Stories of Sex and Crime

edited by
Jonathan Santlofer
and S.J. Rozan

Illustrations by Jonathan Santlofer

B L O O M S B U R Y
LONDON · BERLIN · NEW YORK

First published in Great Britain 2010

'Sunshine' by Lynn Freed originally appeared in *Narrative* magazine.

Bloomsbury Publishing, London, Berlin and New York

36 Soho Square, London W1D 3QY

A CIP catalogue record for this book is available from the British Library

ISBN 978 1 4088 0758 3
10 9 8 7 6 5 4 3 2 1

Typeset by Westchester Book Group
Printed in Great Britain by Clays Limited, St Ives plc

Mixed Sources
Product group from well-managed forests and other controlled sources
www.fsc.org Cert no. SGS-COC-2061
© 1996 Forest Stewardship Council
FSC

www.bloomsbury.com/sjrozan

www.bloomsbury.com/jonathansantlofer

To all the writers who jumped at the chance to cross the Great Divide, and did it with brilliance, this book is affectionately dedicated.

SJR & JS

CONTENTS

Introduction

S.J. ROZAN

SEX, CRIME, AND stories. They've all been with us from the start.

In the beginning was the Word. So says the Good Book, which goes on to tell us that as soon as God had the world pretty much in place, He created Adam and Eve, gave them a garden to live in, and laid down the law. Without missing a beat, they broke the law. And where did it get them, committing that first crime? What came of enjoying that apple?

What came of it was Knowledge: They realized they were naked.

And that naked was Evil.

They felt guilty and tried to cover up their crime by covering up their nakedness, God was not fooled and kicked them out of the Garden, and sex and crime have been skulking around hand in hand ever since. And writers have been chronicling them both.

When we proposed this book to writers from both banks of the stream dividing crime writing and literary writing, we thought we had a particularly alluring idea. Write your heart out on the twin subjects of sex and crime. Define each however you want, take any approach you like. What writer could resist? We were pretty sure the idea was hot, but we wanted more.

That dividing stream, it's a permeable boundary. It hosts much splashing and diving, some skinny-dipping, and a good deal of fording late at night. Writers rarely stick to their own "crime" or "literary" banks, and they don't check each other's visas when visiting. The unclimbable steep banks guarding those categories are inventions of reviewers and marketers. So we thought, let's bring them together. Let's get everyone horsing around in the pool at the center of the stream. We asked accomplished, high-octane writers from both shores, and it turned out we were right. Very few could resist the topic, or the chance to, for once, share the pool with each other.

The writers jumped on the idea, and they're at the top of their games. The stories they gave us range from creepily subtle to in-your-face, from darkly tragic to flat-out hilarious. The sex is here front and center, there barely whispered; the crime is sometimes obvious, other times imagined. What ties these stories together, besides the collection's theme, is their writers' clear joy: in the dual subject matters and in the nature of writing itself.

Stories, sex, and crime. Together, as always, and presented here for your pleasure.

1 2 3
F V L

Dragon's Breath

MADISON SMARTT BELL

A JOURNALIST WAS walking west when he happened to notice a young couple smoking cigarettes outside a bar. Nothing remarkable about it except that between them they framed a sign which declared SMOKING BALCONY AVAILABLE, 3RD FLOOR. They both wore black leather, studded with chrome; their skinny shoulders hunched against the cold.

Was there a story, somehow, in that? The journalist sensed the faintest thread of irony, like a drop of blood unraveling through clear water. It was cold, bitter cold, the west wind blowing. He tightened the string of his sweatshirt hood, pulled the zip of his jacket tighter to his throat, walked on. Night had fallen; and denizens were hurrying in all directions homeward, their capped heads lowered to thrust into the cold. Neon signs all along the street drizzled pools of colored light on the damp pavement. Through these the pedestrians trailed dangling tendrils of their unknown narratives. The journalist felt his familiar urge to catch up one of them, reel it to him, follow it home. Learn it, know it. That was not all.

As blandly sanitized as this new avatar of the city seemed to him, to be there still awakened ancient cravings. Like the head of a hatchet, his life had briefly balanced on its thinnest edge. Soon it must topple, one way or another. The journalist circled the block, turning left, left, left, and paused at a deli to purchase a pack of Marlboro reds.

The couple had gone from the doorway when he returned, and the ground-floor bar was extremely crowded. A hostess gave him a thin smile from her stand; he gestured up the stairs with his numb fingers and she nodded. There was no one in the third-floor bar when he lumbered in, but presently a barmaid appeared and the journalist ordered a vodka on the rocks and waited, cradling the glass until his fingers thawed enough to catch the end of the fine gold ribbon that turned the corners of the box of cigarettes.

His cell phone wriggled against his ribs. He plucked it out, and with some fumbling found his way to a text message which let him know that the celebrity whose biography he had been supposed to ghostwrite had decided to go in another direction.

The journalist held the news at a little distance from him, surveying it with professional objectivity to see how it might harm him before he took it in. He had not expected to get any news until the next day and then he'd been confident the news would be good. Leaning forward, cupping the phone his palm below the level of the counter, he read a few labels on the bottles behind the bar: Absolut. Stolichnaya. Grey Goose. The bar stocked an exotic brand of rum he'd also noticed at the celebrity's studio, where no one offered him a taste. Instead they had sent out for coffee—whatever confection anyone wanted. The meeting had gone well, so it seemed to him, and he believed that he'd come only to confirm an understanding.

He lifted the dead phone to his face and said, "I didn't know there was another direction." The barmaid looked at him with a faint curiosity. She was young, beautiful, maybe just young. A wave of belated comprehension broke over him so that he understood he must have been one of a number of ghosts auditioning and some other ghost had won the part.

The barmaid had turned from him, toward the mirror, where she studied the perfect red curve of her lip. The journalist picked up his glass, walked the length of the room, and let himself through a narrow glass door onto the advertised balcony. There were ashtrays chained to the posts of the canopy and several signs admonishing the customers not to let anything fall to the sidewalk below. The journalist smoked, tucking himself into a corner against the bitter wind, peering now and then through the glass to see that his shoulder bag and cell phone were still where he had left them at the bar. No one came in to threaten his possessions.

It had snowed earlier in the day, or the day before, and there was a crust of ice on the metal floor of the balcony. A buildup of snow on the underside of the fabric canopy now and then let a crystal drop. One tagged his scalp through his thinning hair, so he shrugged up his hood and moved aside. No snowflake ever falls in the wrong place, he thought. This recollection cheered him. In spite of it there was something voluptuous about smoking and drinking all at the same time. He had not smoked for a long while and he was a little dizzy when he stepped back into the warmth of the interior.

"Enjoy?" the barmaid said. The journalist nodded. His glasses had fogged, but she *was* beautiful. She looked at his empty glass and he nodded. She wore extravagantly high heels, like those the celebrity had worn. Perhaps he'd glanced at them, admired them once too often. Perhaps he'd overplayed his expertise. The thing of it was that he truly admired the celebrity, who was celebrated for better reasons than most. Well. He looked up and down the bar for a newspaper; there was none. Soon there would be none whatsoever, it was told.

Smiling, the barmaid handed him his drink. "You missed a call," she said. A hubbub drifted up the stairs. The journalist wiped his glasses on his shirttail so he could see the phone's display when he picked it up. After some fumbling he found his way to the callback feature.

"Yo," William said. "How's the city?"

"Safer than church," said the journalist. "And duller than ditchwater."

William laughed. "I mean like . . . really."

Really. "Not like it was," the journalist said.

"How's business?"

"Brilliant," said the journalist. Don't bleed in the water.

"So," William's voice grew faintly teasing. "You don't want to take a walk on the dark side."

"The dark side is only the other side," the journalist said. "We call it dark because it's the other. If we cross over to the dark side, when we look back it's the side we just left that looks dark."

"All right, professor," William said, and this time the journalist laughed with him. He had in fact been William's professor, once upon a distant time. Since then William had been through many changes, most recently managing a chic restaurant which had, not so long before, been sucked down in the widening whirlpool of economic disaster.

"So you wouldn't be interested."

"I'm interested in everything," the journalist said. "It's a matter of degree."

"You remember Etheridge Elliot?"

The journalist patrolled a desert in his mind. "Hum me a few bars," he said, and passed his glass up to the barmaid. It flashed on him before his drink was served.

"The Jamaican Jerk!" he said in a rush.

"You always used to harsh on him that way," William said. "He's got a package."

"A package," the journalist said.

"Jesus, don't say it like that. We're on the phone."

"Okay," the journalist said slowly. "There's a story in here somewhere, but I don't know how I like it."

"I'll call you back," said William, and the journalist's phone went off.

The crush downstairs had squeezed three or four people up into the third-floor area and the barmaid was attending to them. Beautiful people, spending their substance. Bright contrails that they left behind . . . The journalist cast about for a newspaper again before he remembered there wouldn't be one. From either corner of the bar a flat-screen television flickered down at him. He wiped his glasses to read the crawl, then forced himself to look away. The phone was a warmish lump in his palm. He flipped it open, thinking he might call his agent to discuss other prospects but before he pressed send he inventoried what prospects he had and concluded it would be better not to discourage the agent by compelling her to discuss them. He handed the barmaid a credit card and waited, mildly conscious of his respiration, until the charge went through.

The phone rang as he hit the street—displaying a different number but still presenting William's voice, at roughly the same place in the conversation.

"I'm getting too old for this kind of—" The journalist interrupted himself as he flattened his body into a doorway, out of the biting wind. "Is it bigger than a bread box? Does it need airholes? Do I have to wipe it down for fingerprints? Do I need to taste it to be sure it's good?"

"Just bring it," William said. "It's on Elliot if it's wrong, I guarantee you. We'll meet your train."

Far Rockaway. *Far Rockaway!* the journalist had blurted into the phone, and William said, *So take a cab, you can afford it*, and the journalist killed the call, looked at his watch, leaned back in the doorway and watched the frosted feathers of his breath diffusing in the multicolored lights along the street.

At Forty-second Street he got the A train. The rush-hour scrum had already thinned enough that there was breathing room, and by the time the train had left Manhattan he had no trouble finding himself a seat. A wing of newsprint drifted across the floor, stirred by the scissoring legs of a descending passenger. The journalist leaned to catch it up, and glanced at the top headline: TRY TO LIVE IN THIS TOWN ON 500K. Smirking in the shadow of his hood, he rolled the paper and slapped it on his knee.

Half drowsing as the train dragged from stop to stop through Brooklyn, he recalled the panhandler who'd accosted him that morning, when he'd set his satchel down for a moment on the sidewalk just outside Penn Station. The man had cadged a couple of dollars (the journalist gave up the money for luck), then described, apropos of nothing but with a peculiar shuddering relish, an event of fellatio he had once experienced. Was the story in exchange for the dollars? the journalist wondered—if so, he didn't think he wanted it. He took a couple of steps away, but the panhandler closed the distance softly, saying, "It's nicer to ask—I don't like to rob people." Not until much later in the day had the journalist processed this statement as a threat; at the time he had not felt menaced in the least.

"You're a good man," the panhandler said. "I see it in your eyes." The journalist must have cocked an eyebrow above the aviator sunglasses he wore, for the panhandler then added, "I see your eyes around your glasses."

The subway lurched around an underground bend and the journalist came half awake, for an instant unsure where he was—clinging to a rail of a truck or the strap of a bus rounding hairpins in the highlands of Rwanda, or maybe in the mountains of Jamaica where he had once gone to report on a two-hundred-year-old community of maroons. He opened his eyes completely: The vodka was draining out of his system, leaving behind it little claw marks of despair. He was riding an empty car, with only his reflection—leather jacket and face in shadow under the hood—accompanying him from the window across the way. The journalist checked his phone, his knife, his keys, the slack black bag on the seat beside him. He closed his eyes. Elliot would be expecting him, William had said, but most likely wouldn't call.

The Jamaican Jerk. He'd been a student at the same time as William, give or take, but Etheridge Elliot was unique in that little pond where he had floated to the surface, though south Florida and the whole Caribbean were choked with hustlers of his style. Elliot was a blithe and effortless liar, con to the marrow of his bones. He'd cut extraordinary swaths through the suburban white girls who populated that place, had smoked faculty and administration alike for an almost limitless series of free rides, but it was a rather small institution in the end and Elliot had worn through its possibilities before obtaining a degree.

Then put himself into the wind. The journalist was surprised, now, to find how clearly he remembered Elliot. In the years between he had used a good many such types as guides and drivers and informants, had become quite friendly with a couple, but trusted them only to his sorrow.

He came fully awake again as the train began to traverse

Jamaica Bay. On the north shore, a jetliner lowered toward the tarmac; the journalist felt his belly tighten, then release when it safely touched down. A few years previous he'd been one of a pack rushing out to cover the plane that had flamed out and flown straight to the bottom of the dark water he was studying now. Or no, it was only the tail cone that had landed in the bay, while the rest of the plane slammed into shore to raze a dozen houses and kill all aboard: nine crew, 241 paying passengers, five lap children. The journalist remembered these statistics plainly. He had a convenient faculty for that sort of thing. Two hundred and fifty-five disparate tales hurled forward to the same rough jolt of an ending. He went on peering out the window into the water below the filament of track. There were glints reflected from chunks of ice floating in the chop raised by the wind. At the time of the Rockaway plane crash he'd been in the full-time employ of a journal now defunct.

It was not his reflection across from him after all, he realized, as the train rattled into the Sixty-seventh Street station, but another autonomous human being, yin to his yang, dressed in a similar scuffed leather jacket and black hoodie beneath, but with light-colored pants where the journalist's were dark, and blond Timberlands where the journalist wore a cheaper, knockoff brand of shoe. The other clung to him, tight as his shadow, as the journalist stepped onto the platform and moved toward the caged stairs that led down to the street. At the first landing an arm wrapped around his trunk from behind—reaching toward the front jacket pocket where the phone was (why not the wallet on the hip?). Half prepared for something like that, the journalist spun his shoulder into the other man, checking him into the wire of the cage.

A hand came toward him and he managed to catch it by its thumb and forefinger and roll the wrist clockwise, pulling the trapped arm straight so the lock went straight from the shoulder into the spine. But when he heard the other man grunt, doubling over as the pressure forced him down from the waist, he released the hold and jumped down the remaining stairs. A bolt of pain from a soggy landing on his right knee. He ran, in his heavy, ill-fitting boots, till he was breathless, which turned out not to be very far.

Definitely getting too old for this sort of thing. He could feel the single cigarette he'd smoked, telling on him with a wheeze. No one had followed him, however. He had managed to jog as far as the south-side beach and now he sagged, gasping, against the pipe rail of the boardwalk, looking across the blocks of scrubby waste ground between the strand and the lights of Edgemere Avenue, thinking confusedly of the fields of fire surrounding various third-world palaces where he had once reported.

All this beachfront somehow undeveloped—and likely to stay that way, now, for a good while longer. When he had caught his breath enough he lit another cigarette in the shelter of his hood, then turned to face the wind and water. There was surf, beating down to white foam on the waterline. Perhaps a mile to the east were the lights of the high-rises. Westward, the dull glow of the city lit a sagging belly of snow-filled cloud.

When the cigarette had burned to the filter he flicked it out onto the sand and turned in the direction of the address William had given him. It was astonishingly cold and there was no one else on the street. The attack on the subway stairs had been random, he thought. Just a blast from the past—from the city he used to live in thirty years ago. He remembered that he hadn't remembered his knife, and that he was lucky he hadn't been shot.

* * *

Etheridge Elliot had lost his two top front teeth but his smile exuded the same überconfident charm as before. He wore a blue bandanna secured at the center of his forehead with a row of gnarly little knots of a style once favored by a certain Flatbush Crips set. Or so the journalist seemed to recall; it was ten years or more since he'd reported that one. A blast of heat swirled out of the basement door Elliot had opened and the journalist stepped gratefully into it, clenching his teeth so they wouldn't chatter.

"Ragamuffin!" Elliot cried. The journalist fumbled a hipster handshake. They were standing in a square of partially finished basement; a drape of kente cloth hanging from the ceiling tiles divided them from what must have been the larger part of the space.

"Wattagwan wid wi?" Elliot said, expanding his smile around the black gap of the two missing teeth.

"Same as it ever was," the journalist said, after a moment of bewildered cogitation. The patois he'd picked up among the maroons had long since rusted away, and to the best of his recollection Etheridge Elliot had spoken reasonably standard English the last time they had met. They had never addressed one another as "ragamuffin," so far as he could recall. Still, the overwrought accent touched him, like a warm breath of the island wind.

Elliot held up one finger and stepped through the kente cloth. The journalist waited, still on his cold feet. The only seating option was a pair of bucket car seats, still bolted together. From above, footsteps crossing a floor broke up a steady throbbing of bass. There were also some other people besides Elliot in the space behind the kente cloth, the journalist thought, though he was unsure of his reason for thinking so.

Then Elliot came back with two bottles of Red Stripe and a short dog of Bacardi gold. He offered the rum first.

"Cut de col', mon."

Gladly, the journalist took a belt from the bottleneck, then chased it with the beer Elliot proffered. They sat down side by side in the twinned car seats. The length of Elliot's legs put his knees up somewhere around his ears. He and the journalist clicked their beer bottles, then Elliot passed him the short dog again. The warmth of the rum restored to the journalist a glimmer of optimism.

"Lessee wheh dot ting." Elliot twisted over the arm of the car seat to scrabble in a beer box mostly full of shiny old newspaper advertising inserts. The back of his shirt rode up to disclose the grip of a nine sticking up from his waistband, along the pale knobs of his spine. The journalist took the opportunity to probe the flesh around his jarred knee joint—a little tender but he thought there'd be no long-term consequences.

Out from under the litter Elliot fished an oblong bundle about the size of a telephone book, wrapped in black plastic and silver duct tape. The journalist accepted it into his lap, then, after a discreet pause, zipped it into his shoulder bag. He leaned forward and set his empty Red Stripe on the concrete floor.

"Okeh den," Elliot said. "Yuh wanna ride inna town?"

The journalist thought it over. What if the jump at the subway hadn't been random after all? Or he might draw another piece of random. If Elliot wanted to take him off he could do it anywhere and besides that play didn't make any sense.

"If you can drive me to Canarsie," he said, "I could catch the double L."

He hefted the bag and stood up, wrinkling his nose. From behind the cloth divider came the scent of scorched foil and burning resin.

"Deh chasen de dragon," Elliot half whispered. "Doan you wanna taste?"

"I don't think so," the journalist said with a pain like the pang of lost love.

"Still yuh would do, mon," Elliot said, his voice turning wistful now. "Back in de day."

Surely the dragon had opened its maw and would smother the journalist in its vapors. Neurons were standing up all over his system, like the hair of a terrified cat. He had the odd and distant thought that maybe Elliot was only pretending to have recognized him when he came in, that in fact he did not know him at all. Or that he did know him, but not from experience.

"No," he said finally, uncertain whether he was declining the proposition of the moment or just the idea that Elliot had ever seen him accept it. Back in the day when they'd known each other the journalist was a tenure-track prof at a cozy East Coast college and he would not have swapped his shot at security for this. Later on he had traded it for something else, he couldn't now remember what.

An associate of William's met him at the Baltimore station, not in the empty, elegant lobby but on the second level of the parking garage below. His headlights swept over the journalist as the car rounded a bend of the garage, and the journalist stepped aside from the beams as the tinted driver's side window slid down. The associate had once been a waiter at the restaurant William used to manage before it went down. The journalist didn't recall his name but was sure enough of his identity to pass the package on to him. In return, the associate flipped him an old campus-mail envelope folded three times over and snapped tight with a rubber band. The journalist tucked it quickly into the inside pocket of his jacket.

"Who loves you, baby?" the associate said. The associate had not shaved recently; the journalist wondered if that might be a new style open to him now that he was no longer employed as a waiter, or the result of a drop in morale.

"Only my mother," he replied, but the associate had already driven away. "And she's dead."

The journalist drifted toward the southern face of the garage, thinking. I ask myself: What is a stable commodity in a time of deep recession? I answer: whatever the consumer can't stop wanting. This solution was congruent with the gritty, powdery feel of the package through its plastic, and with the sum of money William had offered him for bringing it down. The journalist touched the thickness of the envelope through the leather of his jacket but he didn't want to look at it yet, in case it should prove to be only dried leaves.

He stopped at the vertical bars that closed off the garage, wondering if they were meant to stop people going out or coming in. Out, most likely, as there was a two-story drop to the expressway below. He took out the cigarettes and stuck one in the corner of his mouth and tossed the box out through the bars, watching its red and white edges flashing end over end until it had disappeared into the slow current of night traffic.

No snowflake falls in the wrong place. The journalist lit his last cigarette and flicked the match pack after the box. As he exhaled he seemed to feel a warm breath on the back of his neck but he knew all that was mere illusion, only the idea of the dragon, snuffling at him one more half-interested time before it moved on. He felt that he missed the dragon already, although he knew it would surely return.

Scenarios

LAWRENCE BLOCK

THE ROAD VEERED a few degrees as it reached the outskirts of the city, just enough to move the setting sun into his rearview mirror. It was almost down, its bottom rim already touching the horizon, and would have been somewhere between gold and orange if he'd turned to look at it. In his mirror, some accident of optics turned it the color of blood.

There will be blood, he thought. He'd seen the film with that for a title, drawn into the theater by the four uncompromising words. He couldn't remember the town, or if it had been weeks or months ago, but he could summon up the smell of the movie house, popcorn and musty seats and hair spray, could recall the way his seat felt and its distance from the screen. His memory was quirky that way, and what did it matter, really, when or where he'd seen the film? What did it matter if he'd seen it at all?

Blood? There was greed, he thought, and bitterness, and raw emotion. There was a performance that never let you forget for a moment that you were watching a brilliant actor hard at work. And there was blood, but not all that much of it.

The sun burned bloodred in his rearview, and he bared his

teeth and grinned at it. He could feel the energy in his body, the tingling sensation in his hands and feet, a palpable electrical current surging within him. The sun was setting and the night was coming and there would be a moon, and it would be a hunter's moon.

His moon.

There would be a woman. Oh, yes, there would be a woman. And there would be pleasure—his—and there would be pain—hers. There would be both those things, growing ever more intense, rushing side by side to an ending.

There would be death, he thought, and felt the blood surging in his veins, felt a throbbing in his loins. Oh, yes, by all means, there would be death.

There might even be blood. There usually was.

Yes. This was the place.

It was the third bar he'd walked into, and he stepped up to the rail and ordered his third double vodka of the evening, Absolut, straight up.

As far as he could tell, all vodka was the same. He ordered Absolut because he liked the way it sounded. Once in a liquor store window he saw a vodka that called itself Black Death, and he'd tried ordering that for a while, but nobody ever had it. He didn't suppose it would taste any different.

The bartender was a short-haired blonde with hard blue eyes that took his measure as she poured his drink. She didn't like what she saw, he could tell that much, and under the right circumstances he'd enjoy setting her straight. She had an inch-long scar on her sharp chin, and he let himself imagine giving her some new scars. Breaking some bones. Driving the heel of his hand into her temple, right next to the eye socket. If you did it just right, you got the eye to pop out. If you did it wrong, well, there was nothing to stop you from trying again, was there?

He didn't like her, didn't think she was pretty, wasn't drawn to her. But he was hard already, just thinking of what he could do to her.

But all he did was pick up his glass and drain it. On nights like this the only effect alcohol had on him was to energize him. Instead of taking the edge off, it honed it. The anticipation, the heightened excitement, caused his body to metabolize alcohol differently. It coursed in his veins like amphetamine, but without the overamping, the jitters. Picked him up and straightened him out, all at once, and a pity they couldn't use that in their ads.

The bartender had gone off to make a drink for somebody else. He thought again of the hard look in her eyes and pictured her eye popped out. He put his hand in his pocket and touched the knife. Let her keep her eyes, at least for a while. Cut her eyelids off, put her in front of a mirror, let her watch what happened to her. Cut her lips off, cut her ears off, cut her tits off. Teach her to look at him and size him up, teach her to judge him. Teach her good.

He couldn't pick her up, no chance of that, but he could easily wait for her. Lie in ambush, be there in the shadows when she closed the bar and walked to her car. Next thing she knew she'd be naked, wrists and ankles tied, mouth taped, watching herself in the mirror. Like that, bitch? Happy now?

Then he turned away and saw the girl and forgot the bartender forever.

What other men would see, he supposed, was a pretty woman. Not supermodel looks, not heart-stopping beauty, but an exceptionally attractive oval face framed with lustrous dark-brown hair that fell to her shoulders. He saw all that himself, of course, but what he saw most clearly was her utter vulnerability.

She was there for the taking, there to be taken, and it was almost too easy, like shooting tame animals at a game farm. Not that he ever considered letting that dissuade him from scooping her up. Her vulnerability had a powerfully erotic effect on him. He was rock hard and knew he'd stay that way until dawn. He'd be able to fuck her all night long, he wouldn't stop until she was dead. And maybe not even then. Maybe he'd throw one more fuck into her afterward, just for luck. What was death, after all, but the ultimate submission?

He watched her, felt the energy flowing, and willed her to look his way. He knew she'd be unable to resist, and sure enough her head turned and her eyes met his. He put everything into his smile and knew the effect it would have. At moments like this his face turned absolutely radiant, as if lit from within.

She answered with a tentative smile of her own. He walked over to her, and didn't she look like a bird hypnotized by a snake? One hand holding her stemmed glass, the other resting on the bar, as if for support.

"Hi," he said, and dropped his own hand on her free hand. Her hand was small beneath his, small and soft. If he pressed down hard he could break all the bones in her sweet little hand, and he could picture the look in her eyes when he did, but for now his hand rested very lightly upon hers.

"My name's Jerry," he said. "Actually it's Gerald, with a G, but people call me Jerry, with a J."

None of this was true.

You know where this is going, don't you? Of course you do. Why, you could probably write the rest of it yourself.

Clearly, there's going to be a twist, a surprise. Otherwise there's no story. Boy meets girl, boy fucks girl, boy kills girl—that's not a story. However dramatically you might present it, however engaging their dialogue, however intense his pleasure and her pain, it just won't work as fiction. We might hang on to the very end, completely caught up in the action, but by the time it was all over we'd hear Peggy Lee singing in the background: "Is that all there is?"

No, that's not all there is. We can do better than that.

For example:

He didn't need any more vodka. But she poured drinks for both of them, and another would do him no harm. He tossed it back and had just enough time to register the thought that there was more in it than alcohol. Then the lights went out.

They didn't come back on all at once. Consciousness returned piecemeal. He heard music, something orchestral, harshly atonal. He was seated on some sort of chair, and when he tried to move he found that he couldn't, that he was tied to it, his wrists to its arms, his ankles to its legs. He tried opening his eyes and discovered he was blindfolded. He tried opening his mouth and discovered it was taped.

And then she was touching him, caressing him. Her hands knew their business, and he responded almost in spite of himself, desire shoving fear aside. Her hands, her mouth, and then she was astride him, engulfing him, and God knows it wasn't how he'd planned the evening, but then the evening wasn't over yet, was it? They'd do it her way for now, and later it would be his turn to tie her up, and what a surprise he'd have in store for her!

But for now this was fine, this was more than fine, and she took him right up to the edge and held him there, held him there forever, and then tipped him over the edge.

The climax was shattering, and it sent him away somewhere,

and when he came back he was no longer wearing the blindfold. He opened his eyes and she was there, naked, glistening with perspiration, and he would have told her how beautiful she was but his mouth was still taped shut.

"You naughty boy," she was saying. "Look what I found in your pocket." And she held out her hand and showed him the knife, worked the catch to free the four-inch blade, turned it to catch the light. "Now tell me, Gerald with a G or Jerry with a J, just what were you planning to do with this?"

But he couldn't tell her anything, not with his mouth taped. He tossed his head, trying to get her to take off the tape, but all that did was make her laugh.

"That was a rhetorical question, sweetie. I know what you had in mind. I knew the minute our eyes met. Why do you think I picked you? I wasn't sure you'd be bringing a knife to the party, but it's not as though I don't have a knife or two of my own."

She turned, put the knife down, turned back to him, and her hand reached out to take hold of him, the soft little hand, the one he'd had thoughts of crushing. She stroked and caressed him, and if he could have spoken he'd have told her she was wasting her time, that he wasn't capable of response. But his flesh had ideas of its own, even as the thought went through his mind.

"Oh, good," she said, using both hands now. "I knew you could do it. But sooner or later, you know, you won't be able to." She bent over, kissed him. "And when that happens," she murmured, "that's when I'll cut it off. But whose knife shall I use, yours or mine? That's another rhetorical question, sweetie. You don't have to answer it."

That's better, isn't it? The only thing wrong with it is the predictability of it. The biter bit, hoisted upon his own petard, and what's the use of a petard if you're not going to be hoisted upon it? He's on the hunt, he finds Little Miss Vulnerability and makes off with her, and in the end he's the vulnerable one, even as she turns out to be Diana, goddess of the hunt. Perhaps this particular Diana makes it a little more interesting than most, but still, we saw it coming. A surprise ending is more satisfactory when the reader as well as the protagonist is taken by surprise.

How's this?

They took his car, drove to the dead-end lane he'd scouted earlier. Earlier there had been another car parked at the lane's far end, and he'd crept close enough to identify its occupants as a courting couple. He'd entertained the idea of taking them by surprise, and some day he'd have to do that, but he'd stayed with his original plan, and had had the great good fortune to find this girl, and the other car was gone now and they could be alone together.

He parked, killed the engine. He took her in his arms, kissed her, touched her. He noted with satisfaction the quickening of her breath, the heat of her response.

Good. She was turned on. Time now to show her who was in charge.

He took hold of her shoulders, moved to press her down on the seat. She didn't budge. He put more into it, and she pushed back, and how could such a soft and yielding creature be so strong?

Her lips parted, and he saw her fangs, and got his answer.

Now that might work, if we weren't up to our tits in vampires these days. The undead everywhere, curled up in their coffins, guzzling artificial blood in Louisiana, being the coolest kids in a suburban high school, so many vampires it's clear Buffy never made a dent in their ranks.

So what's left? Werewolves? Cannibals? How many ways can we spin this? And to what end?

Ah, the hell with it. I could go on, but why try to dream up something?

Here's what really happened:

Her apartment, her bedroom, her bed. Soft lighting, soft music playing.

Soft.

"Jerry? Is there, you know, something I should do?"

Dematerialize, he thought. *Vanish, in a puff of smoke.*

"No."

"I mean—"

"It's not gonna happen," he said.

"That's okay."

"I think that last vodka put me one toke over the line, you know?"

"Sure."

Dammit dammit dammit dammit . . .

"But here," he said. "Let's see if we can make the magic happen for you, huh?"

"You don't have to—"

"Please."

He used all his tricks, his mouth on her, a finger in front, a finger in back. It took time because his own failure held her in check, but he was patient and artful and he found her rhythm and took her all the way. At one point he thought her own excitement might be contagious, but that didn't happen.

"That was wonderful," she assured him afterward. And offered again to do something to arouse him, but seemed just as glad when he told her he was fine, and it was late, and he really ought to be on his way.

He got out of there as quickly as he could, and on the way to his car his hand dropped to feel the knife in his pocket. Its presence was curiously reassuring.

He drove around, thinking about her, thinking of what he could have done, of what he should have done. He found a place to park and thought of what might have been, if he were in life the man he was in his fantasies. The man who didn't let his knife stay in his pocket. The man who acted, and reacted, and lived as he wanted to live.

The scenario played in his mind. And he responded to it, as he'd been unable to respond to her, and he touched himself, as he had done so many times in the past, and as he'd known he would do from those first moments in the bar.

Afterward, driving home, he thought: Next time I'll do it. Next time for sure.

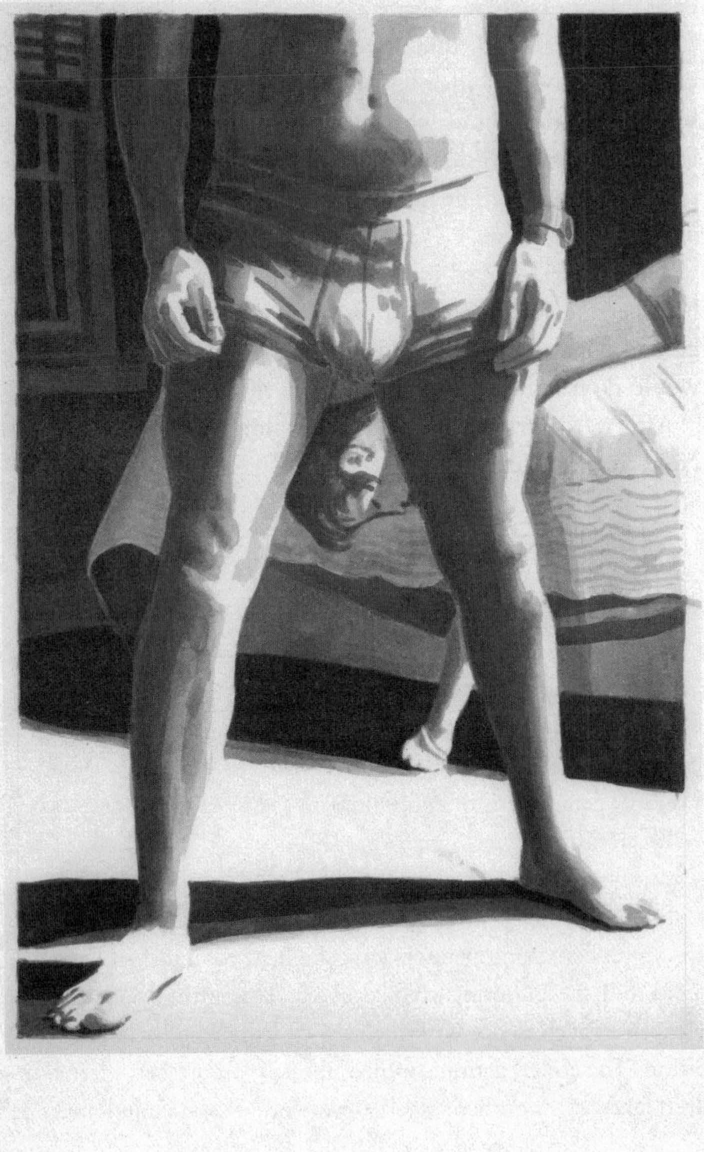

The Hereditary Thurifer

STEPHEN L. CARTER

I

AMANDA SEAVER TRACED the sign of the cross above the bread and wine and waited for the magic. There had been a time in the yet recent past when the act of consecration had sparked in her an elemental tremor, as though in response to a raw electric shock, followed by a prayerful buzzing in her ears, damping the sound of Sunday shoes on thick carpet and creaking pews as parishioners rose and gathered at the altar rail with its heavily polished dark surfaces that had known the folded hands of generations of communicants.

But no longer.

Candles flickered to either side. The chalice winked gold. The vestments lay heavily along her slim arms. Arranging her face in an expression of proper sobriety, she held the Host in her right hand and the glittering chalice in her left, lifting both toward Heaven in accordance with the rubric of the Anglo-Catholic tradition. The congregation shuffled uneasily before her, three hundred faces, most of them black, observing, assessing, judging. She chanted the litany with care, reading the prayers rather than reciting from memory because the Episcopal Church of Trinity and St. Michael, here in the heart of Washington, D.C., disdained the contemporary Eucharist with which Amanda was familiar. Beside her, the deacon, yellowy face locked in permanent disapproval, turned pages in the 1928 Book of Common Prayer and pointed to the proper lines. Amanda felt grateful and angry at once, worrying about her own feelings when she should have been thinking about the consecrated Host she was about to distribute. Today was her first Sunday as rector of TSM, as the younger members called it, and she knew she had not been these people's first choice, nor their second, nor their tenth. They had sent the bishop of Washington a list of a dozen traditionalists they could accept as their new leader.

The bishop had sent them Amanda.

They're good people, the bishop had instructed her. *They just need to be shaken up a little.*

Meaning: *Teach them to think like we do. Bring them into the twenty-first century.*

"And although we are unworthy, through our manifold sins, to offer unto thee any sacrifice," Amanda reminded the flock, secretly begging God to restore the magic, and, at the same time, avoiding the gaze of the deacon, whose ability to read her innermost thoughts she found both appropriate and scary, "yet we beseech thee to accept this our bounden duty and service, not weighing our merits, but pardoning our offenses, through Jesus Christ our Lord"—frantically signing over the bread and wine, as though the intricate gestures of her craft could conjure afresh the faith that had slipped behind her with the years.

But she felt nothing. No stir, no magic, no miracle. A thin, tasteless wafer and heavily watered wine. Calling the congregation to the altar, preparing to offer the consecrated Host on its gleaming silver tray, Amanda Seaver imagined that the greatest mystery facing her was how long she could pretend to possess the belief she lacked.

She was pardonably mistaken.

II

Amanda slipped out of her vestments in the sacristy, laying them in the waiting hands of a trio of older women, two black and one white, who represented the altar guild. At her former church, a dying all-white congregation near Boston, she had counted herself lucky to scrounge a single sixty-year-old acolyte for Sunday services. Here, the mass was choreographed with a precision that would have done credit to Westminster. Leaving the sacristy via the narrow hallway behind the altar, she overheard the women whispering.

"When they said a woman, I didn't know they meant white."

"So what? I'm sure she won't stay long. You know what I'm talking about."

"Oh, pooh. You can't believe every story—"

"It was terrible, what happened."

"It was a long time ago."

Then Amanda was out of earshot.

The hallway exited into the Lady Chapel, a room arranged with altar and pews in mimicry of the larger sanctuary where she had just celebrated, so ineptly, the mass. In the chapel Amanda found, off its hook, a thurible: the container for the incense Trinity and St. Michael no longer used. She lifted the small vessel, felt a twinge of sadness at the dust that had accumulated on its golden surface, and the several deep dents that made it unfit for service. She wondered who had pulled the thurible down and left it sitting on a pew. One of the children, she decided: the younger acolytes, unable to sit still, who relaxed in the Lady Chapel when their presence in the sanctuary was not required.

She returned the thurible to what she hoped was the proper hook, then climbed the short stair to the parish hall for coffee hour. She put on a smile and stood very straight, because nobody here seemed to slouch. She shook hands, accepted stiff and formal welcomes, said how happy she was to be here. She wished it were true. At thirty-nine, with a decade of ministry behind her, Amanda had longed for the barricades. The idea of being thrust into the midst of an African-American congregation had thrilled her. But she had never before been around so many black people: not black people like these. They had, most of them, money and breeding, in many cases generations of both, and if their expensive clothes didn't tell you, the parking lot full of German imports would. They voted Democratic, but their politics verged the other way. Few described themselves as "black," or even "African-American." They seemed to prefer unusual formulations, chief among them "darker nation."

Making her, Amanda supposed, a representative of the paler nation.

Roaming the parish hall, she sought out and thanked the choirmaster and the deacon, the chalice bearers and the acolytes, but only the children so much as smiled. The adults looked at her askance, maybe because of her color, or because she had been imposed on them, maybe because—

I'm sure she won't stay long. You know what I'm talking about.

—because they knew what the woman in the sacristy was talking about. Trinity and St. Michael had gone through three interim priests in just over a year before the bishop chose Amanda. She had talked to two about their experiences, and both had hinted that all was not well at TSM, but they were older white men, and she had put down their furtiveness to an uneasiness around people of color. Now, crossing the room toward the coffee cake, she remembered how one of them had complained that the congregation was too protective of its secrets. She had taken him to refer to, say, finances, or even gossip; only now did she wonder whether the secret was something else.

It was terrible, what happened.

Amanda supposed that whatever they were talking about must be written down somewhere. The church kept meticulous ledgers. Surely anything horrific enough to drive the new rector away would have been recorded—

Then she was cornered by Mrs. Routledge and Mrs. Madison, black women of a certain age and class, who sized her up from beneath their oversize Sunday hats and explained that she should not take it personally, theirs was just a congregation unused to newcomers. Amanda naturally wondered what they meant by "it," but found herself too cowed to inquire. And this attitude would have astonished her classmates back at the divinity school, for her outspokenness on every issue under the sun, whether the authenticity of the epistle to the Hebrews or the racial diversity of the reading list for systematic theology, had been a legend around the quad.

Somebody else drew her away, wanting to discuss her reasons for choosing the contemporary rather than the traditional form of the blessing at the end of the service. Stumbling through an explanation of how, through force of habit, she had said "among" rather than "amongst," Amanda heard the two women murmuring behind her:

"I don't think anybody's told her."

"It's such a shame, poor lamb. Well, she'll find out."

III

After ninety minutes—the coffee hour lasting nearly as long as the service—Amanda escaped gratefully to her office, a cramped, sunlit chamber whose three leaded windows overlooked the pretty churchyard. The walls were lined with shelves, and most of the books seemed to belong to the church: Amanda had little room for her own. There was a fireplace but it was sealed. There were several closets, most of them stuffed with peeling hymnals and ancient lists of prayer requests. One closet featured a mouse-trap in the corner, a discovery she did not consider auspicious.

Hunting for personal space, she opened a drawer in one of the shelves, and found candles. In another she discovered several small cans. She opened one and took a whiff of the clayey powder inside then thanked Whoever was possibly paying attention that TSM, for all its reputation as a church in the old "bells and smells" tradition, had forsaken the use of incense, which secretly gave her headaches.

"It's agarwood," said a voice from behind her. "Made by Benedictine monks. The finest incense available."

She turned to find a fortyish man in slacks and dress shirt and tie, but no jacket. His hair was sandy in color, and at first she thought him one of the church's few white congregants. Looking closer, she realized that he was black, but with skin so light in hue that he might easily have passed.

"I don't think I've had the pleasure," she said, fumbling to close the can like a child caught searching for Christmas presents.

"Christopher Taite." His grip was strong yet somehow patient, the gaze of his light-gray eyes steady yet appraising. Despite willing herself not to, she noticed that he wore no wedding band.

"I saw you at the service," Amanda said, a bit stupidly. "You sat in the back."

He had no comment on this intelligence. He had managed, in a single smooth movement, to transfer the canister from her hands to his. Now he unscrewed the top and inhaled.

She waited for his head to snap backward. Instead, he nodded approval. "Seems fresh," he said.

"Perhaps you might consider reinstating the use of incense during mass. It seems unfortunate to let it go to waste." He gestured toward the door. "I believe that the congregation would be appreciative."

"I'm a little surprised that they ever stopped using it. This seems"—she searched for an inoffensive way to put the point—"a place where traditions are important."

The visitor nodded, handed the container back to her. The solemn expression on his pale features never flickered. "The traditions are indeed important, but the traditional use of incense ended because of a rather trivial misunderstanding."

Amanda held on to the jar, not sure whether returning it to the drawer required some ritual with which she was unfamiliar. She sensed that Christopher Taite was the sort of man who would correct her, patiently and ruthlessly. "Which misunderstanding is that?"

"They stopped using incense," he said, "after the murder."

IV

They were walking in the churchyard, Amanda and her new acquaintance. The graves, she soon realized, were laid out mainly along the high outer wall, on either side of the cinder path. In the middle were trees and flowers, lovingly tended. It occurred to Amanda that none of her tours of the facilities had taken her deeply into the cemetery. She had peered from the door and pronounced it beautiful. She wondered whether her hosts had sensed her silent shirking when confronted with what Professor Gyver, back at the div school, used to call the Big E and the Big O, Eternity and Oblivion.

Christopher Taite seemed comfortable here. He walked with his hands linked behind his back, ear cocked toward her like a professor listening to a slow but promising student. He explained that his family had provided for over a century hereditary thurifers at Trinity, and later, after the merger, at Trinity and St. Michael. Trinity, she knew, had been an all-black Episcopal church, founded before the Civil War. It had merged with St. Michael, a dying but upscale white congregation, in the pandemonium of the 1960s.

"Do you by any chance happen to know what a hereditary thurifer is?" he asked with insulting patience.

"I know the thurifer carries the incense."

A brisk shake of the slender head. Traditionalists liked their traditions perfect. "The thurifer carries the thurible. The thurible holds the incense. In the strict Anglican tradition, the title of thurifer was often hereditary. It ran in families, devolving usually upon the first-born male child."

"Like primogeniture," Amanda murmured, working hard to get a smile out of him.

"Precisely," said the thurifer, never missing a step. "Here." He pointed to a wide patch of earth set off by a low metal rail. Easily two dozen headstones were encompassed within the border, with room for several more. "This is where the Taites are buried. My older brother." He pointed. "My father." He pointed, again and again. "Two uncles, my grandfather, his older brother, their father. All served as thurifers at Trinity, or here. I was the eighth in the line, and, as I have no children of my own, I may be the last."

"I would assume it's permissible to select a new thurifer." Again she smiled. "Even if he—or she—isn't a Taite."

The frown on the unlined face deepened without shifting. "That would be up to the rector."

His use of the title in the abstract rather than a simple pronoun—say, *up to you*—solidified Amanda's fear that Christopher Taite was among those unready to accept, even after all these years, that women could be properly ordained as priests. She wondered, sometimes, whether the traditionalists were traditional enough to endorse *Apostolicae Curae*, Pope Leo XIII's late-nineteenth-century bull proclaiming all Anglican ordinations null and void.

"I see," she said. Then, as directly as she dared: "The congregation thinks I was forced upon them."

"You were." He waved aside her squawked objection. "You have no cause for apology or explanation. The canons are clear. The authority rests with the diocesan bishop."

She nearly sagged with relief. "Not everyone agrees."

"Once the bishop has acted, the matter is closed. It makes no difference what others may prefer."

"It makes a difference to me."

The hereditary thurifer said nothing. He had them walking again, now along the crumbling stone wall, eight feet high, shielding the cemetery from the side streets. Beyond stood the staid, expensive houses of the black rich, the neighborhood of the city known as the Gold Coast: the heart of the opposition to her appointment.

"Tell me about the murder," the priest said finally.

"An affair of the heart, I'm afraid." He uncurled his hands

briefly, plucked a leaf from a tree, sniffed it, dropped it. The wind carried it before them along the path. "I find it fascinating," he said, "that no one has mentioned the story to you. Or perhaps you read an account in the newspapers."

"No."

"The victim was a man named Bauer. Joshua Bauer. Killed, I'm afraid, just outside the office presently assigned to you." Again choosing his words carefully, the way many members of the congregation did, leaving in abeyance whether she was, or was not, their actual rector.

"In the hallway?"

"In the passage between the rector's office and the sacristy."

"Near the Lady Chapel."

Christopher Taite nodded. He hooked a thumb over his shoulder. "Joshua is buried back there with the other Bauers, beneath the two dying elms. You can see the grave from your window."

Amanda shivered at the casualness with which the thurifer spoke of murder and death and burial. She was a thorough materialist. The bishop knew it, and she suspected that the members of Trinity and St. Michael knew it. At her former church, she had preached rarely about the afterlife, or, indeed, about anything requiring an acceptance of the supernatural. She could do war or climate change at the drop of a hat; she would happily deconstruct images of women's sexuality in the Book of Esther; she could demonstrate how the Gospels mandated national health insurance. But the Big E and the Big O were well outside of matters she felt comfortable discussing from the pulpit.

"Who killed him?" she asked.

"Nobody knows. Not for sure." He slowed. They had reached the far corner of the cemetery, the church building entirely hidden by the thick copse of trees. The wind was harsher here, flattening her hair, and she wondered whether it was some trick of the foliage and the walls, a tunnel effect. The bricks were newer, too, as if they had started repairing this section of wall before running short of funds. "A young man was believed to have committed the crime, but there was never a trial, and there has always been some doubt about whether he really did the deed. Would you care to sit?"

There was a stone bench, and a pretty little fountain. Water spouted from a jug held by a maquette of a cherub. Brightly colored fish glistened as they wiggled and darted.

"I've never been to this part of the cemetery," she said.

"The rectors often come here for reflection. You might have noticed the quiet." And she did. Birds chirped. Water gurgled. Breezes fluttered the leaves. That was all: Not even traffic noise from the side streets penetrated the magical shield of trees and walls. "I think you will find this spot conducive to prayer and meditation."

"Thank you," Amanda said, and meant it. For some reason she felt close to tears, perhaps because she had at last met a congregant who, for all that he might judge her failings—gender foremost among them—did not seem to regard her as an interloper sent by a left-leaning bishop to subvert the traditions of Trinity and St. Michael.

Christopher Taite seemed to read her mind. "You have to understand the people here," he said. "We have fought all our lives to change the rest of the world, to open it up for members of the darker nation. We have battled our way to great fortunes, to positions of influence, to places in society. We have no wish to battle within the church as well. We need an island of stability, a place we can come for renewal, a place that is the same for us as it was for our grandparents. Can you understand that?"

"Of course," Amanda said, although she couldn't, really.

Her well-off family had gone from hard right to hard left in two generations. Like most people of strong conviction, she saw no reason other than sheer pigheadedness for anyone not to trace with joy the steps of her own journey.

The thurifer nodded his head. "Well, you'll learn. Give them time. Give yourself time."

"I will," she said, quite unpersuaded. "Thank you, Christopher. Or do you prefer Chris?"

"Mr. Taite," he said. "My family is rather old-fashioned—"

Embarrassment burned. "Yes, I understand. I'm sorry."

But he continued in the same tone precisely, and it occurred to Amanda that he had corrected her not out of annoyance but as a means of assistance. "Trinity and St. Michael is full of old-fashioned families. I suppose you know that. You'll get used to them. The Hennefields will criticize you behind your back, but they do that to everyone. They're all bark and no bite. The Madisons are probably the worst. They're a power in the church. You'll want to stay on their good side. Chamonix Bing was a terror, but she's gone. The one to watch out for is Mrs. Corning. Have you met her, by any chance? Janet Corning?"

Amanda frowned, trying to remember. She lacked the facility with names and faces that usually marked pastors of large congregations. She knew to the penny the cost of a single F-35 fighter, and how many hungry mouths the money could feed, but people had always defeated her. "I might have. I'm not sure."

"Well, you will. Mrs. Corning is head of the Lectors Guild. The one you'll complain to if nobody shows up to read the Epistle appointed for the day." A pause. "Her cousin was the reason for the murder."

"The one outside my—outside the rector's office."

"Yes. I suppose you'd like to know the details."

She hesitated, not sure which answer he wanted. "I heard some of the women talking," she finally said. "They seemed to think that some incident from the past would drive me away. Did they mean the murder?"

"Probably."

"Why would it bother me, Mr. Taite? From their tone, I assume it was a long time ago."

"Thirty years." Christopher Taite climbed to his feet. "The rain is coming," he said. "We can continue tomorrow. I will meet you in the Lady Chapel at ten sharp."

He strode off among the trees.

V

The Lady Chapel was placed, quite properly, to the right of the altar from the perspective of the congregation. Its low gothic arches reminded her of divinity school. There were six wooden pews and a high altar of cut stone and a low altar of very fine wood. When Amanda stepped inside at five minutes to ten, Christopher Taite was already there, clad once more in tie and shirtsleeves, examining a thurible.

"It hasn't been polished in some time," he said with soft reverence. He ran a fingernail over the gold surface. "The altar guild used to polish both the thurible and the boat, but I suppose they no longer see the need. Another tradition dies." He put the thurible back on its hook and turned toward her, his face in the shadows. "The thurible should always be gold. And it must always shine. Revelation 5:8. The boat is for the incense, usually carried by a youngster, often a son or brother of the thurifer. The thurifer puts coals in the thurible and lights them, then takes the thurible to the priest, who spoons incense from the bowl onto the coals and blesses the thurible. The rising fumes signify the prayers of the congregation wafting toward heaven."

"Why are you telling me this, Mr. Taite?"

"Because I believe that you will decide to reinstate the tradition, and you have to know how it is done."

Again she tried a smile. "I assume I would have the hereditary thurifer at my side, showing me what to do."

He showed nothing. No amusement, no perplexity, no offense. "Perhaps. One should not anticipate." He turned back to the shelf, tugged another thurible from its hook, shook his head and clucked. "You must be sure that the thurible used in the service is properly polished."

"Of course," she said. "That one is dented. I noticed it yesterday."

"It should have been disposed of." Again his fingers ran gently across the surface. "Desacralized, melted down, proceeds given to the poor."

"I'll see to it," Amanda said, hoping she sounded decisive. Then: "I went on the Internet last night, Mr. Taite. I didn't find anything about a murder at Trinity and St. Michael. Joshua Bauer seems to have died of an undisclosed illness, back in the late 1970s."

He nodded, not turning. The airless room seemed to grow darker. "They would say that, of course. That he was ill. The police were never called, you see. The church could hardly endure a scandal. We had several doctors in the congregation. They knew what to do. Whom to contact."

"You said it was in all the papers."

"A figure of speech," he said in that same solemn tone. "I meant only that the facts were widely known, at least among the congregation. Do you ever pray for the dead?"

The sudden change of subject momentarily threw her. Once

again the Big E and the Big O reared their scary heads. "I'm not sure what you mean."

The thurifer nodded, as if to say he had expected as much. From a side table he lifted an aging volume he must have brought along, the *Oxford Movement Centenary Prayer Book*. "The Litany for the Dead," he announced, then read aloud: "Have mercy, O Lord, upon the souls which have no especial intercessors with thee, nor any hope save that they were created after thine own image; who from age, or poverty, or the unbelief or negligence of their friends, are forgotten and whose day of departure is never remembered." He glanced at her. "Nobody prays for the dead anymore."

"We pray for the dead every Sunday."

His stern eyes rejected this cant. "We pray for the dead we know. The dead we cherish. The dead we miss. We are really praying out of our own pain, not for an easing of the pains of those who have passed on."

Amanda said nothing. She wondered how an otherwise intelligent man—a member of so accomplished a congregation—could possibly believe in this nonsense. Dead was dead, and that was all. But another part of her, standing in the drafty chapel, surrounded by the chalices and crosses and thuribles and candles, was terrified by the yawning possibility.

Christopher Taite, meanwhile, had laid the book in her hands. "You might have need of this one day," he said. "Perhaps quite soon."

She flipped to the title page. "This book was published in 1933."

"In England," said the thurifer. "And it is not officially recognized by the Episcopal Church. But, given some of the nonsense that passes for liturgy nowadays, I do not see why that should matter." He lifted his chin, in the direction of the hallway: the site of the murder. "The Litany goes on at some length, but that is appropriate. The dead, too, have need of your prayers."

"Let's go out and walk," she said. Not adding: This place is starting to spook me.

VI

They were in the churchyard again, sitting on the same bench. She had examined the parish register that morning, confirming Christopher Taite's story about his own family. She discovered that no fewer than three of the hereditary thurifers had been named Christopher. She judged the Christopher sitting beside her to be about forty. That meant he could hardly have been much older than ten or twelve at the time of Joshua Bauer's death, or murder, or whatever it was. Amanda did not see how he could have been thurifer, any more than she saw how the congregation could have hidden the murder. She began to have the feeling that somebody was playing a terrible joke on her, a sort of hazing, meant to drive her away. She would not give in. Not to the ladies of the altar guild, not to the Madisons or the Routledges or Christopher Taite, or any of the others who hated her being white, and female, and not the right kind of Episcopalian.

"An affair of the heart," she prompted.

"Yes."

When nothing more was forthcoming, she threw out ideas. "Meaning what? A jealous husband? A rejected suitor? A fatal attraction?"

"An angry young man," he said after a moment. The gray eyes lifted toward the church spire, the only part of the building visible from the secluded bench, then went higher, perhaps seeking out Heaven itself. "Joshua Bauer ran what was at the time perhaps the largest chain of funeral homes in the area. The second largest in the country owned by a member of the darker nation. His family began the business during the Civil War. That's when most of the larger mortuaries began their work. Collecting corpses from the battlefield, preserving them, sending them home to their parents for burial. That's how they all got started, black and white alike."

"I see."

"Mr. Bauer was always a member of the vestry. Senior warden, junior warden, treasurer. Always held an important position. He had this daughter—Theresa, known as Terry—who was, by common consent, the most beautiful young woman in the church." For the first time, a tinge of emotion colored Taite's tone. A warmth, perhaps, but mixed somehow with awe, even fear. "The Bauers were not particularly religious, you should understand. Mr. Bauer did the vestry because that was how one maintained one's position, both social and commercial. But his commitment to the enterprise was entirely financial. He gave generously, but also collected greedily. I daresay half or more of the congregants in those days buried their relatives through his funeral home."

"I see."

"The Bauers had several children, but Terry was their pride and joy. She had the easy charm so many young women just miss. The boys, I fear, chased her—at times literally. Even when she was a little girl, here at the church, they would chase her around the parking lot. When she grew older—well, as I say, the Bauers were not particularly religious. Their children mostly ran wild, but Terry they shielded. They wanted her unsullied by the world. One might have described their attitude toward her as idolatrous. Certainly they loved that child more than they loved their God."

"I see," Amanda said again, trying to understand the

disapproval in his voice. She would have assumed that a traditionalist such as Christopher Taite would approve of a daughter being overprotected by her family.

"Terry, however, was quite faithful. She never missed a Sunday, even when the rest of her family chose not to attend. She was the first girl to serve as acolyte at Trinity and St. Michael. She even talked about becoming a priest, if you can imagine. In the seventies."

When the national church was first fighting over the same issue, Amanda marveled. Terry sounded like a battler. The priest realized that she liked her.

"Despite the vigilance of her parents," Christopher Taite continued, "Terry naturally had her suitors. There was one young man in particular who coveted her. Wally. He, too, was from an important family in the parish. They might have made precisely the sort of marriage for which the older families of the darker nation yearn, a merging of two senior clans. Wally, however, never met the approval of Terry's parents. He was a bit of a ne'er-do-well, what we might call, if you will forgive the allusion, the black sheep of an otherwise successful family. Did poorly in school. Often in trouble. The Bauers barred him from their house. They wanted no contact between Wally and their precious Terry. The congregation chose up sides. It was very nearly open warfare."

"And that's what led to the murder?"

"You are getting ahead of yourself, Miss Seaver." It was the first time he had referred to her by any name. Most of the congregants called her "Amanda." A few were willing to venture "Reverend Seaver," in Episcopal terms a vulgar neologism. Nobody would attempt "Mother Mandy," the affectionate name by which she had been known in Massachusetts.

"Remember what I told you about the incense," the thurifer continued. "Everything is methodical. First the coals, then the incense, then the blessing, then you cense the altar. You return the thurible to the thurifer. He censes the servers and the congregation. You must get the order right, or the entire effect is ruined."

She apologized, but softly, so as not to break the flow.

"The passion that stirred between Wally and Terry was the coal," he said. "The hot coals are always the symbol of sin, you see. Sin, then the layering balm of repentance, then prayers. The addition of incense and blessing would mean solemnizing their union in Christian marriage."

"Which never happened."

"Correct, Miss Seaver. It never happened. They ran away together, Wally and Terry. Not for marriage. Simply for—oh, in those days we simply called it intimate relations. They ran away, and that was the coals being lighted, but without the blessing. Her parents of course were furious, and Wally's family was not much happier. The Bauers had money. They hired detectives. Finding the kids wasn't that hard. They were just out of high school. They had no skills. The detectives tracked them to Pittsburgh, beat Wally quite badly, and dragged Terry back. When she turned out to be pregnant, her family packed her off to relatives in Atlanta, who arranged a hasty marriage to an unsuitable young man."

Christopher Taite was off the bench now, crouching near the pond. He had gathered small stones from the path and was plinking them into the water, smoothly, the way a younger man might have.

"Wally must have been angry," she said gently.

"He was. He came back to town. He tried to see her, and was

refused. He tried again and again, and was refused." Another stone. Plink. Another. "When they sent her South, I suppose the young man snapped. He confronted Mr. Bauer in the church."

"Outside the rector's office."

Plink, plink, plink. "I'm afraid their argument grew violent. There was a bit of shoving back and forth—" He glanced up at the clouds. "More rain," he announced.

She was beside him. "Wally hit him with the thurible. That's why it has that terrible dent."

"One would think it would have been repaired by now. Or, as I said, desacralized and melted down. Alas." Plink.

"He was carrying the thurible because he was the thurifer, wasn't he? Or maybe the boat bearer, learning from his father, say, what being the thurifer entailed." Christopher Taite said nothing. Standing so close, Amanda saw the faint crinkling around his eyes. She supposed she could have been wrong about his age. Maybe late forties. "With all those Christophers in the family, you would all need nicknames—"

The thurifer turned toward her, his face as blank as before, the youthful excitement gone. "I can see why you would think what you're thinking," he said. "But Wally, I fear, took his own life a couple of days later."

"No." The pain almost bent her over. She was unaware until now of how the story had affected her.

He nodded. "A grievous sin. Perhaps they still teach the fundaments in divinity school? You'll have read Augustine on suicide?"

"I might have missed that day," Amanda began, struggling to lighten the mood, but his frown reminded her once more that levity was unwelcome. "Yes," she murmured meekly. "I know that suicide is a sin."

His gray eyes held hers for a long moment. Then he turned

away. "The peculiar part is that Wally denied that they ever in fact were intimate. He told anyone who would listen. He had stolen Terry away to protect her, not to defile her. That was his word, Miss Seaver. Defile."

"Protect her from what?"

"Nobody believed the poor boy. The baby had his crooked eyebrows." The thurifer touched his own forehead. "The Taite eyebrows. Very distinctive." He was on his feet. "Same time tomorrow," he said, and left her.

VII

Amanda dined that night at the home of a younger family in the congregation, Patsy and Lawrence Morrow. Although members of the darker nation, the Morrows lived not along the Gold Coast but in a small, nicely appointed town house in Georgetown. Lawrence was something important at the White House; Patsy was a congressional aide; the children were delightful, and spoiled. Three other couples were at dinner, along with a single man, obviously invited with matchmaking in mind, and just as obviously not interested in Amanda; nor, for that matter, interesting to her.

He left early, pleading another engagement.

Over dessert—a slightly soggy tiramisu—Amanda mentioned that she had met Christopher Taite, who had been filling her in on some of the recent history of the church.

Silence around the table.

"Which history is that, exactly?" asked Patsy, alarm in her eyes.

"He didn't *scare* you, did he?" murmured somebody else.

"Are you sure he said *Christopher*?" demanded a third voice.

Amanda was taken aback by the chorus of dubiety. She had

hoped to discuss the murder from thirty years ago, not the bona fides of her informant.

"Is there something I should know about him?" she asked.

"There's an old Trinity and St. Michael's tradition," said Lawrence Morrow, his tone thoughtful. "A new rector shows up. A few days later, Christopher Taite drops by to frighten him. Pardon me. Her. Nobody takes Mr. Taite seriously."

"Some people do," said Patsy, glaring at her husband.

"Three other rectors left," Amanda objected. "Did he scare them all away?"

"They were interim," said Lawrence, before anyone could get a word in. Plainly he wanted to put an end to the topic. He was a lawyer, and had the lawyer's precision with sophistry. "They were leaving anyway. Hence the word *interim*. Whereas you"—he was on his feet, signaling an end to the evening—"you, Mother Seaver, we hope will be around TSM for many decades to come."

The use of the honorific was meant to reassure. But as she said her goodbyes, nobody would meet her eyes.

VIII

Home was an apartment on Sixteenth Street, backing on Rock Creek Park, but Amanda decided not to return there. Not yet. Instead she drove up to the church. Although the building was shuttered and locked, a light burned, as always, in the spire. Exterior floodlights illuminated the facade on the street side.

She let herself in through the garden entrance, shut off the alarm, flipped on the lights, headed for her office. She spent a moment examining the dented thurible, then pulled from the shelf two volumes of the church registry, immense leather-lined folios in which, by hand, deaths and births and other significant events were recorded. She found the year that Joshua Bauer had died, then the month, finally the week.

Sure enough, there was the handwritten entry, in the beautiful script of Granville Dean, in those days the rector. Most of the names of the departed had a cause of death inked alongside, but not Bauer. He had been sixty-one when he passed away. In the margin was a small glyph, also handwritten, a cross, ornately drawn but turned at an angle, like the letter X. The symbol stirred a memory from divinity school.

The angled cross was called a saltire, or crux decussata: sometimes known as a Saint Andrew's cross because church tradition held that Andrew, the second Apostle to be called, had been martyred on one. Father Dean had been recording the murder without seeming to, sneaking it past whoever was reading over his shoulder.

A new rector shows up, Lawrence Morrow had said. *A few days later, Christopher Taite drops by to frighten him.*

She flipped the pages. One week later. Two.

There it was.

An eighteen-year-old dead "by his own hand." A further notation: "*Not cons. gr.*" Amanda recalled the thurifer's emphasis on the sin. In those days the Episcopal Church must have taken the rules very seriously, or at least this one did. *Not consecrated ground*, Father Dean's brief note meant. The dead teenager could not be buried in the churchyard.

"Christopher Wallace Taite," the line in the ledger read.

Known, she was sure, as Wally.

Three hereditary thurifers named Christopher, and Wally, a suicide at eighteen, who never succeeded to the post. A ne'er-do-well. The black sheep of the family. Unlikely to have been chosen as thurifer of Trinity and St. Michael, even had he lived.

But the church would not have left the succession to chance. There had to be another candidate: someone in training.

And the congregation of today, when the national church had long resolved the issue, was unalterably opposed to women as priests.

Not weighing our merits, but pardoning our offenses.

Amanda took a flashlight from her desk and stepped out into the hall, then jumped against the wall because she heard the creak of footsteps. But she had locked the door behind her, so it had to be the building settling.

Right. A hundred-fifty-year-old church built of solid stone, choosing just this moment to settle.

She listened. No more creaking.

Amanda took a moment to slow her breathing, reminding herself that the supernatural did not exist. There was only this life, this planet, this existence. The rest was repressive bunk.

Fortified by her own denials, the priest made her careful way to the end of the hall and opened the heavy wooden door to the churchyard. In the darkness, nothing stirred. She clicked on the flashlight and tried to remember the path. She walked slowly, turning neither to the left nor to the right. The ghosts in the trees were only the night sounds of the material world. The watchful Heavens above were empty space. She recited this mantra, her desperate dying faith, as she reached the Taite family plot.

There were the headstones.

Not weighing our merits . . .

She played the flashlight beam over the names, one by one. No Christopher Wallace Taite. Of course not. Wally was not buried in consecrated ground.

But pardoning our offenses.

The other grave she was looking for: The other one was there.

For a moment Amanda was dizzy, the world shifting on its

axis. She stumbled and found herself on her knees in front of the headstone. She scrambled up again, but her thoughts were whirling in twelve directions at once. Her doggedly materialist faith began to slip from her grasp. Meditate long enough on the Improbable, Professor Gyver used to say, and you will come to accept the Impossible.

There had been two murders thirty years ago, not one; and the second, not the first, was the church's dirty secret.

IX

At ten the next morning, she sat in the Lady Chapel, the 1928 Book of Common Prayer open on her lap. She was trying to memorize the traditional liturgy so that the deacons would stop looking askance as she read past their fingers. She felt, more than saw, Christopher Taite slip in. He settled beside her, so lightly the loose wooden pew never budged.

"Are you staying?" he asked without preamble.

"Staying where?"

"Here. At Trinity and St. Michael." He sat very still in his tie and shirtsleeves. "I would imagine you suspect a conspiracy to force you out."

She shut the book, leaving one of the attached ribbons to hold her place. "If I leave," she said, "you probably won't visit me anymore."

He considered this. "Would you stay if I said I shall continue to visit?"

"Will you?"

He tapped a finger against his pale lips. "I doubt it. No. I've done my job, I think."

"I know what happened thirty years ago," she said.

"Please."

"Wally wasn't the father of the baby, was he? It was his uncle. Another Christopher. The hereditary thurifer." When he said nothing, Amanda continued. "That's why Wally took Terry away. He was protecting her from one of the most powerful men in the church. And that's why the church stopped using the incense, isn't it? Not because Joshua Bauer was killed with the thurible. Because the hereditary thurifer had impregnated a teenager."

"She asked to be trained," he said after a moment. "The church had never had a female thurifer."

"But Terry was your first female acolyte."

"Yes. And of course the national church was busily fighting about the same time over female priests. The earth was moving under our feet." He stood up, walked over to the rack of thuribles, pulled out a modest-looking one. "Start small," he advised. "A thurible of this size will hardly be noticed at first. Remember, the coals are the sin, and the incense is the balm. And the smoke—"

"The prayers of repentance, rising to Heaven. I remember."

"It was a terrible temptation," he said, still turning the golden vessel this way and that. "It was so terribly wrong, but, as St. Paul says, we are at every moment slaves to Christ or slaves to sin. And the thurifer was, for a time, slave to his sin. To desire. To the needs of the flesh. Theresa Bauer was very beautiful. She and the thurifer worked together closely. Still, he had no excuse for his behavior."

"But he let them blame his nephew." A pause. "Your nephew."

"Yes. And then, when Wally killed himself—" He shook his head. "The families eventually learned the truth." The thurifer's voice was fainter, as if he was drifting from her. "I have tried to tell each of the interim rectors the story. None would listen. None would believe. Father Bishop succeeded Father

Dean. He laughed at me. Father Greely was here for four years after Father Bishop died. He listened now and then, but never took me seriously. Father Dean, however—well, he was a man of true belief. He confessed me, you see. Gave me penance in the orthodox manner."

"But that didn't help."

"It was too late. Scripture teaches the existence of the too-late repentance. Our Savior preached to the dead, but the orthodox teaching of the church is that they were not able through repentance to secure salvation. They learned the truth but could not act on it."

"That hardly seems fair."

"You forget yourself, Mother Seaver. It is not our place to judge the will of God." He put the thurible back in its place, straightened, and seized her with those grave gray eyes. "You, Mother Seaver, are the seventh rector of Trinity and St. Michael, or, counting back to the beginning of Trinity Church, the eighteenth. The decisions are yours. Will you reflect on all that I have told you?"

"I will," she promised, and meant it.

"Thank you," he said gravely, and, for the last time, left her.

X

She opened the Prayer Book and, for a while, sat alone in the Lady Chapel. She considered visiting whatever Taites were left to check her conclusions, but there was no point; and besides, none of them attended TSM any longer. The rest of the congregation would tell her nothing, and contacting the authorities was out of the question.

She was the rector. The decisions were hers.

She decided to take a walk through the grounds of her church.

In the bright morning sunlight, the birds sang noisily. Beyond the tumbledown wall, cars shuddered and honked and squealed. She heard playing children. The cemetery was utterly unthreatening. By trial and error she found the little bench, cracked in the middle and overgrown by weeds. The fountain was empty, clogged with years of vegetation. Too bad. She would have enjoyed this place of reflection.

She picked her way along the unkempt path until she stood in front of the Taite family plot, as she had last night. There was the grave, nearly hidden by brush. The Improbable lay before her, lighting the way to the Impossible. Christopher Standish Taite, aged forty-four, date of his passing a year after Wally's. No cause of death written in the ledger, no words of affection or praise carved into the tombstone.

Of course not.

But beside his name in the ledger Father Dean had inked a small St. Andrew's Cross.

Amanda wondered who had killed him. Terry's family? The other Taites? Some unknown member of the church, determined to equalize the balance? The one thing she knew for sure was that the last hereditary thurifer had not taken his own life, or he would not be buried here. Trinity and St. Michael was a stickler for excluding suicides.

Odd how one could grow so tangled in theology that justice became inverted. Wally rested in unhallowed ground. His uncle rested here.

Uneasily.

Repentant, but not seeking forgiveness; seeking instead to restore Trinity and St. Michael to what it had been before the wave of violence unleashed by his sin.

Amanda understood what the suffering Christopher Standish Taite did not, that you could move only forward in time. The church could never be what it had been in his lifetime. It could only be something new. But the traditions would help. Of that she was now sure.

She would have to find Wally's grave. It should not be that hard. She would find his resting place and pray to God to have mercy on his soul. But that would come later.

Amanda had carried the thurible from the Lady Chapel. She lit the coals, sprinkled incense from the boat, and murmured a blessing. She censed the graves before her. The cemetery was large, and the work would take her all year. No matter. She knelt in the grass, opened the book Christopher Taite had given her, and began chanting aloud the Litany for the Dead.

Me & Mr. Rafferty

LEE CHILD

I CAN TELL what kind of night it was by where I wake up. If I've been good, I'm in bed. If I've been bad, I'm on the sofa. Good or bad, you understand, only in the conventional sense of the words. The moral sense. The legal sense. I'm always good in terms of performance. Always careful, always meticulous, always unbeatable. Let's be clear about that. But let's just say that some specific nighttime activities stress me more than others, tire me, waste me, leave me vulnerable to sudden collapse as soon as I step back into the sanctuary behind my own front door.

This morning I wake up on the hallway floor.

My face is pressed down on the carpet. I can taste its fibers on my lips. I need a cigarette. I open one eye, slowly, and move my eyeball, slowly, left and right, up and down, looking for what I need. But before we go on, let's be clear: However haltingly you read these words, however generously you interpret the word *slowly*, however deep and 16-RPM and *s-l-o-w* your voice, however much you try to get into it, you are certain to be racing, to be galloping insanely fast, to be moving close to the fucking *speed of light*, compared to what is actually happening in terms of my ocular deployment. The part with the eyelid alone must have taken close to five minutes. The eyeball rotation, four points of the compass, at least five minutes each.

A bad night.

I am pretty sure I have a fresh pack of cigarettes on the low table in the living room. I concentrate hard in that direction. I see them. I am disappointed. Not a fresh pack. An almost-fresh pack. A pack, in fact, in the condition I like least: recently unwrapped, the crisp little cardboard lid raised up, and one cigarette missing from the front row. I hate that for two reasons: First, the pack looks violated. Like a dear, dear friend with a front tooth punched out. Ugly. And second, however hard I try to prevent it, the sight sends me spiraling back to grade-school arithmetic: There are twenty cigarettes in a new pack, arranged in three rows, and twenty is *not fucking divisible by three*. I see a pack like that and instantly I am full of rage and paranoia: The tobacco companies are lying to me. Which, of course, they would. They have an accomplished track record in that department. For forty years I have been paying for twenty, and all along they have been supplying me with eighteen. Eighteen is divisible by three. As is twenty-one, but are you seriously suggesting the tobacco companies would supply *more* than a person pays for?

So I lie and pant, but again, let's be clear: The oldest, tiredest dog you ever saw sighs a hundred million times faster than I was panting. We're talking glacial inhalations and exhalations. Whole species could spark and evolve and go extinct between each of my morning breaths.

I had left cigarette butts at the scene. Two of them, Camels, close to but not actually mired in the spreading pool of blood. Deliberately, of course. I know exactly how the game is played. I'm not new to this. The police need the illusion of progress.

Not *actual* progress, necessarily, but they need something to tell reporters, they need smug smiles and video of important things being carried away in small opaque evidence bags. So I play along. It's in my interests to give them what they need. I give Mr. Rafferty things to smile about, and I'm absolutely sure he knows they're gifts.

But they're useless. A cigarette smoked carefully in dry air retains almost no saliva. No DNA. No fingerprints, either. The paper is wrong, and most of it burns anyway, at a temperature close to two thousand degrees. So the gifts cost me nothing, and they give me the satisfaction of knowing I am playing my part in keeping the whole show on the road.

I move the fingers of my right hand and make a claw and start to scrabble microscopically against the resistance of the rug. I have future events to plan: getting to my knees, standing upright, stripping, showering, dressing again. A long agenda, and many hours of work. No breakfast, of course. Long ago I decided that respect for minimum standards of propriety forbade eating after killing. I am hungry, make no mistake, but the promised cigarette will help with that. Plus coffee. I will make a pot and drink it all, and compare its thin fluidity to blood. Blood is less viscous than people think, especially when generated in the kind of volume that my work produces. It splashes and spatters and runs and drains. It is spectacular, which is the point: Obviously Mr. Rafferty does not want to work cases that are mundane, or trivial, or merely sordid. Mr. Rafferty wants a large canvas, and a large canvas is what I give him.

I push with my left palm and ease my shoulders an inch off the floor. The pressure is relieved from my cheek. I am sure the flesh will be red and stippled there. I am not young. My face is doughy and white. Tone has gone. But I can pass it off as razor burn, or bourbon. I focus again on the almost-fresh pack ten feet from me. Tantalizing, and for now as distant as the moon. But I will get there. Trust me.

I have no clear recollection of last night's events. The details are for Mr. Rafferty to discover. I sow, he reaps. It is a partnership. But lest you misunderstand: My victims deserve to die. I am not a monster. I have many inflexible rules. I target only certain kinds of repulsive criminals; I never hurt women or children. I look for the people Mr. Rafferty can't reach. And not hapless, low-level street pimps or escort bookers, either: I set my sights a little higher. Not too high, though: for that way lies frustration. Neither Mr. Rafferty nor I can get to the real movers and shakers. But there is a wide layer of smug, culpable people between the two extremes. That is where I hunt. For two reasons: I can feel a glow of public service, and, more importantly, such careful selection puts Mr. Rafferty in a most delicious bind. He wins by losing. He loses by winning. The longer he fails to find me, the more the city is relieved of bad people. The reporters he deals with understand, although they don't say so out loud. Everyone—me, Mr. Rafferty, citizens, inhabitants—benefits from perfect equilibrium.

Long may it continue.

Now I have to decide whether to roll right or left. It has to be one or the other. It's the only way I can get up off the floor. I am not young. I am no longer agile. I decide to roll left. I stretch my left arm high so that my shoulder goes small and I push with my right. I roll onto my back. A significant victory. Now I am well on the way to rising. I know that Mr. Rafferty is getting up, too, ready to start his day. Soon he will get the call: another one! Hung upside down, as I recall, zip-tied to a chain-link fence that surrounds a long-abandoned construction zone, gagged, abused, eventually nicked in a hundred places, veins, arteries, throat. I don't recall specifically, but I imagine I finished with the femoral artery, where it runs close to the surface in the groin. It's a wide vessel, and, given adequate pressure from a thumping heart, it spurts high in a wonderful ruby arc. I imagine the man jerked his chin to his chest to look up in horror; I imagine I asked him how he was enjoying his BMW *now, asshole*, and his big house and his Caribbean vacations and his freebies with the poor Romanian girls he imports with all kinds of false promises about jobs with Saks Fifth Avenue before turning them loose to perform disgusting acts for six hundred dollars an hour, most of which he keeps, until the girls grow too addicted and haggard to earn anything anymore.

Not that I care about either Romania or the girls. I have no enthusiasm for any part of Eastern Europe, and prostitution has always been with us. Although I know the man I tied to the fence also runs Brazilian girls, and I care for them to some slight extent. Sweet, dark, shy creatures. I partake regularly, in fact, in that arena, which is what led me to the man himself. A girl I rented, less than half my age, recited on request the menu of services she offered, some of which were truly exotic, and I asked her if she really liked doing those things. Like all good whores she faked great enthusiasm at first, but I was relentlessly skeptical: You *enjoy* sticking your tongue deep into a stranger's anus? Eventually she confessed she was obliged to, at risk of getting beaten. At that moment the man's fate was sealed, and I imagine I used a stick before I used the knife. I care about justice, you see, and the whole what-goes-around-comes-around thing.

But mostly I care about the equilibrium, and the partnership, and keeping Mr. Rafferty in work. He is a veteran homicide cop, my age exactly, and I like to think we understand each other, and that he needs me.

It is time to sit up. And because written narrative has its conventions, let me again be clear: A long time has passed. My thoughts, however presented on the page, have been halting and disconnected and have taken a long time to form. We are not talking about a burst of decisive energy here. This process is slow. I walk my hands back above my waist, I raise my head, I twist and lever, I sit up.

Then I rest.

And I confess: It is about more than just equilibrium and partnership. It is about the contest. Me and Mr. Rafferty. Him against me. Who will win? Perhaps neither of us, ever. We seem to be perfectly matched. Perhaps equilibrium is a result, not a goal. Perhaps we both enjoy the journey, and perhaps we both fear the destination.

Perhaps we can make this last forever.

I scan ahead through my morning tasks. The ultimate objective, as for so many, is to get to work on time. My day job, I suppose I should call it. Punctuality is expected. So less than an hour after sitting up I gather my feet under me and rise, hands out to steady myself against the walls, two staggering steps to establish balance, a lurch in the general direction of the living room, and the prize is mine: my morning smoke. I pull a second cigarette from the pack and close the lid so as not to see two busted teeth; I gaze around, trusting in the eternal truth that wherever cigarettes may be, there will be a lighter close by. I find a yellow Bic a yard away and thumb its tiny wheel; I light the smoke and inhale deeply, gratefully, and then I cough and blink, and the day finally accelerates.

The shower is soothing: I use disinfectant soap, a carbolic product similar to medical issue. Not that I carry trace evidence; I am not new to this game. But I like cleanliness. I check myself in the mirror very carefully. The carpet burn on my cheek is noticeable, but generalized, like a normal Irish flush; it is entirely appropriate. I part my hair and comb it flat. I unwrap a shirt and put it on. I select a suit: It is not new and not clean, made from a heavy gabardine that smells faintly of sweat and smoke and the thousand other odors a city dweller absorbs. I tie my tie, I slip on my shoes, I collect the items a man in my position carries.

I head outside. My employer provides a car; I start it up and drive. It is still early. Traffic is light. There is nothing untoward on the radio. The abandoned construction zone is as yet unvisited by dog walkers.

I arrive. I park. I head inside. Like everywhere, my place of employment has a receptionist. Not a model-pretty young woman like some places I have seen; instead, a burly man in a sergeant's uniform.

He says, "Good morning, Mr. Rafferty."

I return his greeting and head onward, to the squad room.

The Perfect Triangle
MICHAEL CONNELLY

IT WAS THE first time I had ever had a client conference in which the client was naked—and not only that, but trying to sit on my lap.

However, it had been Linda Sandoval who had insisted on the time and place to meet. She was the one who got naked, not me. We were in a privacy booth at the Snake Pit North in Van Nuys. Deep down I knew it might come to something like this—her getting naked. It was probably why I agreed to meet her in the first place.

"Linda, please," I said, gently pushing her away. "Sit over there and I'll sit here and we'll keep talking. And please put your clothes back on."

She sat down on the changing stool in the booth's corner and crossed her legs. I was maybe three feet away from her but could still pick up her scent of sweat and orange-blossom perfume.

"I can't," she said.

"You can't? What are you talking about? Sure you can."

"No, if my clothes are on I'm not making money. Tommy will see me and he'll fine me."

"Who's Tommy?"

"The manager. He watches us."

"In here? I thought this was a privacy booth."

I looked around. I didn't see any cameras, but one wall of the booth was a mirror.

"Behind the mirror?"

"Probably. I know he knows what goes on in here."

"Jeez, you can't even trust the privacy booths in a strip club. But look, it doesn't matter. If the California Bar heard this was how I conduct client conferences, I'd get suspended again in two seconds. You should remember that yourself when you start practicing. The Bar is like Tommy, always watching."

"Don't worry, I'll never be in a place like this again—if I get to practice."

She frowned at the reminder of her situation.

"Don't worry. I'll get it handled. One way or another, it'll work out. The information you've given me should help a lot. I'll crack the statutes and check it out tonight."

"Good. I hope so, Mick. By the way, what were you suspended for before? I didn't know about that when I hired you."

"It's a long story and it was a long time ago. Just put your clothes on, and if Tommy gets upset I'll talk to him. You must have guys that come in here and just want to talk, don't you?"

"Yeah, but they still have to pay."

"Well, I'm not paying. You're paying me. This was a bad idea, meeting here."

I picked up her G-string and silk camisole off the floor and tossed them to her. She put a false pout on her face and started getting dressed. I took one last look at her surgically enhanced breasts before they disappeared under the leopard-skin camisole. I imagined her standing before a jury someday and thought she was going to do very well once she got out of law school.

"How much will this cost me?" she asked.

"Twenty-five hundred for starters, payable right now. I can take a check or credit card. Then I go see Seiver tomorrow, and if it ends there, that will be it. If it goes further, then you pay as you go. Just like it works in here."

She stood up to pull on the G-string. Her pubic hair was shaved and cropped into a dark triangle no bigger than a matchbook. There was glitter dust in it so the stage lights would make that perfect triangle glow.

"You sure you don't want to take it in trade?" she asked.

"Sorry, darling. A man's gotta eat."

Once she snapped the G-string into place in the back, she stepped toward me and leaned down in an oft-practiced move that made her brown curls tumble over my shoulders.

"A man's gotta eat pussy, too," she whispered in my ear.

"Well, that, too. But I still think I'll take the money this time."

"You don't know what you're missing."

She stood up and raised her right foot, removing her spike. She wobbled for a moment but then steadied herself on one foot. From the toe of her shoe she pulled out a fold of cash. It was all hundred-dollar bills. She counted out twenty-five and gave them to me.

"I'll write you out a receipt. Did you make all of that tonight?"

"And then some."

I shook my head.

"You're going in the wrong direction if you're going to give this up to practice law."

"Doesn't matter. I need something to fall back on. I'm about to hit the big three-oh. And when you lose it, it goes fast."

I appraised her flat stomach and thin hips, and the agility with which she raised her leg and put her spike back on.

"I don't think you're losing anything."

"You're sweet. But it's a young girl's game."

She bent over and kissed me on the cheek.

"You know what?" she said. "I bet it's the first time in the history of this place that a girl paid a guy off in a privacy both."

I smiled and took two of my hundreds and slid them under the garter on her thigh.

"There. A professional discount. You being in law school and all."

She quickly slid back onto my lap and bounced a few times.

"Thank you, Sweetie. That'll make Tommy happy. But are you sure I can't do something for you? I think you're feeling the urge."

She bounced up and down a couple more times centered on me. She was feeling my urge all right.

"I'm glad Tommy'll be happy. But I better go now."

Late the next morning, I walked into Dean Seiver's office in the district attorney's office in the Santa Monica Courthouse annex. I carried my briefcase in one hand and a bag from Jerry's Deli in the other. More important than the files I had in my case were the sandwiches I had in the bag. Brisket on toasted poppy-seed bagels. This was what we always ate. When I came to Seiver about a case, I always came late in the morning and I always brought lunch.

Seiver was a lifer who had always called them like he saw them, regardless of the whims of politics and public morals. This explained why after twenty-two years in the DA's office he was still filing misdemeanors off cases spawned in the unincorporated areas in the west county.

This is also why we were friends. Dean Seiver still called them like he saw them.

I had not been here in a while but his office had not changed a bit. He had so many cases and so many files stacked on and in front of his desk that they created a solid wall that he sat behind. He looked up and peered over the top at me.

"Well, well, well. Mickey Haller."

I reached over the wall and put the bag down on the small workspace he kept clear.

"The usual," I said.

He didn't touch the bag. He leaned back and looked at it as if it was a suspicious package.

"The usual?" he said. "That implies routine, Haller. But this is no routine. I haven't seen you in at least a year. Where you been?"

"Busy—and trying to keep away from misdemeanors. They don't pay."

I sat down on the chair on the visitor's side of his desk. The wall of files cut off most of his face. I could only see his eyes. Finally he relented and leaned forward and I heard him open the bag. Soon a wrapped sandwich was handed over the wall to me. Then a napkin. Then a can of soda. Seiver's head then dropped down out of sight when he leaned into the first bite of his sandwich.

"So your office called," he said after taking some time to chew and swallow. "You're representing one Linda Sandoval on an indecent exposure and you want to talk about a dispo before I even file it. Remember, Haller, I have sixty days to file and I haven't used half of them. But I'm always open to a dispo."

"Actually, no dispo. I want to talk about making the case go away. Completely. Before it's filed."

Seiver's head came up sharply and he looked at me.

"This chick was caught completely naked on Broad Beach. She's an exhibitionist, Haller. It's a slam-bang conviction. Why would I make it go away? Oh, wait, don't tell me. I get it. The sandwich was really a bribe. You're working with the FBI in the latest investigation into corruption of the justice system. I didn't know it was called Operation Brisket."

I smiled but also shook my head.

"Open your shirt," Seiver said. "Let me see the wire."

"Settle down, Seiver. Let me ask you, did you pull the case after my office called?"

"I did indeed."

"Did you read the deputy's arrest report and did you compare the information to the statute?"

His eyebrows came together in curiosity.

"I read the arrest report. The statute is up here."

He tapped a finger on his temple.

"Then you know that under the statute the deputy must visually observe the trespass of the law in order to make an arrest for indecent exposure."

"I know that, Haller. He did. Says right in the report that she came out of the water completely naked. Completely, Mick. That means she didn't have any clothes on. I think it's safe to say that this academy-trained deputy had the skill to notice this distinction. And by the way, do you know how cold the Pacific is right now? Do you have any idea what that would do to a woman's nipples?"

"Irrelevant, but I get the picture. But you miss the point. Read the report again. No, wait. I have it right here. I'll read it to you."

I took the first bite of my own sandwich, and while chewing it pulled the file from my case. Once I swallowed I read aloud the arrest summary, which I had highlighted when I had reviewed the case file the day before.

" 'Suspect Linda Sandoval, twenty-nine years of age, was in

the water when responding deputy responded to call. Multiple witnesses pointed her out. R/D told suspect to come out of the water and suspect refused several times. R/D finally enlisted help of lifeguards Kennedy and Valdez and suspect was physically removed from the ocean where she was confirmed as completely naked. Suspect willingly dressed at this time and was arrested and transported. Suspect was verbally abusive toward R/D at the time of her arrest and during transport.' "

That was all I had highlighted but it was enough.

"I've got the same thing right here, Haller. Looks like slam-dunk material to me. By the way, did you see that under occupation on the arrest sheet she put down 'exotic dancer?' She's a stripper and she was out there getting rid of her tan lines and she broke the law."

"Her occupation isn't germane to the filing and you might want to look again at the report there, Einstein. The crime of indecent exposure was created by your own deputy sheriff."

"What are you talking about?"

"It doesn't matter if multiple witnesses pointed her out to him or that they saw her frolicking naked in the surf. Under the statute, the deputy can't make the arrest based on witness testimony. The arresting officer must observe the actual infraction to make the arrest. Pull down the book and check it out."

"I don't need the book. The deputy clearly met the threshold."

"Uh-uh. He clearly didn't observe the infraction until he had those two brave lifeguards pull her out of the water. He clearly created the crime and then arrested her."

"What are you talking about, an entrapment defense? Is this a joke?"

"It's not entrapment but it's not a valid arrest. The deputy created the crime and that makes it an illegal arrest. He also humiliated her by having her dragged out of the water and put on public display. I think she's probably got cause for civil action against the county."

"Is that a negotiating ploy? Public display? She's a stripper, for God's sake. This is ridic—"

He stopped midsentence as he realized I was right about the deputy creating the trespass upon the law. His head dropped down out of sight, but I don't think it was to take another bite of his sandwich. He was reading the arrest report for himself and seeing what I was explaining to him. I waited him out and finally he spoke.

"She's a stripper, what's she care? Maybe if you take the conviction and then ran an appeal on it you would get some media and it would be good for business. Have her plead nolo pending the appeal, and meantime I'll make sure she only gets a slap on the wrist. But no civil action. That's the deal."

I shook my head but he couldn't see it.

"Can't do it, Deano. She's a stripper but she's also second-year law at USC. So she can't take the hit on her record and gamble on an appeal. Every law firm runs background checks. She can't go in with a ding on her record. In some states she'd never be allowed to take the bar or practice. In some states she'd even have to register as a sex offender because of this."

"Then what's she doing stripping? She should be clerking somewhere."

"USC's goddamn expensive and she's paying her own way. Works the pole four nights a week. You'd have to see her to believe this, but she makes about ten times more stripping than she would clerking."

I momentarily thought about Linda Sandoval and the perfect triangle moving in rhythm on the stage. I had regretted not taking her up on her offer. I was sure I always would.

"Then she's going to make more stripping than she will practicing law," Seiver said, snapping me back to reality.

"You're stalling, Dean. What are you going to do?"

"You just want the whole thing to go away, huh?"

I nodded.

"It's a bad arrest," I said. "You refuse to file it and everybody wins. My client's record is clean and the integrity of the justice system is intact."

"Don't make me laugh. I could still go ahead with it and tie her up in appeals until she graduates."

"But you're a fair and decent guy and you know it's a bad arrest. That's why I came to you."

"Where's she work and what name does she dance under?"

"One of the Road Saints' places up in the Valley. Her professional name is Harmony."

"Of course it is. Look, Haller, things have changed since the last time you deigned to visit me. I'm restricted in what I can do here."

"Bullshit. You're the supervisor. You can do what you want. You always have."

"Actually, no. It's all about the budget now. Under some formula some genius put together at county, our budget now rises and falls with the number of cases we prosecute. So that edict resulted in an internal edict from on high which takes away my discretion. I cannot kick a case without approval from downtown. Because a nol-pros case doesn't get counted in the budget."

This sort of logic and practice did not surprise me, yet it surprised me to be confronted with it by Seiver. He had never been a company man.

"You're saying you cannot drop this case without approval because it would cost your department money from the county."

"Exactly."

"And what that means is that the interest of justice takes a backseat to budgetary considerations. My client must be illegally charged first, in order to satisfy some bureaucrat in the budget office, before you are then allowed to step in and drop the charge. Meantime, she's got an arrest on her record that may prevent or impede her eventual practice of law."

"No, I didn't say that."

"I'm paraphrasing."

"I still didn't say that last part."

"Sounded like it to me."

"No, I told you what the procedure is now. Technically, I don't have prefiling discretion in a case like this. Yes, I would have to file the case and then drop it. And, yes, we both know that the charge, no matter what the outcome of the case, will stay on her record forever."

I realized he was trying to tell me something.

"But you have an alternate plan," I prompted.

"Of course I do, Haller."

He stood up and moved what was left of his sandwich from the clear spot on his desk.

"Hold this, Haller."

I stood up and he handed me a file with the name Linda Sandoval on the tab. He then stepped up onto his desk chair and used it as a ladder to step up onto the clear spot of his desk.

"What are you doing, Seiver? Looking for a spot to tie the noose? That's not an alternative."

He laughed but didn't answer. He reached up and used both hands to push one of the tiles in the drop ceiling up and over. He reached a hand down to me and I gave him the file. He put it up into the space above the ceiling, then pulled the lightweight tile back into place.

Seiver got down and slapped the dust off his hands.

"There," he said.

"What did you just do?"

"The file is lost. The case won't be filed. Time will run out and then it will be too late for it to be filed. You come back in after the sixty days are up and get the arrest expunged. Harmony's record is clean by the time she takes the bar exam. If something comes up or the deputy asks questions, I say I never saw the file. Lost in transit from Malibu."

I nodded. It would work. The rules had changed but not Dean Seiver. I had to laugh.

"So that's what passes for discretion now?"

"I call it Seiver's pretrial intervention."

"How many files you have up there, man?"

"A lot. In fact, tell Harmony to put some clothes on, get down on her knees, and pray to the stripper gods that the ceiling doesn't fall before her sixty days are run. 'Cause when the sky falls in here, then Chicken Little will have some 'splaining to do. I'll probably need a job when that happens."

We both looked up at the ceiling with a sense of apprehension. I wondered how many files the ceiling could hold before Seiver's pretrial intervention program came crashing down.

"Let's finish our sandwiches and not worry about it," Seiver finally said.

"Okay."

We resumed our positions on either side of the wall of files.

It was early evening and still bright outside. When I walked into the Snake Pit North I had to pause for my eyes to adjust to the darkness inside. When they did, I saw my client Harmony was on the main stage, her perfect triangle glittering in the spotlights.

She moved with a natural rhythm that was as entrancing as her naked body. No tattoos as distraction. Just her, pure and beautiful.

That's why I had come. I could have delivered the good news by phone and been done with it. Said, See you around the courthouse in a year. But I had to see her one more time. Her body had left a memory imprint on me in the privacy booth. And I had started dreaming about being with her now that the case was closed and it could be argued—before the Bar if necessary—that she was no longer a client. Bar or no Bar, I wanted her. There was something intoxicating about having the smartest girl in the room moving up and down on you.

The song was an old one, "Sweet Child o' Mine," and had just started. I stood in the crowd and just watched and after a while she saw me and gave me the nod without breaking her rhythm. It might be a young girl's game but I thought she could give lessons for the next twenty years if need be. She moved with a rhythm that seemed to push the music, not the other way around.

I looked around and found an open bar table along the back wall. I sat down and watched Harmony dance until the song ended. While another dancer took the next song, she stood by the stairs at the back of the stage and put her orange G-string and zebra-striped camisole back on. The garter around her thigh was flowered with money—ones, fives, tens, and twenties. She walked down the steps, stopped at a few tables to kiss heavy donors on the cheek, and then came to me.

"Hello, Counselor. Do you have news for me?"

She took the other stool at the table.

"I sure do," I said. "The news is that your research was superb and your strategy excellent. The prosecutor bought it. He bought the whole thing."

She held still for a moment, as if basking in some unseen glow.

"What exactly is the disposition of the case?"

"It goes away. Completely."

"What about the record of my arrest?"

"I go back in a couple months from now and expunge it. There will be no record."

"Wow. I'm good."

"You sure are. And don't forget I had a little part to play in it, too."

"Thanks, Mickey. You just made my night."

"Yeah, well, I was hoping you could make mine."

"What do you have in mind?"

"I was thinking about what you said last night."

"About what?"

"About a man needing to eat pussy."

She smiled in that way that all women have, that way that says it isn't going to happen.

"That was last night, Mickey. Tonight it's a whole new world."

She slid off the stool and came around the table to me. She kissed me on the cheek the way I had just seen her kiss the big donors, the schmucks who had put twenty-dollar bills in her garter.

"Take care, baby," she said.

She started to glide away from the table.

"Wait a minute. What about the privacy booth? I thought maybe we could go back there . . ."

She looked back at me.

"It takes money to go back there, sugar."

"I still have the money you gave me last night."

She paused for a moment, her face hard in the red light bouncing off the mirrors in the club.

"Okay. Then let's go make Tommy happy."

She came back and took hold of my tie. She led me toward the back rooms and the whole way there I thought that there was no doubt that she was going to be a better lawyer than she was a stripper. One day she was going to be a killer in court.

Sunshine

LYNN FREED

THEY TOLD GRACE they'd found her curled into a nest of leaves, that since dawn they'd been following a strange spoor through the bush, and then, just as they'd begun to smell her, there she was, staring up at them through a cloud of iridescent flies.

They peered through the mottled gloom. Flies were clustered on her nose and eyes and mouth, and yet she didn't move, didn't even blink. "It's dead," said one of them, stretching out a stick to prod her.

That's when she sprang, scattering the flies and baring all her teeth in a dreadful high-pitched screech. They leapt back, reaching for their knives. She was up on her haunches now, biting at the air between them with her jagged teeth. But with the leaves and flies swirling, and her furious, wild hair, it took some time before they understood that it was a girl raging before them, just a girl.

"Hau!" they whispered, and they lowered their knives. She was skinny as a stick—filthy and naked, and the nest smelled foul. One of the men dug into his pocket for some nuts. "Mê," he said, holding them out to her. "Mê."

She lifted her chin, trying to sniff at the air. But her nose was swollen and bloody, one arm hung limp at her side.

"It will be easy to catch her," the older man said. "How do we know the Master won't pay? Even half?"

Julian de Jong stormed out into the midday sun. "What on earth's the matter out here, Grace?" he said. "Why've you locked the dogs away?"

One of the men held the girl up, the other lifted her hair so that the Master could see her face.

"They found her in the bush, Master," Grace said, not looking up. She never wanted to see the girls when they were brought in. "They say if they put her back, maybe the jackals will get her."

The girl writhed and twisted to free herself from the grasp of the men. She bared her teeth, screeching pitifully. All the way up the hill, she had screeched and struggled like this, and all the way baboons had come barking after her.

De Jong stepped out into the yard and the men dropped their eyes courteously. Everyone knew he was not to be looked at when he was inspecting a girl, even an ugly one like this, even their own daughters. Even the girl stopped her squirming when he walked up, as if she, too, knew what was good for her. She stared at him as he questioned the men, breathing lightly through her mouth like a dog.

He put his monocle to his eye, and, for several minutes, examined the girl in silence. And then, at last, he stood up and said, "Grace, clean the creature up. Here," he said to the men, digging around in his pocket for change. "Take this and divide it between you."

"Bring me the scissors!" Grace said to Beauty. "Bring me the Dettol!"

Beauty held the girl down while Grace took the scissors to her hair. "Ag!" she said, handing the tangle of hair and grass and blood to the garden boy. "Burn that," she said. "And bring me the blade for shaving. And the big tin bath."

By the time the bath was filled with hot water, the girl was almost bald, her scalp as pale as dough, and bleeding here and there from the blade. When they tried to lift her in, she struggled even more, twisting and thrashing and working one leg free so that she slashed at the flesh of Grace's arm with a toenail.

"Be *still*, you devil!" Grace cried, giving her a hard slap on the flesh of her buttock. "You want to go back to the bush? You want the jackals to get you?"

But the creature would not be still. By the time she was clean, the kitchen floor was awash with dirty water and she was cowering against the side of the bath, shivering, the teeth chattering. Now that she was clean, they could see that the nose and arm had been badly broken, and that the skin was sallow where the sun had not caught it. It was covered in scratches—some old, some new—and her hands and feet were calloused as hooves.

"He'll send her back after all this trouble," Beauty said. She was standing in the kitchen doorway with an armful of clothes. They were the same clothes each time, flimsy things that the girls loved to wear. "They will only be spoiled," she said. "It's a big shame." She put them on the kitchen table.

Grace pulled a small chemise out of the pile. She didn't understand these clothes, she hadn't understood them when she'd had to wear them herself. "Hold up her arms," she said to Beauty.

But it was hopeless. One by one, the clothes were tried, torn, bitten, abandoned. The best Grace could do was to pin a dishcloth onto the girl as tightly as she could. And then once it was on, the creature only squatted on her haunches like a monkey and clawed at the cloth with her good hand, drawing blood in her madness to have it off.

"It's too cruel," said Grace. "Let's take it off."

And so the girl was carried onto the veranda, naked and bald, to be presented to the man who would decide what would become of her.

Over the years, there had been rumors in the local villages of children living with baboons in the forest—of children snatched by baboons if you left them outside unguarded. Some children the baboons ate, the rumor went, some they kept for themselves. But only the old women ever believed this.

"Look again," Julian de Jong said to the local administrator. "See if anyone reported a baby missing—six or seven years ago, white, half-breed, anything you can find. I don't want any trouble later."

But no one had reported such a thing, not in the whole province. No one would challenge his claim.

"She could have been thrown away as a newborn and left for dead," said Doctor McKenzie, leaning over to examine the arm. "Some desperate teenager, who knows? I suppose it's not out of the question that baboons could have taken her up. But it hardly seems plausible, does it? Mind you, these fractures could very well be the result of a fall from a tree. She could have grown too big, I suppose. And she's malnourished, which would make her prone to fractures. Anyway," he said, straightening up, "there it is, and something needs to be done about the teeth. Don't mind telling you, old boy, I'm glad *I'm* not the dentist. Oh, and here—don't leave without the worm powder. Sure you're up for this one, Julian?"

* * *

The first night, de Jong had Grace lock the girl into the storeroom in the servants' quarters. But all through the night, the creature screeched and wailed, keeping the servants awake. The next morning they found that the sling on her arm had been bitten away, the bandage torn from her nose. Even her calloused hands and feet were bloodied and raw from trying to climb to the small, barred window above the door.

"It's cruel to lock her in there, Master," said Grace. "She's like an animal. We must train her like a dog."

De Jong looked at the girl. All night she had visited him in dreams—more like presences, really, than dreams—but, when he woke up, he could still put not face to the creature. Usually he knew just what he had. At first they'd cry and beg to be sent home. Sometimes it would go on for weeks, and then he'd have to punish them. But in the end Grace always managed to have them ready for him, cleaned and oiled and docile.

If there was a principle that drove Julian de Jong, it was never to obscure his motives. And so, from the outset, there'd never been a question of theft. He was doing the girls a favor, everyone knew that, even their families. How else could it be that old McIntyre the missionary had never got any of them to talk? They'd just shake their heads when he came calling, press their lips together. They knew that when de Jong was finished with them, the girls would fetch a decent bride price regardless. There was the money, of course, but there were other things, too, things they'd learned from Grace—how to lay the table and mend the sheets, and sometimes even how to make a pudding or a soup. And so, when he finally sent them home, they seemed not to know where they'd rather be. And who was the worse for it then?

He stretched out his hand to touch the rough skin of the creature's cheek. He wanted to stroke it as he would stroke one of the others when she was new, for the pleasure of the life under his hand—grateful, warm, blameless. But just as his fingers came near her, she whipped her head around and tore at the flesh of his thumb with her teeth.

"Good God!" he cried, watching the blood well into the wound. He grasped the wrist tightly with his other hand as if to restrain it from grabbing her by the throat. And all the while she was staring at him, panting, waiting, ready.

Grace lowered her eyes. She had seen him take the riding crop to a girl for staring. She had seen him take the crop to a girl for doing nothing at all.

"I'll call Beauty to fetch the gentian, Master," she said quickly.

He turned then, as if he had forgotten she was there. A breeze was up, playing with his frizzy gray hair. But there was nothing playful in his face, she knew. It was flushed with fury, ready for the Lord knew what.

"Grace," he said, "I want you to tell the rest of them that no hand is to be laid upon this girl, not even if she bites. You will treat her like any of the others. Do you hear me?"

"Yes, Master."

"De Jong," McKenzie said, smoothing down the last of the plaster of Paris, "she will need to be restrained to a board if this is to do any good. And I'll have to fashion a bucket collar so that she can't get at the nose. No one come forward to claim her?"

"No one."

"Well, the word is out, you know. The papers are bound to dig it up sooner or later."

"Let them dig. I have Dunlop's word he'll fix things. Anyway, who'd want her? She's an animal—just look what she did to my hand this morning."

McKenzie took the hand and turned it over. "It'll need a stitch," he said, "and we should test her for rabies. Here, keep still."

Grace took the girl to the chair in the corner. She held her there by the wrists, securing the girl's hips between her own copious thighs. But still the girl strained forward, as if she wanted another go at de Jong's hand.

"How long till the bones knit?" de Jong said.

"Bring her back in four weeks, and we'll take a look."

For four weeks, the girl was kept strapped to a board on the sleeping porch of the upstairs veranda. There Grace fed and cleaned her, and there, every night, de Jong himself slept in the bed next to hers, talking softly to her, telling her things he wouldn't have told the others. The hot season was beginning to die down, but when he tried covering her with his knee rug, she gasped and gagged, straining against the straps that held her head in place. So he took it off again.

After a while, he began to sit at the edge of her bed, and then place a hand on her forehead, almost covering her eyes. He'd hold it there until she stopped struggling, and, when she did, he'd run his fingers around the coil of an ear and under her jaw, down into the curve of her neck and shoulders. And then, if she was quiet, he'd feed her a piece of raw liver, which she loved best of all.

And so, soon he had her suffering his touch without struggling. She would lie still, staring at him around the plaster on her nose. Once, as his hand slipped itself over her rump, she even closed her eyes and fell asleep, he could hear her breathing settle. But when he stood up to leave, she was instantly awake again, following him with her eyes through the fading light to his own bed.

As the fourth week approached, de Jong had a cage built and placed at the back of the sleeping porch. Inside, Grace placed a tin mug and bowl, his knee rug and a driving glove that had lost its pair. The girl was to be lifted so that she could see every stage of the preparations, and Grace was to hold the bowl for her to sniff before she put it inside, and then the rug, and then the glove.

"Master," Grace said, "maybe she's not so wild now. Maybe we can let her walk for herself when the arm is better."

But the minute the plaster was off and the girl was given the freedom of the cage, she began to rage and screech again as if she had just been caught. With both arms growing stronger, she began to climb and swing and leap as well. She bit and tore at the blanket until it lay in shreds on the floor of the cage. The glove she examined carefully, turning it this way and that way, and then testing it with her teeth. The teeth themselves had been drilled and cleaned before the plaster came off. But they were still brown, and a few had been pulled out, giving her an even wilder look.

No one could work out how old she really was. Certainly, she was the size of most of the girls they brought to him. But the dentist seemed to think she was a bit older, which made the whole thing a little more urgent. All night and much of the day, de Jong stayed up there, talking softly to her. The servants watched and listened. It was the voice that he used for the dogs, and for the girls when they were first brought in. Never for anyone else. After a while even the girl herself seemed to listen. She would stare at him through the bars of the cage, frowning her baboon frown. And then he would pour some water into her mug, showing her how to drink it without lapping.

Over the weeks, she became quiet for longer and longer stretches of time. Even when de Jong went away and Grace came up to sit with her, she would wait quietly for her water, for her food. It was Grace herself who found a way to stop the girl tearing up the newspaper that was placed there day after day for her mess. And then one day, when the girl messed on it by chance, Grace began to sing. "You are my sunshine," warbling in her high-pitched vibrato, and the girl cocked her head like a bird, this way and that way. She ran to the bars and hung on, waiting for more. But Grace just waited too. And the next time the girl messed on the newspaper, she sang the song again, adding a line or two. And so, with singing, Grace managed to coax the creature into a pair of pants and a vest, and by the time de Jong returned, she'd learned how to pull them off and put them on herself.

"Master," Grace said, "maybe we can unlock the dogs now."

And so the dogs were led one by one to the cage, ears back, straining at the leash. When the girl heard them coming, she ran wildly for the far corner of the cage, upsetting the bowl, climbing the bars and hanging there, screeching with all her teeth. The dog itself would jump up, wagging, barking wildly, only to be scolded, corrected, made to sit and stay.

Day after day the ritual was repeated until dog and girl could stare at each other without fright. After a while, de Jong could trust the dogs to approach the cage unleashed. And then, at last, when the girl was ready to be taken out, the dogs ran beside her without incident.

"Master," Grace said, "I can't make her stand straight like you said. She still wants to bend over like a baboon. I think she was living with the baboons over there. I think she can still be like them."

De Jong smiled down at the girl. Thick black curls were beginning to cover her head. And her face was beginning to reveal itself, the nose long and straight, a high forehead, small ears, olive skin, and the wide black eyes of a gypsy. Considering only the head, she could be any child, any dark, silent girl, no breasts yet, no body hair either. If she still stooped, what difference would it make? She was ready, baboons or no baboons, he could see it in the way she looked at him. It was Grace who was trying to hold her back for some reason.

"You'll bring her to me tomorrow evening," he said. "The usual hour."

Grace bowed her head. Usually, she was only too glad to hand a girl over because then she'd have her two weeks off. When she did return, as often as not the girl would be over the first fright of it. So what had come over her this time? "Maybe a few more days?" she said.

He smiled at Grace. It was almost as if she'd known from the start how it would be with this girl. And now that he was taking pride—well, not so much pride in the girl herself as in the things she could do, the way he could make her obey him—now that he was waking each morning to the thought of what he might make the girl do for him next, now came Grace with her suggestions.

"She does not even have a name yet," Grace said.

They were walking down to the river, which the girl always liked to do. Once he'd thought he heard her laugh—laugh or bark, it was hard to tell which. The sun was shining brilliantly on the muddy water, and she'd looked up into his face, her mouth and eyes wide. And then, freeing her hand from his, she'd bounded down the hill with the dogs, down to the water's edge.

"Tomorrow evening. In the atrium. The usual time."

Grace had dressed the girl in a simple silk shift. There was a pool in the middle of the atrium, with a fountain at its center. Most of the girls couldn't swim, but the pool was shallow, and he'd be sitting in it, naked, waiting for them with his glass of whiskey. The girls themselves always stopped at the sight of him there, the pink shoulders and small gray eyes. And then he'd rise out of the water like a sea monster and they'd make a run for it, every one of them, never mind how much Grace had told them there was no way out.

Men in the village liked to say they'd come to the house one night and cut off his manhood like a pawpaw. But Grace knew it was all talk. Without his money, where would they all be? Where would she be herself? The Master himself knew that, standing there, shameless, before her. But when he had finished with this one, where would she go? Usually, they'd run home with the money, and then, sooner or later, they'd be back at the kitchen door, wanting work. But what about this one? Where *could* she go except back to the baboons?

Quickly, Grace turned and walked out of the atrium.

He held his hand out to the girl, but she didn't take it. She was leaning over the low wall, splashing one hand into the water. He caught it in his own then, and took her under the arms and lifted her in. She didn't struggle, she was used to his lifting her here or there. But this time he was lifting her dress off her, too, throwing it aside. She wasn't wearing any panties, he never wanted them wearing panties when they came to him. So now there was nothing but her smooth, olive skin. He ran his hands down her sides and cupped one around each buttock—small and round and girlish, the rest of the body muscled like a boy's.

She let him coax her down into the water, lapping at it happily. And when he moved one hand between her legs, she just glanced down there through the water with the frown she always wore when Grace tried to show her how to wipe herself after she'd used the toilet. But he was stroking her, prodding into her with a finger so that she jumped away and stared hard at him. And still he came after her, taking her by the arms before she could scramble up onto the fountain. He was pushing her backwards to the side of the pool and his smile was gone, he was holding her arms wide so that he could force his knee between her legs.

Caught like that, she slammed her head wildly then from side to side against the edge of the tiles, shrieking piteously. A trickle of blood ran down her neck, and when at last he had her legs apart and was thrusting himself into her, she was bleeding there, too. He knew from her narrowness that she'd be bleeding properly when he'd finished with her, that her blood would cloud out beautifully into the pool, turning from red to pink. It was the moment he longed for with every new offering, first the front, then the back, and always the mouths open in astonishment like this, the eyes wild and pleading, and for what? For more? More?

By the time he was finished with her and resting his head against the side of the pool, she was moaning. They all moaned like this, and what did they expect? What did this one expect after all these months she'd kept him waiting with her grunts and squawks? He stretched out an arm to grab her neck. Usually that's all it took to shut them up. If it didn't, he'd duck them under the water until they were ready to listen. "Quiet," he'd croon in his deep, soft voice. And if that didn't work, he did it again, and for longer. "Do you hear me now?" he'd whisper. "I said quiet!"

But with this one words were useless. And, just as he was about to push her under, she slipped free, twirling herself into the air, twisting, leaping, springing out of reach until, at last, he had caught her by an arm. But then she only doubled back, sinking her teeth into his wrist, and, when he'd let her go, into an ear, and, at last, as his hands flew to his head, she took his throat between her jaws. And there she hung on like a wild dog, only tightening her bite as he bucked and flailed for air. But the more he struggled the deeper she bit, never loosening her jaws until he was past the pain, past the panic. Only then, only after the last damp gurgling of breath had left him limp, did she rip away the flesh and gristle she'd got hold of, and, gulping it down as she ran, leap out through an open window.

When they came in with the tea things, the whole pool was pink, pinker than they'd ever seen it, even the fountain. At first they'd just stood there, staring at what was left of his throat. But then they remembered the girl, and they ran, one for a kitchen knife, another to lock the doors and windows of the house.

But she never returned. And the generations that followed were inclined to laugh at the whole idea of a baboon girl—of *any* girl killing that demon like a leopard or a lion. They were inclined to doubt the demon himself as well. Surely someone would have reported him to the authorities, they said? Surely one of his girls would have told her story to the papers?

Midnight Stalkings

JAMES GRADY

Erin wore a stolen maid's uniform as she walked up the grand staircase from the Manhattan mansion's first-floor party preparations. She carried a stack of white towels as if they hid nothing. Kept her thighs from brushing together and breaking the glass tubes of acid tucked into her garter-belted midnight stockings.

Forget acid: She worried someone might discover she wore no panties.

Not my style, but when she'd stood in her one-room Brooklyn walk-up and used her lone window to the night as a mirror, that dark glass reflection of her social worker's white underpants over the black garter belt and stockings made her look like a joke. She refused any such role.

Better to be bold than a buffoon.

Her borrowed black high heel climbed another step in the mansion.

Just this once and I'm free. Erin reached the third-floor landing where firelight flickered beyond the study's open sliding doors.

He deserves it. Cowgirl hips swayed her maid's skirt. Floating up from downstairs came a radio voice turned on by the caterer to track time:

"—as this is *the* most exciting cultural moment of 1939, we shall now broadcast *live* our opera selections timed to end *precisely* at midnight."

A closed downstairs door muffled the radio.

A clock went GONG! eleven times as she entered the study. A flat oak desk ruled that room. Wall sconces and the fireplace blazing behind the desk created undulating waves of golden light and warm shadows. A crystal vase held blossoming red roses.

Above the mantel hung a painting of dogs playing poker.

Erin stacked the white towels on the otherwise bare desk.

Rolled the double doors shut.

Leaned her back against them with wrists crossed behind her as if they were handcuffed. *You can still change your mind. Run.*

But she moved between the tycoon's leather chair and the fireplace.

A wall's huge mirror caught her removing the white cap of a maid.

Ordinary earth-dark hair tumbled to cup her pale face like twin half moons. *Of course* she knew her jaw was too long, her mouth too big, and she had freak-show indigo eyes.

The mirror reflected her unbuttoning the maid's blouse. Underneath she wore a silver-sequined knee-length black gown lent to her—*"Just for tonight, Cinderella!"*—by the Broadway seamstress who lived in her building. Erin pulled off the maid's skirt. The bunched-up gown fell from her waist like the curtain at the end of Act One.

Erin gave herself a shake to become who the mirror said she might be. The black gown swooped low in the front, bared her back. Her breasts swayed free inside the night fabric of twinkling stars.

Nobody knows about the panties.

The maid's uniform got tossed into the crackling fire and buried under the weight of a thick log the flames licked.

She took the top white towel off its stack and set it alone by the side edge of the desk. A purse waited atop the remaining stacked towels.

Erin lifted her gown and *oh so slowly* plucked the two tubes of acid from her stockings. Laid the acid tubes beside each other on the lone white towel like a terrified first-night honeymoon couple.

From the purse came a silver tube of lipstick. She twisted the tube and stroked her lips with the round tip of a color called ruby.

Not my sensible shade.

She put the lipstick in the purse, sprayed perfume on her wrists, her neck, cool puffs into her bare underarms to mask any odor of secret work.

Or fear.

I can do this. By myself! No one will see me. I'll get away clean.

She looked at the image caught by the room's mirror.

Is this how I'll remember tonight?

Bloodred lips. Roses. Musk perfume. Burning logs. No panties.

A glance showed the study doors still closed to the outside world.

Erin faced the fire. Spread her arms high and wide as if she were nailed to some invisible cosmic cross.

Lifted the painting of the dogs playing poker off the wall. Put it on the leather tycoon chair she shoved across the room.

The dial on a now-revealed wall safe stared at her like a Cyclops.

Her dad's Colt .45 revolver hid in the towel stack on the desk.

Won't need it.

She inhaled deep into her belly. Reached toward the wall safe—

"WHOA!"

Behind me!

Erin whirled—

Saw him standing there. The hulk of a man. Backlit in the *so silently slid-open* double doors. Wearing a black tuxedo jacket, open white shirt. The fireplace beyond her flickered in his ice-blue eyes.

"*Whoa*," he said again. Only softer. A stunned whisper.

He glided into the room like a boxer.

Said: "I didn't know anybody was in here."

Saw her all alone. Asked: "Would you help me?"

More like a farm boy than a scion of Park Avenue, he smiled and raised his hand that held an ebony ribbon. "I've never been good with ties."

"*Mr. Daniels!* I thought you were at the opera with your guests!"

"Guess I'm running late." Standing near the open doors, servants just a shout away, he frowned: "How about you?"

"Me?" *Don't stammer!* "I guess I'm early, I'm always early."

"That's a refreshing quality of leadership for a woman—"

Sexist pig!

"—that doesn't get its just due. Good for you."

He moved deeper into the room's flickering light.

The press called him handsome, and he *might* have been—

though he looked rough. Short hair. Lines along his mouth: Call them . . . not dimples . . .

Heart scars leapt into Erin's mind: lines of laughter, lines of sorrow.

None of the newspaper articles mentioned those.

Keep him looking at you! Focus him on you! Trick him!

Erin's lying smile surprised her with its honest, self-conscious curl.

"Better go," she said. "You don't want to miss your opera."

"Well," he said, taking a step closer, "*Tosca* is impressive—"

Pretentious snob!

"—but I'd rather go see Billie Holiday."

"In the Village!" blurted Erin. *Don't let his focus drift! He'll notice!* "Have you heard her 'Strange Fruit'? Can you believe—"

"—that people think she's singing about swings on trees or . . ."

"Or sex."

"But it's not, is it," he said. "That song. About sex."

"No," she said. "It's not."

His eyes narrowed: "I've never seen you down there."

A quick lunge would let her grab the revolver from between the white towels stacked on the desk, but he'd shout and those doors were still open.

"I've never seen you anywhere," said this man she officially loathed.

"Maybe you just weren't looking. I'm easy to not notice."

"No," he said. "And no."

She stood between the desk and the crackling fire. Her legs felt like rubber. She wobbled on those borrowed high heels. *This isn't me.*

He turned and rolled shut the doors but before she thought to grab the gun, he'd turned back, taken one, *two* steps toward her. Stopped.

"You don't know me," he said. "I don't know you. Yet here we are."

"For your party. After the opera. I'm early. Came to meet someone."

"Found me." He grinned. "Isn't luck the damnedest thing?"

Then he looked past her to the wall with its exposed safe.

She saw him spot the poker-dogs painting in the shoved-away chair.

Maybe I can talk my way out of this! Maybe I won't need the Colt!

"You're . . . a thief!" He scowled. "Are you working for Nick?"

Huh?

He stepped closer to the desk. "No, Nick's a loner."

Keep him talking! Erin stepped from behind the desk but stayed by it. Closer to him. To the stacked towels. To the gun. "Who's Nick?"

This man who was about her age shrank with his answer.

"Nick Cole and I . . . Mr. Blue Blood and Mr. Blue Sky. The only person I let call me Bernie instead of Bernard. Bernard Daniels the *third*. He said he didn't like me being trapped by all that weight."

Keep him distracted! "So why does he want to rob you?"

"He thinks he's owed. Or he wants to knock me down. Or both."

"Because . . ."

"Nick and Bernie go to Vera Cruz. Black-hair-to-her-waist Carmelita. May the best man win. We blunder into somebody else's cantina brawl. Knives. Blood. Blame the gringos. Bought my way out of jail. Nick doesn't have my bucks. I closed the deal with Carmelita."

"You left him in jail?"

"Well . . . technically, *yeah*, but he was in the fight, too. He just couldn't pay the tab. Not my fault."

"Besides, there was Carmelita. She should have made you help him."

"Every transaction has its goals. She got her ticket to Hollywood. Before I got around to more bribes, Nick lock-picked his way out. *Poof!*"

"Would he have left a friend behind?"

"He's not the good man he wants to be." A long strong finger aimed straight at her heart. "And you're more than a thief."

"I'm not a—"

"Too late," he said. "You took the dogs off the wall. That's enough for the law, even if it were honest. Robbery like this is a low blow."

And she heard her father after the banks had taken the ranch telling his motherless little girl: *"Just once I wish one of them sons a bitches would get what's coming to 'em."*

"You deserve it," she said.

"What did I ever do to you?"

"Personally, nothing."

"But for you, this is more than business."

She stood as tall as she could beside the desk.

Said: "Is business what you do with the refugees on the Lower East Side? You hunt them down. Give them a dime on the dollar for what they managed to save from the goose-steppers."

"Diamonds," he said.

"In a lockbox," she told him. "In that safe."

"Guess too many people heard those stories." He shook his

head. "So you're going to steal diamonds I bought fair and square and give them back to the people who were grateful my deal let them eat?"

"There are charities I know." *That's true.*

"I hope you were planning to keep some for yourself."

She didn't answer.

Said: "Why do you do it? You don't need the money."

"Life is action. Money is just one currency. And when a dime is still big-time, when it's personal: That's the sweetest."

Think! I've got to think! What—

"How were you going to do it?" He eased closer. "I don't see you sneaking across rooftops, then burgling a window. I figure you tricked your way in here. Dressed like that, once the party started, you could escape. In and out is easy, but there's a safe with a combination."

"You love your birthday. It's your limo license plate: 02-21-06."

"Smart *and* brave." He stalked toward her.

The gun, the heavy gun hid in the stack of white towels that along with her purse and the honeymoon bed for acid tubes was all that waited on the slab of a desk. The gun, a Colt Peacemaker, was her only inheritance from a father who'd died whispering: "*Somebody should get shot.*"

In that study, Erin knew: *I can grab the gun and . . .* And.

"But then what?" said the man she came to rob. "The diamonds in the safe are in a lockbox."

Her eyes flicked to the two glass tubes on the white towel.

"What's that?"

"Acid."

"You were going to pour acid on the box lock?"

"Or the hinges." She shrugged. "Sometimes there's more than one way to do something."

He sighed. "Sometimes I wish there was no way to do what I want."

Asked: "Which is worse, regretting what we can't resist, or regretting what we wish we'd dared?"

"What are we talking about?" she said.

"How we got here." As he draped the black tie around his neck, she wondered if his cheeks gave a soft scratch of straight-razor-shaved stubble. He walked like he was following the curve of a noose until his back was to the huge mirror and hers was to the desk. Said: "What comes next?"

The clock gonged the quarter hour.

"Why does the opera end at midnight?" *Why am I whispering?*

"Because everybody wants tomorrow to be a party."

"Is that what you want?" she said.

Realized how he looked at her *then* had *changed* how he looked.

Suddenly he'd gone from *Lon Chaney* to *werewolf* and *I*—

—she thought—

I can be his silver bullet.

The werewolf never wins.

Maybe this can all be a movie. So maybe whatever I do, want . . .

"You make me want to say something corny," he told her.

"Like what?"

"Your dress is made out of stars, but the light inside you is dazzling."

They stood staring at each other.

"*Wow*," she finally said. "But you're not a sentimental guy."

"*Corny* is one thing Bernard Davis *the third* is not."

"So what would Bernard Davis *the third* say at a moment like this?"

The fireplace crackled.

He said: "*Come here.*"

"Make me!"

"What—*no*, I mean: I was saying what Bernie'd normally say."

"Oh! Me, too." Her tongue wet her lips. "This is no normal moment."

"I knew we'd agree on something."

"Is that what you're looking for? Agreement?"

"You came here to get the diamonds, right?"

"And to get away free."

"No such thing," he said. "You pay for what you do and you pay for what you want. The best you can hope for is that those two things join up. But that's rare magic. So rip the best deal you can out of what you got."

"Spoken like a true rogue."

"I feel like I want to be in a truthful mood."

"Really." Her heart pounded against its cage of ribs.

Her voice said: "What else do you want?"

Erin took a step toward him. Heat from the fire baked her bare back. Shallow breaths made her gown rise and fall, rise and fall. Scents of musk perfume. Roses. Burning wood. Lemon polish that had turned the slab of a desk into a brown-mirror dance floor for reflected flickering flames.

She heard herself say: "We're both after the best deal, right? For me, that means getting what I came for. For you, that means treasure."

"What treasure?"

"A memory worth more than law or silver or diamonds."

A fate better than murder.

They stood so close they could see only each other's faces.

Whisper from her: "What would a truthful rogue do here? Do now?"

His hands. Floating up from his sides like he was going to clap. Or strangle. She couldn't move. Could barely breathe. Her parentheses of hair brushed aside as molten steel bands circled her neck *oh!* so softly became warm fingers cupping her face . . .

. . . as he leaned close . . .

. . . as her eyes closed . . .

She felt the kiss.

Not at all like that first kiss stolen with her silent blessing by a boy who blew away in the Great Winds that came with the Depression.

Not at all like the wet slobbers from the drunk college frat rat who bumbled his first attempt at *doing it* with Scholarship Girl and then a half hour later almost passed out before he could contribute the pain of Erin making sure she didn't die a virgin.

And not at all like the angry peckings that accompanied *always with the lights off* bedroom events with Mister Mistake who turned out to have *zero* intention of leaving the wife he neglected to disclose to Erin.

No, not like any such kiss. Like . . .

Lips burning moist melting to fly MORE kiss.

Couldn't help it, she realized: *This is a man I could kill.*

Their eyes blinked open. She saw the smear of her ruby on his lips.

He whispered: "You sure you know what you're doing?"

She said: "Show me."

Stood before him with her hands at her sides.

Waiting.

Trembling.

He lifted the gown's black straps off her white shoulders. Let go. The sequined garment fell. Fireplace heat glowed her bare breasts. The straps slid down her loose arms, the gown brushed past the black garter belt circling her hips, fell to a crumpled nothing around her shoes. No panties.

She filled his eyes and he whispered: *"Jesus!"*

Heard her whisper back: "No. *Me*."

She grabbed the black ribbon circling his neck, pulled him to her parted lips as his hands circled her hips, pulled her closer, his grip sliding up her sides along her stomach to cover and cup *oh!*

Like dancers they moved, for her backwards, stepping out of/on the black dress as he fought free of the tuxedo jacket. She threw away his black tie but he stayed kissing her mouth her cheeks and she ripped open his white shirt, him shrugging it gone *black undershirt* and he stops, leans back—

—they're staggering in front of the roaring fireplace—

—and he pulls off the black undershirt *muscled lean* drops it. She arches her back, guides his face to her heart his hands fill *squeezing* as he kisses her *there* then *there* his lips suck in *oh!* electricity jolts up her spine to tingle her tongue.

They bump into the desk, her left leg his right then somehow she's sitting on that hard wood as he's stepping away, kicking off his shoes.

Stands back to the fire, facing her.

He drops his pants.

Watches quick breaths slide in and out of her smeared ruby lips.

Off come his boxer shorts.

Even in the flickering shadows, she saw all of him.

He stepped toward the V made as she felt her knees move apart.

Stopped.

A shy grin as he told her: "I want to take off my socks."

Laughing, both of them, as he hopped on one leg, then the

other. Stepping to her barefoot, her nylons crackled sliding along the outside of his thighs. He pushed himself as near to the desk as all the laws of physics allowed, his hands plowing her hair as his eyes devoured her.

She whispered: "*What about my stockings?*"

"Leave them on."

Kissing her as she leans back onto the wooden desk, as he climbs on there, too, as his weight presses to her, covers her as her hands stretched up behind her along the desk wood—

Knocked her purse—

—and the white honeymoon towel of acid tubes—

—off the desk.

Erin heard glass *crack*. Acid hiss. Volcano chemical clouds billowing up from the floor vanished in heat from the fireplace, vanished in smells of burning wood, of roses, of musky perfume salty sweetness and *them*.

Her right hand brushed the stack of white towels.

Brushed the hiding place of her gun.

She gripped his shoulder blades and he kissed her cheek, her neck, oh *there* and *there*, *yes* filling his mouth with her *yes* kissing her heaving breastbone *down* kissing her belly button and *What is he doing?*

Standing on the floor at the end of the desk grabbing her waist pulling her along the sweat-slick wood, her high heels off the edge of the desk, her knees curl up and back and he's with her but he's down there kissing and *oh! NEVER READ ABOUT THIS IN ANY BOOK* oh oh *OH!*

Erin grabbed his skull, pulled him onto the desk as she heard herself say: "*Kiss me, kiss me!*" and he does, pressing her against that hard wood his right hand sliding down her side . . .

She rolls sideways. *Don't knock over the stack of towels. The gun.* He's on his back, *straddle him* and after all the yesterdays of awkward or ignorant or counterfeit or mechanical moves, she knows *how* for this triumph and she's atop him *fill me* her stockinged legs knelt bent along his chest, his hands caressing her breasts her hips, try to kiss *can't stop gasping*, she rises curves tall over him hears their *clap clap clap* of flesh sees—

—in the huge wall mirror—

—them on the desk—

—them, *me, yes, me, yes* LOOK: his face gasping like he's in pain.

Reflections in the dark wood of the desk alongside the white towels, *them* and fireplace flames flickering and . . . and . . .

Nnnh!

Feel him buck beneath her fighting crying out shudder *taut* . . . He sinks onto the desk. She drapes over him, her right cheek pressing his, his breath panting in her ear, her hands pressed on the hard wood as strong arms circle around her back, hold her tight and she is right there, here, *now*.

The universe took a breath.

Let it go.

GONG! sounds the clock.

Trapping her to him, he says: "I lied."

GONG!

What?

GONG!

"I can't let you get away," he says.

GONG!

Slowly. GONG!

So he won't feel her doing it. GONG!

So he won't know until it's too late. GONG!

Her left hand glides above the dark-wood mirror of the desk. GONG!

Her fingertips brush soft fabric. GONG!

Find the gully between white towels. GONG!

Slide into cloth warmth. GONG!

Touch cold steel.

At the midnight GONG! Erin heard him say: "But now you should open the safe, then let me pick that lock so we can steal Bernie's diamonds and get ourselves gone."

Greed

AMY HEMPEL

MRS. GREED HAD been married for forty years, her husband the cuckold of all time. A homely man with a notable fortune, he escorted her on errands in the neighborhood. It was a point of honor with Mrs. Greed to say she would never leave him. No matter if her affection for him was surpassed by her devotion to others. Including, for example, my husband. If she was home at night in her husband's bed, did he care what she did with her days?

I was the one who cared.

Protected by men, money, and a lack of shame, Mrs. Greed had long been able to avoid what she had coming. She had the kind of glee that meant men did not think she slept around, they thought she had joie de vivre. They thought her a libertine, not a whore.

She had the means to indulge impetuous behavior and sleep through the mornings after nights she kept secret from her friends. She traveled the world, and turned into the person she could be in other places with people she would never see again.

She was many years older than my husband, running on the

fumes of her beauty. Hers had been a conventional beauty, and I was embarrassed by my husband's homage to it. Running through their rendezvous: a stream of regret that they had not met sooner.

He asked if she had maternal feelings for him. She said she was not sure what he wanted to hear. She told him she felt an erotic mix of passion and tenderness. If he wanted to think the tenderness maternal, let him.

When they met, he said, he had not hidden the fact that she looked like his mother, a glamorous woman who had been cruel to him and died when he was a boy. He had not said this to underscore her age, nor did she think it a fixation. She would have heard it as she felt it was intended: as a compliment, an added opportunity to bind them together. She would have been happy to be the good mother as well as the ultimate sensate. And see how her pleasure seeking brought pleasure to those around her!

A thing between them: green apples. Never red, always green. I knew when my husband had entertained Mrs. Greed because a trio of baskets in the kitchen would be filled with polished green apples. My husband claimed to like the look of them; I never saw him eat one. As soon as they would start to soften and turn brown, I would throw them out. And there would be the basket filled so soon again.

He told me he got them from the Italian market in town. But I checked, and the Italian market does not carry green apples.

What the green apples meant to them, I don't know, don't want to know. But she brought them each time she entered our house, and I felt that if I had not thrown the rotting ones out, he would have held on to every one of them. The way he fetishized these apples—it made him less attractive to me.

Mrs. Greed convinced her young lover, my husband, that she

was "not the type" to have "work" done, but she had had work done. She must have had a high threshold for pain. She could stay out of sight for the month or more of healing after each procedure. She had less success hiding the results of surgery on her spine. She claimed her athleticism had made it necessary, claimed a "sports injury" to lessen the horror of simple aging. But she could not hide the stiffness that followed, a lack of elasticity that marked her an old woman who crossed the street slowly in low-heeled shoes. I watched her cross the street like this, supported by my husband.

Maybe that was why she liked to hear complaints about his other women, that they were spoiled and petty, gossips who resented his involvement with her. Because he would not keep quiet about such a thing. At first, she felt the others had "won" because they could see him at any time. Then she saw that their availability guaranteed he would tire of them. They were impermanent, and she knew it before they did. So however much he pleaded with her to leave her husband, or at least see *him* more often, Mrs. Greed refused. It galled me that he wanted her more than she wanted him.

I listened to them often. I hooked up the camera to the computer when I was at home alone. For two hundred dollars I'd bought a hidden surveillance camera that was fitted into a book. I did not expect it to work. I left it next to the clock on the nightstand. I did not pay the additional seventy-five dollars that would have showed them to me in color. But the 90-degree field of view was adequate for our bedroom, and sound came in from up to seven hundred feet. Had this not worked so well, I would have stood in line for the camera that came hidden in a ceiling-mounted smoke detector.

Usually the things they said were exchanges of unforeseen delight and riffs of gratitude. But the last time I listened to them, my husband said something clever. Mrs. Greed sounded oddly winsome, said she sometimes wished the two of them had "waited." My husband told her they could *still* wait—they could wait a day, a week, a month—"It just won't be the *first* time," he said.

How she laughed.

I said to myself, "I am a better person!" I am a speech therapist who works with children. Parents say I change their lives. But men don't care about a better person. You can't photograph virtue.

I found the collection of photographs he had tried to hide. I liked that the photos of herself she brought to him were photos from so long ago. Decades ago. She wears old-fashioned bathing suits aboard sailboats with islands in the faded background. Let her note that the photographs of me that my husband took himself were taken in this bed.

Together, they lacked fear, I thought, to the extent that she told him to bring me to dinner at her house. With her husband. Really, this was the most startling thing I heard on playback. Just before the invitation, she told him she would not go to bed with the two of us. My husband was the one to suggest it. As though the two of us had talked it over, as if this were something I wanted! I heard her say, "I have to be the queen bee." Saw her say it.

She would not go to bed with us, but she would play hostess at dinner in her home.

I looked inside my closets, as though I might actually go. What does one wear for such an occasion? The corset dress? Something off the shoulder? Something to make me look older? But no dress existed for me to wear to this dinner. The dress had to do too much. It had to say: I am the sexy wife, and I will outlast you. It had to say: You are no threat to my happiness, and I will outlive you.

* * *

Down the street from our house, a car waited for Mrs. Greed. I knew, because I had taken note before, that a driver brought her to see my husband when I visited clients out of town. Was there a bar in the back of this car? I couldn't tell—the windows had a tint. Maybe she would not normally drink, but because there was a decanter of Scotch and she was being driven some distance at dusk, maybe she poured herself a glass and toasted her good luck?

This last thought reassured me. How was it this felt normal to me, to think of her being driven home after a tumble with my husband? I guess it depends on what you are used to. I knew a man who found army boot camp "touching," the attention he received from the drill sergeant, the way the army fed him daily. It was a comfort to him to know what each day would bring.

I felt there could be no compensation for being apart from my husband. Not for me, and not for her.

I knew I was supposed to be angry with *him*, not with her. She was not the first. She was the first he would not give up. But I could not summon the feelings pointed in the right direction. I even thought that killing her might be the form my *self*-destruction took. Had to take that chance. I tried to go cold for a time—when I thought of him, when I thought of her. But there was a heat and richness to what I conceived that made me think of times I was late to visit a place that my friends had already seen. When you discover something long after others have known it, there is a heady contentment that comes.

What I heard on the tapes after that: their relaxed relentlessness, impersonal intimacy, the air of resuming a rolling conversation that *we* had not been having. As though living in another dimension, a dimension I thought I could live in, too, once. Just take me there. Just teach me the new rules.

Watching them on camera I thought: What if I'm doing just what I'm supposed to be doing? And then I thought: I am.

The boys said they would give me a sign.

It was money well spent. With what I saved not needing to film in color, and knowing I would not need the standard two-year warranty, I had enough to pay the thuggish teens a client's son hung out with. The kid with the stutter had hinted he needed m-m-money. I will even give them a bonus—I will let them keep the surveillance camera hidden in the book after they send me the final tape.

Mrs. Greed does not live so far away that I will miss the ambulance siren.

And what to make of this? The apples my husband "bought," the green ones from the Italian market that does not carry green apples—I ate one on the front steps of our house and threw the core into the pachysandra. The next morning the core I had thrown was on the top step where I had been sitting when I ate it. I threw it again, this time farther out so it lodged in pine needles alongside the road in front of our house. The morning after that, today, the core was back in place on the top step.

Boys.

I thought: Let's see what happens next.

We have so many apples left.

Deer

JANICE Y. K. LEE

THEY CAME IN through the long, wooded driveway, opening the gate, struggling with their weekend bags, to find a deer at the bottom of the pool.

"What the fuck," Charlie said.

Boxer ran around the edge, barking at the large dark shape shimmering under the blue.

It had struggled. Part of the pool's vinyl siding had come off and was bobbing in the water. There was blood too. You could see it trailing from the wooden decking to the edge and then the water, slightly tinged around the carcass.

"Jesus," Maggie said. "It's Friday night. Who do we call?"

"Deerbusters?" said Frank, who was always making jokes that were not quite funny.

"What about 911?" Maggie said, ignoring him.

"Is this an emergency?" asked Frank's wife, Stella.

"I'll call the police," Maggie said.

They dropped off their bags in the kitchen and Maggie called information. Information always knew everything.

While they waited for the police to show up, Maggie showed

Frank and Stella their room while Charlie made vodka tonics. They greeted the police with drinks in hand, Boxer barking his head off, and watched as the men darted their flashlights across the pool. It was beginning to get dark.

"Oh, I'll get the pool lights," Maggie said. She darted up to the house. She still wasn't quite familiar with where everything was, but she finally located the switch by the barbecue.

"Poor thing," Stella said, when Maggie had come back down. She was looking at the deer. "What could have possessed it?"

"Deer aren't particularly smart, ma'am," said an officer dressed in some kind of brown uniform. The pool lights had come on and the deer was illuminated. It was sprawled at the bottom, with no visible sign of injury, other than the blood that clung around it in a slight mist. Boxer, bored with the nonactivity—all these delicious strangers and no action!—went back into the house.

After some hemming and hawing, the policemen, there were three in all, who had come in two cars—things must be slow up here—decided they would have to deal with it later.

"We'll call someone to pick it up," they said. "In the morning."

"Glad we could provide excitement," said Charlie. "Thanks for coming by."

After the cars left, Maggie and the guests went inside and sat around the dinner table while Charlie hosed off the deck.

"Should we eat?" Charlie said, coming in.

"It's so late already," Maggie said. "Let's just drink."

She was sitting across from Stella. Tired of smudgy brows and chalky pencils, Stella had recently gotten her eyebrows tattooed and now she couldn't go into the sun without a gigantic hat. Her forehead was still slightly inflamed, puffed out like there was excess fluid underneath. Maggie wondered if she pricked it with a pin, pus would seep out. Stella was pretty in a Snow White sort of way, with coal hair and porcelain skin and lips she slathered with red lipstick every five minutes. Maggie didn't really like her. The first time they had all met, some time last year, they had had dinner at a small restaurant and Stella had made a big deal about ordering three Gulf shrimp. "Just three shrimp," she had said imperiously to the waiter. When he had tried to explain that they only came in sixes, as in half a dozen, a dozen, et cetera, Stella had waved her heavily gold-ringed hand. "You figure it out," she said. Maggie had jumped in, saying she'd eat three too, so then they ordered a half dozen and she'd had to eat three shrimp that she didn't want to eat. Later, Charlie got mad at her, saying that she should have just left it alone, that Stella could have just eaten three and left the others. "Why are you always butting in?" he said. "Shut up," she said, but she knew he was right. She let people like Stella bother her.

"I like your shirt," she said to Stella by way of delayed apology for her uncharitable thoughts of the last year.

"Thanks," Stella said. She looked surprised.

"You're welcome," Maggie said.

"What about Scrabble?" Charlie said.

"No," said Maggie.

They sat in silence for a bit.

"Why not?" asked Stella cautiously.

"Oh, fine," Maggie said. "It's just that someone always gets in a fight."

They got out the Scrabble board and set up. Stella went into the bathroom. When she came out, she sidled over to Maggie.

"I changed the toilet roll," she said. "I mean, so that the paper goes over instead of under. I hope you don't mind."

"What?" Maggie said. She wondered if Stella was insane.

"It's just neater that way," Stella said. "It's easier to pull."

"Okay," Maggie said.

"You know, you can't mess around with people's housekeeping," Stella said confidentially.

"Oh, yes," Maggie said. "My housekeeping is very important to me. And to others," she added.

"Well, anyways," Stella slid into her seat. "The house is adorable."

"Shall we commence?" Frank said.

Stella was annoyingly good, one of those players who knew all the two- and three-letter words and kept racking up double digits in every turn. Maggie felt her competitive spirit kick in.

"Isn't it interesting," she said, "that one does not need a big vocabulary to be good at Scrabble."

Charlie shot her a warning look, but she didn't care.

"I'm not good at much of anything," Stella said placidly. "But I'm okay at Scrabble because I figured out all the tricks."

Frank spelled *aurora.*

"Nice," Maggie said. "That's a pretty word." Stella spelled *xray,* decisively plunking down the *x* last, with her crimson-nailed fingers.

"Very dramatic," Maggie said. "The way you put down the *x* last."

Charlie spelled *tax*. Maggie put her hands on her face in mock despair.

"I have all vowels," she said.

Charlie got her another drink.

"Take it easy, tiger," he said.

"What is it that graphic designers do?" Frank asked. "It's one of those jobs I hear about but never really understand what the day-to-day is like."

Maggie looked up.

"Well, it's a lot of sitting in front of Macs and fiddling around," she said.

"What does that mean?" Frank said.

"It's all on computers now," she said. "So it's quite different from the old days with glue and paste."

"Oh," Frank said. "I don't own a computer. Can you believe that?"

"No," Maggie said. "Actually, I can't."

Stella spelled *quick* on a triple word score.

"Sorry," she said, looking at Maggie.

Later, the game lost, Stella decidedly the victor, they all retired to bed. It was almost one.

Charlie massaged Maggie's shoulders like she was a defeated wrestler, hopeful of rewards.

"She's horrible," Maggie said. "And Boxer hates her too."

"Oh, give her a chance," said Charlie. "She's not that bad."

"Excuse me," Maggie said. "*Gi* is *not* a word."

But she gave in anyways. It wasn't Charlie's fault.

Part of the reason Charlie had asked Frank and Stella up was because he needed a favor from Frank. A favor called twenty thousand dollars. Frank was a childhood friend of Charlie's and was making a bundle of money in real estate, even in the current downturn. He hadn't gone to college but straight into his father's lumber business, and then he'd bought a small strip mall, which grew into a dozen. He had moved to the city last year from Baltimore and was trying his hand at property development in the Big Apple, as he called it. Maggie was on the fence about whether that was endearing or not. They lived in an enormous postwar condo on Seventieth and First Avenue. Maggie and Charlie had been to dinner there once, and all the furniture had been black.

Maggie and Charlie had been financially stable, but they had gone a little, okay, a lot, overboard in the stock market and now they were hurting. They were behind in their mortgage payments and maxed out on credit cards and family goodwill. The rental, paid for before the big, big crash, when the market cratered on that terrible Thursday, had sent them hurtling toward actual, real insolvency, and the rental had been nonrefundable. If Frank said no, they didn't know what else they would do. Maggie was not on board for asking him, but Charlie was insistent, saying that it wouldn't be a big deal, that Frank would do it in a second, without any strings or weirdness. Maggie wanted to believe him. She liked to believe in her husband.

Charlie was easygoing, lovely. They had met six years ago—he was that rare thing, a lawyer without an ax to grind, and she was charmed. "I don't know nothin' about culture," he drawled sarcastically on their first date. He thought her job was creative, something she hadn't thought in years. He taught her about calmness, closeness, and, often, human decency.

Over lunch the next day, Frank told them about what a good shopper Stella was.

"She can tell from the actual clothes what size it is. She never has to look at the tag!"

"Only at certain stores," Stella said. "Like at Banana Republic, I know which one is mine, from like a distance of six feet!"

They had set up a little deli line next to the pool, with ham and turkey, white bread, pickles, and mayonnaise. A partially unwrapped Camembert was melting in the sun. Maggie was not a natural host.

"Lunch al fresco," Charlie said. "With a view of the deer. We can go swimming after lunch—it'll be just like nature, swimming with dead things and chlorine."

"Only after fifteen minutes, though," Maggie said.

Everyone looked at her.

"I mean, after our food's digested? Like mothers always say?"

Frank stared at her, then continued to mayonnaise his bread. "Is there any onion?" he asked. Charlie went in to slice some.

Maggie's jaw ached. She wondered if she had cancer. "I have a canciferous jaw," she said to herself. Canciferous. Surely that wasn't a word. She chewed on her sandwich. Boxer came over and sat heavily in front of her. She gave him the rest.

"Frank killed somebody once," Charlie said later, when she was washing the dishes. "Did I tell you?"

Maggie swiveled around, putting her soapy hands on her hips before she remembered, but it was too late. The lather dripped down.

"Uh, *no*," she said. "Did you think you told me?" The pose she was in now felt fake, orchestrated, and completely silly, with her wet pants.

"No," he said. "But I thought I'd try to slip it in." He paused. "It was an accident though. He didn't mean to kill him. It was in high school and we were all drunk. He got in a fight with someone who had started talking to his girlfriend at a party, and then it got kind of ugly."

"Ugly?" Maggie said. "What does ugly mean? Knife? Gun? Naked hands?"

"Bare hands, I guess," Charlie said. "He punched him and the guy fell into a china cabinet and then the glass cut him up and he bled to death on the way to the hospital. It was awful."

"Oh, was it?" Maggie said. "I thought it might have been rather pleasant."

"Don't start," Charlie said. "Just don't start."

Maggie pointed a soapy finger at her husband.

"Don't you 'don't start' me," she said. "Don't you dare." She thought. "Did he do *time*?"

"No," Charlie said. "He was a minor so he had to do some community service. But it was awful. His parents moved away and I didn't see him for many years." He paused.

"But the weird thing was, after the guy was taken away in the ambulance, and the police were there, Frank never looked sorry. I mean, he was drunk off his ass and barely coherent, but even after, when he had sobered up, he never looked like he was sorry he had done it. That's what disturbed people in the community and I think why they had to move, because people began to say he was a sociopath."

"So, he's a hardened criminal . . ."

Frank and Stella came in.

"You are melodramatic," Charlie said to Maggie with a meaningful stare.

"I believe in law and order," she said.

"Do you think we should call to remind the police about the deer?" Stella said. "It's kind of ominous to have it out there."

"Sure," Maggie said.

No one did anything.

In the afternoon, Stella sat out in the sun with a big blue hat—those fragile, puffy eyebrows—and a *Lucky* magazine, and Frank and Charlie went to hit balls at the golf range. Maggie went for a walk around the Ashokan Reservoir and spotted eight live deer. She counted.

Charlie had told her he was going to ask Frank while they hit golf balls but when they came back, she could tell he had not.

She was relieved. She still wanted to talk him out of it. The more she saw of Frank and Stella, the less she wanted to be beholden to them.

She took a shower before dinner and cut herself on a jagged piece of metal in the shower-door frame. The blood welled up from her shin, again and again, forming plump red drops. She blotted with wadded-up sheets of toilet paper and threw them in the garbage, where they looked like scarlet poppies.

At dinner, they drank too much again, Frank making margaritas with the mix and tequila they had brought up with them as a gift. Maggie made a roast with garlic and blood-orange chutney. This, despite the hot weather. Again, she was not a natural host. Frank took half the slices off the plate.

"Hungry?" Maggie said.

"Starving," he said.

Despite all this, Maggie was starting to like Stella. This happened after a third margarita and because she had spied Stella stomping, without panic, on an enormous water bug that afternoon. True, she had had flip-flops on, but it made Maggie feel calm to see her dispatch the bug without any feminine hysteria. Then they had a good exchange about mothers.

"After my mother visited," Stella said, "she destroyed all my relationships with the local vendors. My dry cleaner wouldn't talk to me for a month."

"What'd she do?" Maggie said, intrigued. She spooned more salad onto Stella's plate.

"The usual," she said mildly. "Haranguing, accusing, complaining. She accused the deli of padding my charge account. She doesn't trust the New York way of doing things—she's never lived in a city."

"What can you do?" Maggie said. She was impressed with

Stella's placid face. Maggie talked to her mother once every couple of months and hadn't physically seen the woman in three years.

"Really," Stella said. "Mothers."

"Do you think about children?" Maggie asked.

"Almost never," Stella said.

Frank harrumphed.

"Pretty much never," Stella said.

Frank had been silent for a while and his quiet had become more menacing. Stella chattered on as if she didn't notice her glowering husband.

"A woman I know was diagnosed with lymphoma and after she got out of the doctor's office, she stepped off the curb and was hit by a FedEx truck," she said to Maggie. "Dead as a doornail."

"What's the point?" Maggie said.

"Right," Stella said. "That's really it."

"You know, I didn't like you," Maggie said after a pause. She decided to go on. "When we first met. The shrimp incident."

"What?" Stella said. "Shrimp?"

"You ordered three shrimp when you could only order six or twelve."

"Really?" Stella said, laughing. "I did?"

"Yeah, and I thought you were really obnoxious."

"Oh," Stella said. "I remember now. We were at Dominico's, right? I had gone to my therapist that day and he said I needed to be more assertive and shape the world my way and not shape myself to fit the world. Plus, I was on a diet."

"Oh," Maggie said, overwhelmed. "Good memory."

"Funny how it all leads to something, yes?" Stella said agreeably. "You had a different picture of me."

"When I'm friends with someone," Maggie said, "I like

remembering how I first saw them. I'm only right about people half of the time."

"Well, that's big of you to say," Stella said. "I didn't like you until a few hours ago."

Maggie was quiet.

"But I like you now," Stella said.

"Thanks," said Maggie. She felt abashed.

"You women are annoying me," Frank said. His voice was so quiet that it didn't register for a half beat.

"Stop it, Frank," Stella said.

"You're fucking yammering on and on about this *shit*," he said. His eyes were glittering and he moved slowly and deliberately as he raised his hand up to emphasize *shit*. Maggie hadn't realized quite how drunk he was.

"Frank," Charlie said. "Take it easy."

"You take it easy," Frank said. "College boy."

"Frank is a bad drunk," Stella said. "Aren't you, honey?"

"No, I'm not," he said. "I am not a bad drunk. And I'm not drunk."

"Frank," Stella said, changing tacks. "Please don't."

"I'll make coffee," Maggie said, getting up.

Frank stood up too. They faced each other across the table.

"I don't need coffee," he said. He looked at her with his bright blue eyes, and Maggie realized what a handsome man he was. His cheeks flushed as if he knew what she was thinking.

"You," he said. "You don't like me."

"No," she said. "You're mistaken. It was your wife I didn't like, remember?" She fell into the condescending voice that people sometimes use with drunks.

"No," he said. "You don't like me. I can tell. You think I can't tell?" He swayed forward, caught himself with his hands on the table, getting one partially on a plate so it clattered, loudly. "You think you're too good for me—you and Charlie and your college degrees."

Charlie put an arm around Frank.

"Hey, buddy," he said. "Don't talk silly."

Frank put a hand up and pushed Charlie away. His hand, covered with chutney, left a mark on Charlie's shirt that looked like blood.

"I don't need your pity, guy," he said. "I'm a millionaire!"

"Yes, yes, good for you, honey," Stella said. "Let's go to bed."

Maggie went to the kitchen to make coffee. She filled the pot with cold water at the sink. When she turned around, Frank was right in front of her. He pressed up next to her, pushing her against the sink, his right hip against her left.

"Does that feel safe?" he asked. "Do you feel in danger?"

"Hey," Charlie said evenly. "Get away from Maggie right now."

Frank leaned her back, his hand supporting her back, and kissed her, hard. She melted, as if that might save her. When she opened her eyes he was staring at her, mean.

But it didn't come to anything. Stella appeared, quick as silver, and dragged her husband away. She was very strong, the little woman with her gold rings and her tattooed eyebrows. She dragged him away to their room, shut the door, and they didn't emerge for the rest of the night, even to get a glass of water.

They had sex because they had to. What else to fix the broken night? It was silent, fraught, awful. She looked at the ceiling. In the morning, they brushed their teeth, aware of the stillness outside. They stayed inside as long as they could.

A few months later, long after they had dropped Frank and Stella off, Stella apologizing and apologizing, after they had received a wire transfer of twenty-five thousand dollars from Frank, after they had—outrageously!—been billed by some contractor for the eventual removal of the deer, Maggie was at CVS picking up some film she had had developed from an old camera she had found at the house, one of those disposable ones. She walked outside, opening the white packet. Paging through the snapshots, an office party, a night at a bar to celebrate a friend's birthday, all of a sudden she saw Frank giving the camera the finger. She let out a short bark of surprise. He was in the living room of the summer house and he was laughing. He must have had Stella take the photo while she and Charlie were out of the room, early on in the weekend, before anything happened. It must have been earlier. She looked at the photo, shiny in the sun, already smudged with her fingerprints, Frank's face alive and vibrant, lit by the harsh light of the flash, and she couldn't say why she, of all people, felt ashamed.

The Salon
JONATHAN LETHEM

THE TIME I feel most like a spy is sitting in the hairdresser's chair—I can't be certain why that should be. I suppose it is because it is a place where I both lie about myself and watch others carefully through mirrors. The reason for my prevarications is the same reason I submit myself impulsively and too often to the shears: There is a kind of unbearable intimacy in a haircut, which for me is a kind of guilty secret. I create oversimplifications or whole diversions, falsify my career (which is in fact nonexistent), declare travel plans I never mean to enact. The talk between a stylist or barber and a client is always so insouciantly familiar, and so my response is to shroud myself within a cover story, to reserve something of myself for myself. This also probably explains my tendency to vanish after a year or two as a given hairdresser's client, then to forever avoid returning to the hairdresser in question. I'm a serial monogamist of the salon, faithful before I flee.

In some essay, the title of which I've forgotten, John Updike explored the erotic dynamics of a visit to the dental hygienist; though fascinated, I couldn't empathize. For me, it is under the hands of a hairdresser, whether a sexually ambiguous or plainly homosexual young man or, more agreeably, a young woman, that I feel myself unfold into a luxurious passivity. I myself am no longer young. Yet in my abstemious way, and due to the neatness of my dress, the precision of my carriage, and, of course, the regular upkeep of the boundary of short hairs at my neck and ears, I maintain the outlines of my youthful allure. Few heterosexual men bother, I find, with this sort of effort, making me quietly anomalous. I've observed young women glancing at me on the street at a distance of half a block, only to see their faces tighten at closer sight of the lines around my lips and eyes, unBotoxed disclosers of my vintage.

I find myself most aware of the paradoxes of age and attraction—most pleasantly aware, I should say—when a hairdresser caresses my tipped-back skull in the shampooing or rinsing phases of a visit. No one can argue the sensuality of fingers spidering through wet strands to knead the crown or temples, and I don't think I'm mistaken to detect the lingering, the pleasure-in-giving-pleasure, that invariably accompanies my shampoos. Sometimes this task is relegated to the assistants, those not yet cutting hair—often these are young but relatively unattractive women assisting women more beautiful than themselves, or dapper gay men. The shampoo or rinse, then, is their moment. What would be an unbearably mercenary transaction in the larger erotic sphere—my age traded against their homeliness—becomes charming. For an instant they are lavishing their touch on a man more elegant than would usually even glance at them. For an instant my enjoyment of their touch is undeniable, and total. At the very apex I might feel the soft blurred pressure of a breast or the firmer nudge of a hip bone as the shampooist leans over me. Then a rolled towel is placed under my ears and along my neck, and I am escorted from foamy dreams into the more sustained if less fulsome encounter, that with the murmuring scissors.

The girls at my present salon are expatriate Israelis, rendered enchantingly tough and stubborn by their kibbutz lives, yet sweetly naïve about American life even as they rightly judge their American contemporaries softer, blurrier, less courageous and forthright than themselves. My only previous experience with young Israelis had been with the men and boys who seem lately to dominate New York's intracity furniture-moving companies, and whom I've several times had tramping through my apartments, diligently duct-taping chests and armoires with thin quilts to insulate the corners and feet from damage in stairwells or from the bumping of their truck in potholes. Much like my girls', their English is impeccable and strange, their eyes full of alertness both to opportunity and to the local ironies of New York City, where the lives of the wealthy are pressed in close adjacency to those of the indigent. The young Israelis strike me almost as return émigrés from the moon or Mars, persistently amazed that we feel we can afford to sustain the old rituals back here on earth. The girls of my salon, three of them, Marina, Larissa, and Maja, in the employ of one older and rarely glimpsed whose name I've heard and forgotten, seem to wear their bustiers and makeup like soldiers off duty, on a leave from which they may at any time be recalled. I think it might be fair to say I love them. And yet I am beginning to make myself ready for farewells. I'll try to explain.

Their salon is in the West Village, where I like to stroll. Yesterday, feeling the urge for a cut, I chanced dropping in without an appointment just after eleven, while Larissa and Maja were still preparing the room for the day's first clients, sweeping yesterday's missed clippings, lining shears and clippers in their places. Larissa is the uglier duckling, so of course it was her with the broom; such pecking orders are remorseless. Marina, the star cutter and nearest to glamorous, her column in the appointment book always fullest, hadn't arrived. Maja checked for me and determined that Marina could fit me in at two thirty. Perfect, I told them; I had a lunch date at twelve thirty, and would be free just in time. In fact I sat by the river and alternated between reading Mary McCarthy's *Cast a Cold Eye* and watching Rollerbladers. I bought a hot dog and chunked the bun to toss at pigeons.

I don't know whether I'd detected a trace of pensiveness in my Israelis when I made the appointment or only felt it in retrospect. Certainly, there was no mistaking the ripple of disquiet when I returned. I received my shampoo at the hands of Larissa while Marina finished with an earlier appointment, a woman my age whose hair had of course been steeping in dye while she paged through every magazine in their supply, and now needed a bit of fluffing and teasing for the climax of what must have been nearly a two-hour visit. The other chair was empty for the moment. Placed in her care, Marina was her usual deft lovely self, able to begin turning up wet layers to snip while she commenced our typical small talk, small inquiries the replies to which she didn't attend, jokes about the frequency of my haircuts, her comb and scissors moving with unconscious grace. But when the older woman had paid and stuffed a twenty in Marina's palm for a tip, then departed, Marina took a step backward, as if needing to examine my hair strategically (surely she didn't), while Larissa slipped in with a wide broom to expertly gather the scribble of fallen hairs from around my shoes into a pad like a moist black toupee, which she then scooped off into the trash. Maja, who, without a client of her own at the moment had lingered behind the counter, studying the appointment book, was suddenly attentive too.

"Did you read in the newspaper about the woman who was killed?" asked Marina.

"No . . ." I spoke absently, contemplating in the mirror a minor asymmetry in the contour of my temples, one always exposed by close cropping. "A particular woman, you mean?"

"Yes, last week. The headline of the paper called it JANE STREET CHAIR HORROR. She was one of Maja's clients." Marina approached the subject with that marvelous Israeli bluntness. For these poor girls, I suppose, the New York *Daily News* was "the newspaper."

"Ah, I'm so sorry." I could see the three had knit into a mourning society. I didn't want to blunt their sense of injustice by pointing out how the city periodically thrilled to the death of a single woman of a certain class, milieu, whereas the attention paid would have been almost incalculably less overwrought, and therefore less vicariously interesting to them, had, say, one of them been murdered in the Greenpoint or Kew Gardens neighborhoods they called home—let alone if yet another young black man had been slain near a housing project. Ironically, that the privileges seemingly available to their well-off clients but not to themselves could be so abruptly revoked by violence was perhaps more deranging to the Israeli girls' worldview than had been the kind of everyday urban risk that had likely spurred their emigration.

Marina stepped back in and placed the scissors to one side. She lay a gentle fingertip at the bottom edge of the perfectly squared sideburns she'd created, testing their rightness as a carpenter tests a shelf with a level. "Are you happy with the length? Her name was Jessica Droory."

Was she testing me? "Yes, the length is perfect as usual, Marina, thank you. Could you do something about—?" I waved vaguely around my ears and nose, knowing she'd understand, but also that she'd wait until I asked, never presume. I've long since shed any embarrassment at requesting the pruning of my nostrils or ear canals. In fact I look forward to this moment, another sensual treat, for me if not for Marina. Though, who knows?

"You might remember her," said Marina lightly, or with a semblance of lightness. Was it my imagination that the others had halted their activities to listen? Well, it was a quiet day, and I was undoubtedly interesting to them, nourishment for the starved.

"Yes?"

Marina gestured at the open chair, visible in the wall of mirror before me, along with the whole tableau of Maja and Larissa, the overelaborate, trying-too-hard decor of their workplace, the counter bearing the telephone, computer, and appointment book, and a tantalizing sliver of window onto the wide world outside their door. Passing sidewalkers appear and vanish in this margin as brief, almost strobelike flashes of clothing, flesh, hair, and other clues for the visual cortex to sort in retrospect: Was that a cell phone? Or mirrored sunglasses? "Maja cut her hair right there beside you the last time I saw you."

"Really?" I said.

"Yes."

I shrugged. "You know how often I come here. And I always reserve my attention for you, Marina."

"I thought you might remember."

"Sorry."

This conversation wasn't interesting. Very much my fault; I was quashing any interest. If Marina had been pushing, she'd gone as far as she dared, and now we reverted to platitudes concerning the weather, the desirability of vacations from New York City during blazing summer months, the price of real estate, and my imaginary workdays, which evidently left plenty of time for haircuts, though this as ever went unremarked. After she'd worked a few products into my scalp and rearranged my part a dozen times until sculpted into just the effect she thought best (I always wash the gunk out as soon as I arrive at home and revert to a "dry look"), Marina declared me finished. With all the usual ritual delight at the cut's result and studied affection for Marina and the others I paid, tipped, and departed, only promising—in a mock-threatening way—that they'd sure see me two weeks from now. Thinking all the time that it was probably the last time I'd set foot in the place, or even walk down that particular block of the city.

I remembered Jessica Droory, of course I did. It is another eccentricity of salons such as that run by the Israelis that they fantasize not only about their clients but on their behalves. What I mean to say is that in a career dedicated to the vanity of others, hairdressers understandably become champions of more than hair, but of lives, of yearning bodies made more attractive and confident and then sent out into the world to entice other bodies. Jessica Droory was one who, unlike myself, was surely entirely truthful in her convivial self-revelations to hairstylists, masseurs, pedicurists, anyone. She'd gone months without an interesting date (I'm guessing here); wasn't noticing heads turning as often as previously; wondered if at thirty-seven (this I confirmed in the newspaper's reports) life's romantic parade was getting too far up the road, around some bend beyond sight of her ditched vehicle.

Jessica was healthy, thin, not unappealing—the Israeli girls liked her chances, I suspect, and felt no bad faith in being optimistic on her behalf. Did she want to marry? Where did she go to meet men? Did she use Nerve? Would she consider someone older, more serious? It took men in New York a while to grow disenchanted with the singles scene, but it happened eventually.

Of course, all such talk would have been silenced by the time I walked in that afternoon and filled the second chair. Most of their discussion would anyway have been glancing, peppery, apparently incidental, in no way revealing its underlying purposefulness nor the insinuating force of the identification between the impossibly youthful Israeli women and the older New Yorker who'd begun to wonder if she teetered on the brink of the middle-aged, and had surely, yes, begun to think a man a decade or two older wasn't the worst possibility in the world. He'd only have to be appreciative. And not have a paunch, or some awful gray beard.

So, when I entered my sensorium that day, I found it altered. The girls who'd never once have considered me seriously as a prospect for themselves were more than comfortable with my sexual personhood through the proxy of Jessica Droory. Far from being possessive of the weird edgy air of flirtation that hovered around my presence in their space, the insertion of Jessica Droory as a rather more appropriate focal point relieved them of a certain anxiety, put a good solid normative footing behind it all. They were matchmakers! None of this would have been in the least enunciated, even to themselves. But framed together in that vast mirror, Jessica Droory and I found our chairs subtly angled together. Marina and Larissa were more effusive with me, the fingertips in my scalp and briefly resting on my shoulders even more lingering and enticing, as though their hands could serve in place of hers while Jessica and I, two heads tucked atop pyramidal black aprons, were efficiently serviced while we looked for a place for our eyes to rest other than on one another—and in this effort helplessly failed. I smiled. She blinked surprise, then split the difference, smiling back briefly and shifting her eyes to her hands where they bunched under her apron, or to the furry floor.

And the talk became deliberate, wretchedly obvious. They didn't introduce us, didn't break that mystical fourth wall of their profession, but instead interviewed us in tandem, asking questions the answers to which they perfectly well knew, Jessica's truths, my lies. Career, birthplace, status. The scripted-seeming pauses in these oh-so-casual twin interrogations, intervals devised to make certain the replies were sinking in, revealed the Israeli girls as aspiring directors of a one-act play, one in which Jessica Droory and I were cast both as the audience and, eventually, the star performers, even if the final act was intended to take place out of view of the directors themselves.

Their pièce de résistance, their showstopper, was a piece of timing: By slowing my haircut to a crawl, Marina managed to have us reach a conclusion at nearly the same moment. Jessica Droory was released from her chair, to pay and tip, and then delayed with chatter, a charade with which Jessica cooperated, it seemed to me. Meanwhile I was finished too, and freed to reclaim my jacket and to step to the counter to pay. They'd orchestrated it so that we might leave at the same moment, and then find one another available for conversation on the pavement, leading perhaps to coffee, an exchange of phone numbers or cards—nearly anything was possible, wasn't it?

This I wrecked deliberately, with a pantomime of my own. I keep a no-good credit card in my wallet, just for such occasions, decorated with the name I've assumed, and though I'd always previously paid the Israeli girls with cash, this was obviously the moment to employ it. Most people, I find, are plagued with shame at the refusal of a credit transaction; American class definitions are so insecure that a small plastic failure can threaten to undermine them, and in fact the tradespeople who are forced to deliver the bad news are often drawn into shame themselves. This was not my situation, obviously, but I do find such discomfort both useful and entertaining. When Larissa handed back my card with an apology, I smiled and handed it back to her and insisted she try again. Ripples of awkwardness spread through the salon, as Maja was forced to struggle to delay Jessica Droory further. Jessica Droory already had her coat on. The card failed again, of course. Larissa suggested sheepishly that I might have another one. Jessica Droory, embarrassed to be stalling, moved for the door. I asked Larissa please to call the company and inquire as to the problem, since, I insisted, the card was perfectly good. (It is astonishing, or perhaps not, how few people in her position feel able to refuse such a request.) Jessica Droory at last went through the door, smiling as bravely as she could in my direction, but there was nothing to be done. Perhaps she'd idled on the sidewalk an instant or two, but I made certain enough time passed in my dumb show with the credit card that the Israeli girls could entertain no hope whatsoever that we'd meet outside. Meanwhile, with Larissa occupied on the telephone and Maja washing the hair of Marina's next customer, an older woman (I mean, a woman my age) who'd entered in the meantime, I leaned over the appointment book. Jessica Droory's phone number was written beside her name, as was my own. I memorized it, just for sport.

When I dialed the number at nine the next evening, that was for sport as well. I sometimes think my life is nothing but sport. Likely Jessica Droory was in her robe and pajamas by then (I'd find these later, on the pegs of the bathroom door), settling in to watch *Lost,* but, supposing my guess was right, she had the self-respect not only to let her phone ring a few times but to mute the television in the background. I explained where we'd met, as swiftly and courteously as I could, then interrupted myself and asked if I'd made a mistake, and that it was too late to telephone her? An unfair question: She'd never have admitted so, and by assuring me that no apology was needed Jessica Droory eased herself past other, perfectly valid objections to what was surely a disconcerting call.

I could have made it easier on both of us, I suppose, by calling at seven instead of nine. Yet even as recently as eight o'clock I'd been deaf to the summons of my appetite, while after the passage of barely less than an hour more it had become too clarion to ignore, or even to defer to the following evening. Such is appetite. And I do like to walk a tightwire, sometimes, just seeing what people might actually balk at. They so rarely do. On that same score, who am I to say that Jessica Droory shouldn't have let me inside? I appreciated her self-possession and daring, even, in reaching for what was before her, or seemingly so. That we had in common. Beginning with the really exquisite contents of her liquor cabinet, her apartment, a parlor-level floor-through, was superbly appointed for my purposes, the high ceilings and heavy sashed curtains giving us privacy and making a nice proscenium for my foolish indulgences. Very little of her liquor had to be poured before I was able to beguile the giggling Jessica into a reenactment of "how we met": two chairs in the center of her parlor room, in front of the large framed mirror I'd moved to the floor for this purpose. More drinks, pantomime haircuts, mock Israeli accents. How obvious those girls had been in steering us together—how poignant, really, their surrogate yearning! My hands invaded Jessica's clothes while we parsed the paltriness of the salon, judged the abjectness of the girls' makeup and dress sense, all of it giving sweet sustenance to Jessica Droory's need to believe that youthfulness, that svelte, kibbutz-firmed flesh, wasn't enough to turn the head of a man of substance, rather that style and poise and experience meant something, and that that was why I had called her telephone and arrived at her door and why she was cross-eyed drunk and half undressed in a chair, pretending to let me shampoo her while my cock pressed against her ear. We fumbled along like this until Jessica's eyelids sagged once or twice, then it was time enough. Curtain sashes more than sufficient to bind her limbs to the chair's legs. Her own shredded blouse to muffle cries. Then a search. That it was pinking shears I found was pure accident; I savor those serendipities which distinguish one adventure from another. The rest you know. You read the *Daily News,* don't you?

So it was that I had to find another salon. I'll miss Maja and Larissa and most of all Marina, and I suppose you may wonder why it was necessary to ruin a good thing. Sometimes I wonder this myself. But really, women such as these and myself were never meant for one another; this sort of vicarious transmission is the only thing possible between us. No matter how imperfect our actual encounter, a woman like Jessica Droory and I come from one world, the same world, while the girls at the salon come from entirely another. They're not, finally, my type. In truth, I'd never so much as touch a hair on their heads.

Tricks

LAURA LIPPMAN

HE IS AWARE of the glances they attract as they cross the lobby of the Hotel Monteleone, but doubts she even notices. She is too busy looking at him. Her gaze is like a stray hair on his cheekbone—light yet irritating, hard to brush away. He's much too handsome for her. Everyone sees it. Even she sees it. She clearly cannot believe her good luck.

She shouldn't.

He, however, is flush with luck, the luck that comes only with due diligence and hard work. You don't find a mark like this by accident. It takes weeks and, at first, moving patiently and slowly, building a rapport. It takes a little money, too, to appear as flush as he claims to be. This suit he's wearing, the Hermès tie, the Gucci loafers—those things cannot be faked. Stolen, on occasion, but never faked.

However, that's phase one. Moving on to phase two now, the honeymoon, literal and figurative, where everything will be on her. Also literally and figuratively.

They approach the registration desk and she is all fluttery, old-fashioned enough to think that the hotel cares whether they are husband and wife yet. "Darling, lots of women don't take their husbands' names," he assured her when he told her to make the reservation. "I would," she said. "I can't wait to take your name."

And I can't wait to take whatever you have to give. But there will be time enough. Time enough to settle in, to move into her house in the Pacific Palisades, the one in all the pictures she has sent him. Time, too, to persuade her to tap into the equity, which he will use for his can't-fail business venture. That part is true—it never fails, not where he's concerned. He makes a profit every time, no matter what's going on in the economy.

"Olive Dunne," she says to the clerk in her little mouse of a voice. God, if he really had to live with that voice until death did them part, he would soon be exhausted from leaning in, the better to hear her. She's a timid one. They run to timidity, his brides, but she's especially shy, irritatingly shy. The courtship was an unusually long one, almost three months since he sent his first e-mail, and that doesn't include the start-up costs, the search process on various matchmaking sites. But once he gets her in bed, she will be his.

He hands the clerk his new credit card, the one Olive presented him with just this morning when they met face-to-face for the first time at Louis Armstrong International Airport. She was the one who offered to add him to her account after he explained how the problems in the financial markets overseas were tying up all his accounts, threatening this long-planned rendezvous. The clerk takes them in. The clerk takes *him* in—his tailored suit, the Hermès tie, the Armani sunglasses. All the real thing, purchased with his own scarce dollars, the cost of doing business; he should be able to deduct them from his income tax. Not that he pays income taxes, but why should he, when the system is rigged against the working man? And make no mistake about it, he works hard for his money. He's like a soldier, or someone on an oil rig. When he gets a gig, it's 24-7, no time off for weeks. Sometimes the highlight of his day is his morning crap, the only time he gets to be himself, by himself.

The clerk upgrades them to the Tennessee Williams suite, but it's not quite as grand as he'd hoped. Nice enough, but he's seen better. Olive, however, is overwhelmed by the smallest things—the galley kitchen, which is nothing more than a noisy minifridge and a coffeemaker, the enormous glass box of a shower stall, the fact that there's a dining room table. "It's like an apartment," she says over and over. She flits from window to window, taking in the views of the French Quarter, exclaiming over everything.

"What do you want to do first?" she asks.

He thinks that's pretty obvious, although it's not what he *wants* to do first, but what he knows he should want to do first.

He takes her in his arms, closes his eyes, and thinks of . . . his mind scans several images, actresses, and models, settles on the literal girl next door, Betty. She used to anoint herself with baby oil and offer herself up to the sun, moving her ratty old lounge chair as the shadows crept over her, hour by hour. That was out in Metairie, barely ten miles from here, where he grew up. Betty was always on her back when he saw her, breasts pointing to the heavens, yet her tan was very even. She was five years older; he had no shot, the gulf between twelve and seventeen too huge. When he started out, the women were five years older, ten years older, fifteen years older. He likes older women. Olive is his first younger woman in a long time and she has a trim little figure beneath her dowdy suit. He caresses her promisingly firm little rump and thinks of Betty, wonders if Viagra is going to be added to the list of his professional expenses, but, no, thank goodness, he's going to be able—

"Not now," she whispers, pulling away. "Not yet. Maybe I'm old-fashioned, but I want to wait until I'm your bride. Besides, didn't you say you wanted to call your bank, straighten out what's going on with your credit cards?"

"My bank is in London," he says, "and that's six hours ahead. They're closed for today."

The story, this time, is that he's a victim of identity theft and all his credit cards, even his ATM card, are "locked" until he can talk to his personal money manager. He discovered this problem when he and Olive began planning their trip a week ago, and she quickly agreed—volunteered, in fact—to add him to her credit card account, even procured an extra ATM card for him, which he used this morning to pull out the maximum amount. "Because a man needs to have cash," she said. "Walking-around money, my daddy called it."

Yes, indeed. A man does need money to walk around. And even more to walk out. How much will Olive be good for? Assuming she can get a second mortgage, the house in California must have at least a half million in it. He's looked up the property records and she's owned it for at least ten years.

"Do you want to walk around?" he asks her. "Go shopping? See if we can get a table at Galatoire's?"

"Could we"—she is blushing, furiously—"walk along Bourbon Street? When I was twelve, my church group came to New Orleans to compete in a chorale competition, but they kept us out near the airport, never let us get near the city proper."

"Of course we can, baby. I'll buy you a big ol' drink, if you like, and we'll walk along Bourbon Street."

He's no stranger to Bourbon Street. His life tricking began here, almost twenty-five years ago, and that's how he always thought of it: *tricking*. Not hustling, but engaging in a fantasy with a consenting adult, and how was that any different from someone paying money to go see a magician? Almost too good-looking as a young man, he decided early on to find out what that commodity was really worth, to test how high the sky was, what one could procure with a pretty face and a great body. Back then he had sex with men and women alike, and while he found some good sugar daddies in his salad days, he also discovered that men were a little harder to control. He lived almost six months with an older man, Jacques, in a mansion Uptown. They had an argument one night, and it had been shocking how quickly it escalated. The old queen had beat him up pretty bad—and *he* had ended up being charged with assault somehow, not that he stayed around to face the music. He had decided then and there to stick to women for business.

Besides, with women, there is the possibility of marriage in all fifty states. And with marriage, there is so much more access to whatever wealth they have, and no one in the world can call it a con, what happens between husbands and wives. Sure, some of them made him sign prenups, but prenups didn't matter when a man never bothered with the formality of divorce. He got whatever cash there was, he moved on. He's lost count of how many times he's been married by now. Twelve, thirteen? Yeah, he's pretty sure that little Olive is going to be number thirteen. And she hasn't breathed a word about wanting a prenup. She's a pliable one, a sheltered girl whose parents, before they died, had spent most of their time telling her that she had to beware fortune hunters, that no one would ever love her just for her.

The Internet was both friend and foe in his business. A few ex-wives had set up blogs, tried to spread the word about him, but his name always changed just enough so that a Google search wouldn't kick him out. A background check under his original name—that's what he really lived in fear of, but no one knows his real name or Social Security number. He barely remembers his real name or Social Security number. Besides, the gals never run that kind of background check. They don't want to. They buy into the fantasy willingly. They know themselves, what their prospects really are. They don't want to question too closely why this handsome, rich man is on an Internet dating site, much less why he is interested in them, writing them flowery e-mails.

Relatives, however, can be skeptical. That's why all-alone-in-the-world-Olive, as he thinks of her, is such a prize. A few years back, he dated a woman whose daughter was clearly skeptical of him, based on the e-mails he began to get. "Jordan wants to know—" "Jordan asked me to ask you—" "Jordan thinks I should see some kind of prospectus before I invest." That was one of the ones he didn't take to the end. He got some money from her but decided to skip before marriage, mainly because of that pesky daughter. He's smarter now, makes sure his ladies are isolated. *All alone in the world*, as Olive described herself in her listing on the dating site. Although, come to think of it, who isn't alone in this world? He's been fending for himself all along, his father figuring that room and board to age eighteen were all he was owed, his mother barely lifting a hand to wave him goodbye. He was doing the best he could with what he had. People think it's an advantage to be born handsome, but that's just raw material. No, it's the Olives of the world who have it easy, being born with money. The things she takes for granted. She thinks everyone knows how to eat escargot, for example. Certainly, he does, but that was part of his training. He had taught himself by watching *Pretty Woman*. Something else he should be able to deduct, buying his own copy of *Pretty Woman*, but it has paid off. He learned everything he needed to know from movies—the James Bond films, although only the early ones; *The Philadelphia Story, Bringing Up Baby*. He has better manners than most. Better than Olive, for example, who is openly gawking at the sights along Bourbon Street. She slips her sweaty little palm in his, and he can tell she is nervous, but exhilarated.

"How about one of those?" he says, pointing to a stand where the drinks are served in large plastic cups that resemble grenades.

"Oh, I couldn't," she says, pressing her face into his armpit, which can't be that pleasant. He's a little damp. Who wouldn't be, wearing a suit on Bourbon Street in September? He forgot how long summer hangs on here, but Olive wouldn't be dissuaded. She had never been to New Orleans, she told him, first in e-mails, then in their Skype conversations. Besides, Louisiana makes it very easy for out-of-towners to marry here. That reminds him: They should wander over to the clerk's office in an hour or so, do the deed. Bless his laissez-faire hometown, where most of the rules can be waived by simple request—the waiting period, the requirement to show a birth certificate. Then on to the wedding night, but first a lovely meal, paid for with his new credit card. He would be needing some oysters, for sure.

But the drink has hit little Olive hard. Has she eaten anything today? Imagine how excited she was, how early she had to start to fly here from California. She starts to stagger, complains of feeling nauseous. The wedding will have to wait. He leads her back to the hotel, half carrying her the final blocks, puts her gently to bed, makes a cold compress for her head, runs his fingers gently across her arms and shoulder blades. "Giving chills," his mother had called it. "Come here, Gus, give me chills." She would stretch out across the sofa in the living room, the blinds drawn so the room was dark all the time, the television on but silent, two or three beer cans on the floor. Never more, because if you drank more than three beers in the afternoon, his mother explained, you were an alcoholic. But if you drank three between noon and five and then another three between five and bedtime, you were just honoring the packaging. "Why do you think they sell them six to a pack?" she would say. Did that mean one should eat a dozen eggs in two sittings? Once, he drank a six-pack of Coca-Cola in one sitting and she gave him a spanking for being greedy and wasteful. But he liked giving his mother chills, was happy to stand next to her and provide her a little pleasure. It was, he supposes, how he discovered his vocation.

He will marry Olive tomorrow. In fact, he will insist they spend the morning shopping, purchasing a new outfit for her to wear, as today's suit is now a little worse for wear, crumpled and hanging on a chair. She's sleeping in a full slip; he can't remember the last time he saw one of those. The shopping trip will distract her and she will probably forget about him calling his bank in London until, once again, it is too late. Once they are married, he will tell her—he sifts through the stories he has used over the years. His London-based business manager is a con man, a scoundrel. He made up the story about the attempted fraud, the locked accounts, and used the time to clean him out. Oh, he has other money, but it's so complicated, tied up in a trust, he won't be able to get it right away. It might seem counterintuitive, telling a lie so close to the truth, allowing Olive to consider that there are people in the world who are not what they say, people who will pretend to be on your side but want nothing more than to fleece your pockets. But it works surprisingly well, he has found. Raise the specter of the very crime you are committing and no one suspects you of perpetrating the exact same fraud.

He is restless, though, a performer who had prepared himself to go, only to find out at the last minute that the show has been canceled. The adrenaline has to go somewhere. He thinks about the clerk, the one who eyed him at check-in. Sometimes he likes a little something on the side, something rough and anonymous and nasty. It's tricky, though, finding someone who won't boomerang back, threaten one of his happy marriages. He can't just sit here in this suite all night as Olive sleeps off her one-bomb drunk. He runs a finger along her jawbone. "I'm going to go out for a meal, let you sleep, okay, precious? And then I'll sleep on the sofa when I get back, so you can have your rest. Big day tomorrow. Our wedding day."

He really does consider each marriage a big deal, no matter how many times he does it. The women are so happy at that moment, and who can put a price tag on that? To date, his marriages have netted him as little as fifteen thousand dollars and as much as two hundred thousand, and he's proud of the fact that each woman got the same quality job.

He's disciplined. He doesn't go too wild, stays out just late enough to find someone who wants to rid himself of energy as quickly and anonymously as he does. Then he creeps back in and, true to his word, stretches out along the sofa, doesn't even bother to pull out the foldaway bed. Olive will appreciate the gallantry, he thinks.

Could she really be a virgin? She has been coy about her age, which leads him to suspect that she's actually older than she looks. But even if she is ten years older than she looks, she's still on the young side, no more than her late thirties. He hasn't been with a woman that young since—well, ever. Even when he was young, the women tended to be over forty. It takes a woman a few years to amass a nest egg worth pursuing. But Olive is an heiress and an orphan. He has hit the exacta. He deserves it.

He awakens to a hard knock on the door—crap, he should have put the Do Not Disturb hanger on the knob—but before he can call out to warn the maid away, the door is thrown open and there is a sudden flurry that he can barely process in his sleep-dazed state. Voices, hard and emphatic, a trio of men circling him, calling him by his real name.

Calling him by his real name. The name that comes up on his rap sheet, from back in his hustler days in this very city. The name with a warrant or two, even a few of the earlier marriages. A name he hasn't used for years for that very reason. How do they know his real name?

They cuff him, then begin examining the contents of his wallet, sitting out on the dining room table that so impressed Olive. Olive. Where is she, how has she slept through this? Maybe she went out for breakfast or a café au lait. He will find a way to explain this to Olive. She will bail him out. He just needs to get out of here before she returns, talk to her without any cops around.

"This your credit card?" one of the cops asks, extracting the platinum card that Olive added to her account.

"Yes, and that's my real name, as you see from my ID. I have no idea who Gustave Meckelburg is." God, what a name. No matter his line of work, he would have dropped that handle.

"Really?" says the cop, a detective, probably fraud or larceny. Whatever name he's ever used, he's never done anything violent, after all, and he can't believe the New Orleans PD cares about his old adventures in vice. "Weird thing is, credit card company says you applied for this online a week ago, but the Social you gave belongs to Gustave Meckelburg. And everything else you provided—your address, your income—turns out to be a straight-up lie. That's frowned upon, but it's so minor compared to the other stuff we have on you, we're not going to sweat it. Although you do owe for this hotel room now that the account has been closed."

"That's ridiculous. The primary account holder is my fiancée, and all she did was add me. When she returns, she'll clear all this up."

"Olive Dunne? The one whose name was on the reservation?

She skipped, buddy. Doorman put her in a cab about six A.M. this morning. Told him her mother was ill."

"She doesn't even have a mother."

"We've got a lot to sort out with you," the cop says, putting his hand on his shoulder. "And we'd like to go over the various infractions in our jurisdiction before we hand you over to the feds."

"The feds?"

"They've been advised that Gustave Meckelburg has never filed a tax return. They'd kinda like to talk to you about that."

She has a long layover in the Nashville airport, almost three hours. She changes into jeans and a T-shirt, dumps the suit in a trash can. It smells like him to her, although the odors really belong to Bourbon Street. He smelled okay. Not a surprise, given his line of work. She parks herself in a Starbucks, uses the wireless feed to empty the checking account she set up only a month ago, calls the bank to tell them what's she done. She bends the ATM card she extracted from his wallet early that morning, along with all the cash, and works it back and forth until it breaks in half. She kills out the photos of Olive Dunne's house in the Pacific Palisades, silently thanking the woman for the loan of her name and her home for these last few months, not that the woman will ever know. Then she makes another quick call.

"Hey, Mom."

"Jordan. Where are you?"

"Heading back to Providence. Ran down to New Orleans over the weekend just for the hell of it."

"What prompted that impulse?"

"Feeling restless."

Her mother is a sweet, trusting woman, despite all that has happened, but she knows her daughter well enough to be skeptical of this. Jordan doesn't do much on impulse. "You're still not on that tear about Frankie, are you?"

"Frankie?"

"Thinking he's a con man, or whatever. He loved me, Jordan. You scared him off, making me ask all those questions. He thought I was too suspicious."

"He did take almost twenty thousand from you."

"For that hospital he's building in Brazil, Jordan. I don't mind that. It was a good cause."

"You're right, Mom." She is right. Twenty thousand is nothing in the scheme of things, and it had served a good cause if it kept her mother from marrying that creep. If her mother had married Gustave Meckelburg—then known as Frank Mercer—he would have taken her for much more. But twenty thousand was still too much to Jordan's way of thinking, and she had put a lot of time and effort into finding out who he was and getting him into a jurisdiction where that mattered. She had learned that bigamy may carry a social stigma, but it didn't fetch much in the way of criminal punishment. But she knew how he had found her mother and she assumed he would find her that way, too, if she baited the hook just right. The hard part had been finding out everything she could about him. But she has always been a patient young woman, the inevitable consequence of her father dying young and leaving behind her sweet but silly mother, who never bothers to read the fine print or question anything too closely.

Jordan says goodbye to her mother and takes a much-folded letter out of her purse, a printout of an e-mail. "Dear Angel," it begins. "How can machinery match two souls so perfectly? How can this thing of wires and circuits know what is in my heart?" It is the letter that George Middleberg sent her three months ago. It is also, word for word, the letter he sent to her mother eight years ago. If she ever harbored any doubts about what she was doing, they ended the day she received that e-mail.

"I can't wait to take your name," she told him at the hotel. And so she had. Taken his latest fake name, and returned his real one to him.

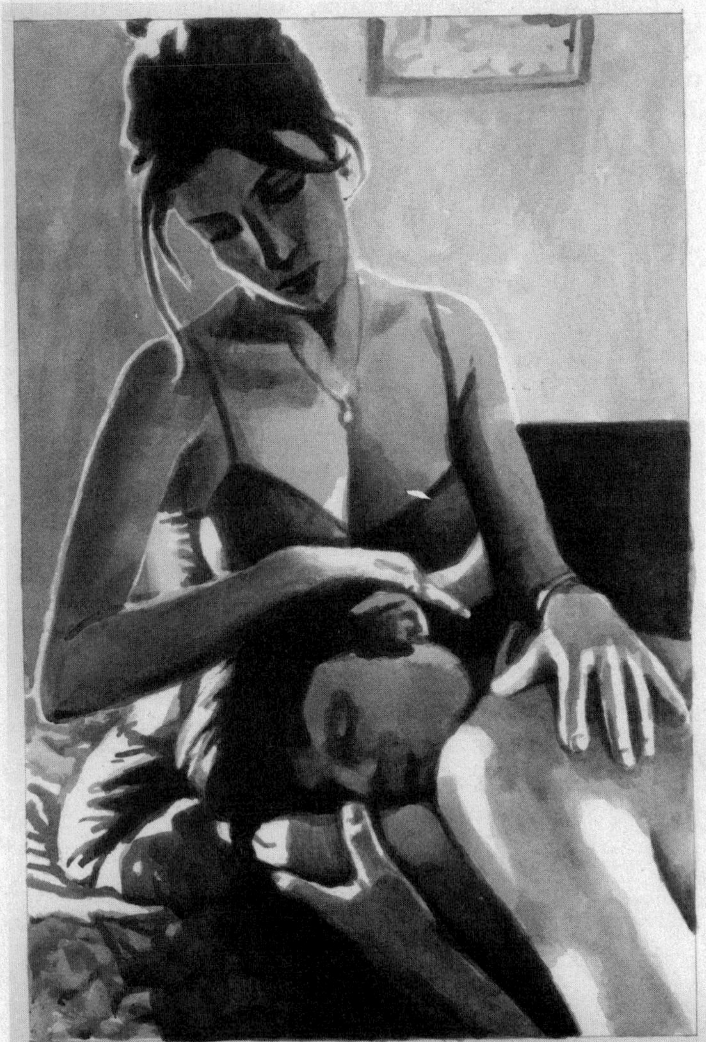

Toytown Assorted

PATRICK MCCABE

YURI GAGARIN WASN'T long in space when Golly decided to go up the town. For just the briefest of moments she thought that she'd forgotten her shop book—but then she remembered.

—Silly me, it was in my handbag all along.

Now as she proceeded across the square, she repeated the various items which it was her intention to purchase.

—I have Brasso to get and half a pound of butter, then there's oranges and a tin of Mansion polish. After that it'll be over to the butcher's for a few tender chops. Thank you, Barney, she heard herself say.

Emerging onto the street, who did she encounter only Blossom Foster—a plump lady in a leopard-print coat and stole.

—This Russian fellow. What do you make of all this talk about space?

Golly's response was that she didn't really have any hard or fast views on the subject. But by now her interlocutor had already moved on and was inquiring of Golly as to what her considered opinion might be of Miami. Golly replied by saying that, regrettably, she'd never been.

There were lots of programs on television—*Dragnet* among them, *The Lucy Show* and *Peyton Place*—but for Patsy Murray and his son Boniface, *Mr. Pastry* was the best of them all. He sported round wire-framed spectacles and had a great big thick gray mustache. Such an amount of idiotic antics as he got up to! Always landing in one complicated situation after another. Even though he was Down syndrome, Boniface had no difficulty appreciating the TV funnyman's idiosyncratic sense of humor. As the twelve-year-old boy fanned his fat fingers and pressed them to his face, rolling around the floor in hysterics—it got so bad that Golly had to go over to wipe the mucus and saliva off his nose.

—*Mittur Pay-twee!* he would squeal—repeating it, falsetto—*Mitter Mitter Mitter Pay-twee*!

Patsy had been watching the television too—but only half-heartedly. Being much too busy perusing his newspaper and thinking about the weekend's football.

—Boo! he heard Golly squealing suddenly as he found himself jumping, instinctively placing his hand over his heart.

—Jesus Mary and Joseph, you put the fear of God in me, Golly!

The giddy peal of his wife's laughter began to amuse him then, however, as she swung her bag gaily, tossing back her auburn curls. She had just come back from space, she told him, where she'd been tumbling about like Yuri Gagarin.

—No! she laughed, I'm only joking—I've just been shopping up the town. Would you like a sandwich? I'm just going in to wet a pot of tea. And what about you, Little Boniface Murray? Would you, perhaps, maybe like a nice little cup?

—Waaay! exclaimed Boniface, and Toytoon Torted!

Which, of course, as she knew, meant: Toytown Assorted.

They were his favorite confection of all. Indeed Golly herself liked them very much too. They came in a family-sized cellophane bag. There were little houses and trees and even a church, all coated in the loveliest of tasty icing sugar.

—I can't wait for my Toytown Assorted! cried Golly, clapping her hands. As Boniface scrunched his eyes, pushing out his lip—squirming and chuckling in a delicious self-cuddle of delight.

Peyton Place was actually on later. But you weren't supposed to watch it—at church the previous Sunday, the parish priest had specifically singled it out.

—Any more of this and Ireland will be in ruins! he had said.

For this reason her hand was seen to twitch whenever it hovered over the dial. Just as she turned it to reveal a hovering of a different kind.

—You can't come in here! protested the woman in the lounge suit—Golly knew it was a lounge suit, for she'd seen them advertised in *Picturegoer*—if anyone hears, don't you know I'm married!

—I know you're married! snapped the man who'd cast the shadow, but darn it to hell I don't care. I'm through with caring, and I know in your heart that so are you!

He grabbed her fiercely as he pressed his lips to hers.

—Let's get away from here—let's go together! she cried.

But already the man had taken off his jacket—and was in the process of tearing at his tie. He was looking at the woman like some kind of wild animal. As he crossed the room and firmly closed the shutters.

—But there's one thing that you and me have got to do first—something I've been longing to do all week!

—Oh, Norman! cried the woman, falling back before him on the bed, scissoring her legs around him as she groaned.

Patsy and Golly were both in bed now—reading. Her husband was inquiring as to whether she wouldn't mind adjusting her position "just a little."

In order that he might maneuver the bolster. She informed him she was more than happy to do so.

Patsy smiled and returned to his pools coupons—chewing thoughtfully on the end of his pencil.

Without thinking, he suddenly frowned and asked his wife did she think that Newcastle would succeed in holding Chelsea to a draw this coming Saturday.

Golly smiled—and, turning a page of her magazine, told him she didn't know.

—I don't really know anything about football, she said.

Patsy laughed.

—But of course you don't. I got carried away there. I don't know what I was thinking, Golly.

Golly returned to the *Picturegoer* article she had been reading about Miami, Florida. Once you have visited you will never be the same, it said. There was a great big photo of an electric blue sea, with an enormous stretch of white sand and some curtseying palms. The apartments were all painted aqua and seashell pink.

It was there that the author and "her lover" had met, she was informed. It was there she had been united with the man of her dreams. In a place which she described as an "Eden on earth."

Golly's nails were making indentations on the margins. She wished they were not—but those were the facts. An urge to switch off the wireless and its dreary monotony then compelled her. Instead she coughed and patted her chest.

—The Fosters are going to America, she told her husband.

But he didn't reply—thinking, as he continued to chew on his pencil. Then, when some time had passed, he said:

—Good night.

—Good night, Patsy, he heard his wife reply.

As, with a soft click, the lamp on his side of the room went out.

As Golly lay there, she found herself not in bed or in Cullymore either but standing in the foyer of a plush hotel. With the bellboy close by waiting with her luggage. She knew that, as her husband, Patsy ought to have been with her—but he wasn't. Patsy was at home.

—Will your husband be checking in with you, the Spanish-sounding desk clerk said with a smile.

—No, she replied, I'm on my own.

—Of course, Madam, she heard him say—handing her her room key, smiling again, even more broadly this time.

She remembered to tip the bellboy generously. Because that was the way they did things in the U.S.

When he had departed she kicked off her shoes and threw herself down on the bed with a sigh—flicking the television on with her toe. It was the biggest screen she had ever seen. And guess who was on it? Yuri Gagarin—grinning out from behind his helmet: CCCP. How happy he looked—away off there, out in the galaxy. Then Golly got up and went down to the bar. There was a foreign-looking gentleman seated at the counter, gazing into a tall, colored glass. In her own town you couldn't approach a foreign gentleman. Indeed dare to go near someone who wasn't your husband. Unless they were bent double and well over sixty. But this was America, not Cullymore.

—I'm looking for Blossom Foster, she told the man.

—I'm afraid I don' know, lady, he said.

How lovely that was, to be courteously addressed as "lady."

—But while you wait, yes—maybe you like a drink?

—Who's offering? astoundingly, she heard herself say. With eyes twinkling.

—Pedro Gonzales, she was told, as the smallish man in the Hawaiian-print shirt treated her to a gentlemanly bow. Why, of course, she told him—she would be delighted to accept his generous offer.

—You're from outta town, no? snapping his fingers as the swarthy barman spread his hands on the marble counter.

—Sure am, she said, again with a twinkle, from *waaay* outta town.

—Me too, said Pedro. In the Siesta Motel on Biscayne Boulevard ees wher' I stay. Every time I come by, that is where I go. They take care of me there. So what's it gonna be? You look like a lady who could use a daiquiri.

—That's exactly what I was going to order.

He made two rabbit's ears of his fingers as she glided effortlessly onto the stool. It was tubular chrome.

—The Siesta Motel, huh? she said.

—Over on Biscayne Boulevard, he replied—and this time it was Pedro's turn to twinkle.

The following day when she woke up, Golly made up her mind to, one way or another, go to Miami. It was to become an imperative—and this was the reason why. It had all begun while she had been blackleading the range. Thinking yet again about what Blossom Foster had been saying about bridge. Her and her stupid cards. What sort of a stupid idea had that been anyway, she asked herself—a bridge session, for God's sake, in the early afternoon. Another stupid plan of Blossom's, what else.

Of course it being the Fosters you were duty-bound to become all excited, as if it was the most original and fascinating idea ever. "Oh, but yes!" you were expected to say. You had to declare yourself privileged because of the invite.

—What a splendid idea! you were expected to squeal.

Then Golly heard the front door closing—it was Boniface, arriving home from school. Which was why she listened with affection as she heard him skidding across the floor. Before bursting into the kitchen with a yelp—tossing his schoolbag into the corner as always, calling out "Babbie! Babbie! Where Babbie!"

He had never been capable of pronouncing *Mammy* properly.

It was a pity about his speech—of course it was, as Blossom Foster had remarked on a number of occasions.

—But I'm sure you have the resources to deal with that, Golly, she had observed.

In spite of herself Golly hated it when Boniface did it—called her "Babbie." Almost immediately becoming overwhelmed by feelings of guilt and shame.

She wondered, did Blossom ever experience such sensations—of abject worthlessness and self-loathing? No—of course she didn't. And if she did, she could always go off to Florida and forget them.

—We can't make up our minds, she had told her, we're such sillies, Bodley and I. One minute it's Miami then the next it's California. Prut! What a pair of old sillies we are, Geraldine!

* * *

After dinner, Boniface ate his rice.

—Do you like it, Bonnie? she asked him as she stood there above him, her son beaming, bright-eyed, from ear to ear.

As he spooned big dollops of the dessert into his mouth. He loved rice almost as much as his favorite biscuits. Which, of course were:

—Toytoon Torted!

Then it was time for his game with his "shooter."

She assisted him with setting up the cardboard box. This was his target. He liked, more than anything, to pretend he was Joe Friday. Joe Friday played in *Dragnet* on the telly. All the men in the barbershop loved it.

—Just the facts, ma'am—that was Joe's catchphrase. That was what Joe was fond of saying.

But Boniface Murray couldn't say that. All he could do was shoot with his shooter, clutching it in a hapless two-handed grip. Scrunching his face as he did so, yelping:

—Whee! he clapped, as the marrowfat pea hit the target, clapping his hands as he squealed: Whee—hooey! Fuck!

Up until now his mother's voice had been a model of restraint.

—Please stop saying that, be a good boy, won't you?

She knew the other boys would make fun when they heard him swearing.

—Fuck! Fuck! Whee—hooey!

The pea went "pop." As down went the target and her son shrieked ecstatically—before skidding across the floor to go and retrieve it.

—Fuckity! Whumph! Me good—pea!

—Stop it, do you hear! Stop it now, Bonnie!

Suddenly the dessert spoon had leaped into her hand. All went quiet in the room.

—Boniface, now listen. There's a good boy. Boniface, love—do you know you're so good, said his mother.

But Boniface, unfortunately, was staring at her, quivering in disbelief. With his face the color of the rice he'd just been consuming. As the enormity of what his mother had just done began to seep into his slow-witted brain. What had she done? She had pressed the spoon's handle quite severely into his arm. Into the soft flesh of his hairless upper forearm. It hadn't actually hurt him—at least not all that much. But Boniface Murray had already begun to whimper—and the more he inspected the faint abrasion which the piece of cutlery had occasioned he began to sob, helplessly. Before flinging his peashooter away in disdain.

For just a fleeting moment a shadow passed across the lace curtain and Golly could have sworn she had just apprehended the outline of her neighbor—Blossom Foster, attired in her leopard print and stole.

She then approached the television—it was time for *Peyton Place*—but all of the sudden heard, or thought she did, the parish priest calling:

—Don't you dare watch that filth, Golly Murray!

And then wept as she retreated, with cries of passion being released by murky figures at the back of her mind. As the woman in the lounge suit swung wild-eyed on her heel, before crying:

—The hell with my husband, he's never understood me! It's you I love, Norman—you! You, and always have! Do what you want to me, anything—just do it!

Once, in the shop, she had seen a countryman with red hands as big as shovels. She wondered was that what Norman's were like, as the woman whimpered and he tore wildly at her flesh—scooping up great big handfuls in the afternoon ecstasy of that shadow-shuttered room.

—Give it to me! she heard her plead, Give me your body, Norman, give it to me until, until I'm ready to die!

As Golly's hands covered her face, her engagement ring briefly scratching her cheek, now fleeing shamefully from the room.

The next day, making their way home from Mass, Golly Murray left her husband at the corner—he was going down to the pub for a drink. Then, all of a sudden, she heard: *Coo-ee!*

Blossom Foster was already making her way across the road.

—I've had this idea, she said, arriving up breathlessly. A fashion show—with Miami as the theme.

—A fashion show about Miami?

—Yes, that will be the subject, if you will. I really do think it's the most marvelous idea, don't you, Geraldine? We'll have it in the hotel over Easter. And maybe we could give the proceeds to the handicapped.

—The handicapped, replied Golly, puzzled—her dry throat rasping a little.

—Yes, to those who are less fortunate. I really think it's the least we could do. Your little fellow—I mean, it's not fair. They need all the help they can get, poor mites. Little fellows like—whatyoucallhim?

—My son? choked Golly.

—Yes! Little Boniface—what age is he now, eleven? Or is it twelve?

—Twelve, choked Golly, he's twelve.

—But of course maybe it's not for me to say. Maybe you mightn't have the time to become involved. I mean he must be difficult . . .

—He's not difficult! snapped Golly, he isn't difficult!

—We could even invite Coco Chanel—we'll be the talk of the place. Well—tottybye, must be off to make the arrangements. Hello, Florida, the Sunshine State! Here we come!

The BBC shipping forecast was just finishing as Golly Murray climbed into bed. Her husband was already busy with his pools coupons. She put on her glasses and began turning the pages of her magazine. If you had the money, it read, there was no problem at all in getting yourself an air-conditioned room, one that was steam-heated to keep you comfortable. On top of that there was a foam rubber bed in every room, with a seventeen-inch television and a Frigidaire ice cube machine. That's if you stayed at the Siesta Motel. With someone like Pedro Gonzales, perhaps. When she went to the motel with him, it turned out that he was the most gentle and lovely man—whose hands, far from being like shovels, were small, in fact, and more like girls'. But which, maybe for that reason, could relax and make her feel things of which no countryman's hands ever have been capable. At first when he had kissed her there—on her "ickle brown nub," as they'd used to call it when they were kids—she had been prompted to laugh. Mischievously, even, like Lounge Suit Woman, to cry out:

—Oo Norman!

But when he had finished—if he was ever going to finish—laughter was just about the last thing on her mind. Because what Golly Murray wanted—she wanted him to do it all over again—circle that ickle nub with the tip of his tongue. And then suddenly—aha!—leaping on it as he had done—giving it most delicious and unexpected bite.

—Ees so sweet, he told her, I could eat it!

—Do it, Norman! Golly had heard herself plead, do it, will you—until I die!

—I not Norman, Pedro had laughed, but believe me, Miss—yes, you will die! I, Pedro, know how to make you do thees.

Then he had proudly presented her with the handle of his stomach, as some of Patsy's pals often called it.

—You like? he had said.

As he set to nibbling her nipple once again. Even when the police's suspicions were made public, she refused to believe it. The *Miami Herald* ran a story claiming he was "the vampire."

The Palm Beach killer the authorities had been searching for for months. And who was reputed to have dispatched fifteen or more victims, most of them women. As the facts filtered out they were accompanied by the most appalling rumors—that the suspect had derived pleasure from actually consuming the nipples of his victims. The detective in charge said that in all his years of experience it was the worst case he'd ever come across.

—We found human hair—and, I regret to say, a female nipple, in the Frigidaire, he was reported as having said.

As she pressed her nails into the magazine's margins, Golly had to remind herself that what she was reading was no more than a story. So incensed did she find herself becoming at the sheer crassness of the detective's lies. But Pedro, of course, had warned her that would be coming.

—For years they try to pin somethееng on me, he had told her—before breaking down in her arms as they danced.

After which they stood together, gazing out through the French windows.

—Those buildings are so beautiful but I know you'll laugh when you hear what I'm going to say.

—I will never laugh, you know that, Golly. Never will I laugh unless it is something that you, as a woman, intend.

—They remind me so much of Toytown Assorted. With the moon's soft light on the greens and pinks and blues.

—I no understand, please, said Pedro.

But he didn't laugh.

—Toytown Assorted, she smiled as she clasped his hand. Boniface loves them. I guess over here you probably call them cakes.

—Toytown Assorted, he smiled, pulling her to him, pressing his tongue inside her mouth as he chuckled.

—Thees the on'y cake that Pedro like right now, Golly cake—yes?

—Yes, replied Golly, tugging at his glossy jet-black curls as she scissored her legs *Peyton Place*–style and cried aloud:

—Tear off my lounge suit, Pedro! Tear it into ribbons, do you hear me!

When she looked up and saw Pedro, baffled, with both arms extended:

—But Golly, you not wearing lounge suit!

As she took it inside her—the handle of his stomach. Trying not to laugh as she thought of the parish priest. Or of Pedro's face as she squealed anew:

—Norman! Do it, will you—until I die! You can even bite it off, if you want to—my ickle brown nub—I don't care!

Golly was in the best of humor when she happened to meet Blossom by chance two days later—this time in the bakery.

—That's a nice dress, Blossom had said with a smile, picking at a full stop of fluff with her finger. It had been located, almost invisibly, underneath the collar of Golly Murray's coat.

—I'm searching for a nice surprise for Bodley's tea, she said, maybe a cream cone or, who knows, even a nice fairy cake.

—A fairy cake, yes, that would be nice, replied Golly.

—With icing, beamed Blossom, with some nice pink icing.

—Like Toytown Assorted, said Golly, without thinking.

As Blossom made a face.

—O no, she said, they're just for children. Much too sugary and sweet for my husband. He likes proper cakes.

—Yes, of course. Bodley would want proper icing.

—Certainly not Toytown Assorted, at any rate. Although of course all the children love them. Does Boniface like them?

—Yes, Boniface loves them, he has always loved his Toytown, I have to say.

In spite of herself, no matter how she had promised herself she would react, once more Golly felt tingly and quite uncomfortable. She could not bring herself to look at Blossom's dress—for she knew how expensive it must have been. But it was more the older woman's imperturbable composure and self-assuredness which, as always, succeeded most in getting under her skin.

—Excuse me, love—if you could just step out of the way. I think I see the perfect little bun.

The older woman's hand was now firmly resting on Golly's shoulder—ever so firmly easing her out of the way. Suddenly Blossom released a small cry:

—Hurrah! she shrieked, leaping up down in an almost childlike fashion, what an absolutely lovely cake—almond!

She had found her holy grail, she triumphantly declared.

—My husband will simply adore this gorgeous almond slice!

To her dismay, Golly found herself becoming hopelessly tongue-tied—with her shoe making shapeless patterns in the tiles that were so vivid she actually had to look away. As Blossom smiled and took her by the hand.

—My garden! You really must come around and see it, yourself and Patsy. You could perhaps take some cuttings—for your own garden, I mean. Is that something that might appeal to you, Golly? You'd be more than welcome, as I'm sure you well know.

It was only after she had fingered the silver half crown onto the marble-topped counter that Blossom Foster was seen to hesitate. Before pressing her gloved hand in mock awe against her lips—as though quite affronted by her own insensitivity:

—But then, of course: You don't have a garden!

She turned away and began to converse with the female assistant. Not that it mattered, for Golly now heard nothing. Making a few halfhearted attempts to rally, galvanize herself into making a reply.

Regrettably, however, she did not succeed.

Instead she found herself bidding goodbye to Blossom Foster.

Who said that now she had to be off, as she had one or two more things to get for Bodley's tea.

The assistant was folding her arms and smiling.

—What a lovely lady, she was saying, before taking out her compact and remarking to Golly from the small oval mirror:

—So what can I get you?

—Some Toytown Assorted, if you please, she heard herself reply—thinking that she had dropped her gloves and then remembering she hadn't even been holding them in her hand. And that, in fact, they had been in her handbag all along. O, and also that they didn't actually sell Toytown Assorted in the home bakery.

—The shop across the road is the place you want for them, the assistant told her in a chillingly disinterested, quite dead monotone.

Or so it had seemed to Golly Murray at the time.

—I have a feeling I'm going to scoop the dividend this time, said Patsy, chewing his pencil, if United can manage a draw against Liverpool. If that happens, then I think I'm in with a very strong chance.

—Perhaps then we can think about going to Florida, said Golly, flicking the pages of *Picturegoer,* smiling.

—Ha ha, laughed her husband as he chewed on his pencil, you really do come out with them, Geraldine. You really do make me laugh sometimes! Would you mind turning the wireless down there, dear—just a teeny little bit?

His wife obliged.

—Thank you, he said, closing one eye as he shuffled his pools coupon, marking in an X for a draw.

But Geraldine "Golly" Murray hadn't, in fact, been joking at all. And the more she thought about it, the more possible it did seem that, if they really wanted to, there would be nothing to stop them from going to Miami. She had read a lot about it now and felt, in her own way, quite at home there. She had even borrowed some books from the library. But her favorite remained the account in her magazine. The Miami Vampire was one of her most-loved stories. Because if it taught her one thing it had shown her that people, worldwide, are essentially the same. For example, the town in which she lived—there weren't any swimming pools or stretches of sand or great tall buildings. But when it came to sex, all men were disappointingly predictable.

—The handle of my stomach, she remembered Patsy's friend saying that day in the shop.

Of course, shutting up immediately as soon as he saw her. What she could not for the life of her understand was how it meant so much to them. Obviously in so many ways her own husband and Pedro Gonzales would have been almost impossibly different. But in this area nothing divided them. Or lantern-jawed Norman from *Peyton Place* either, she presumed. And as she thought of herself laying back in the great expanse of that foam-rubber bed it was difficult for her to suppress a chuckle when she heard Pedro say:

—*Tú eres muy bonita.* If you say you love me I'll do anything. An'ting!

The laugh, of course, was that she knew he would. But it wasn't because of love that he did it. It was on account of, when it jumped, the handle of his stomach.

—Bury it in there, up to her kidneys, she had overheard Patsy's friend continuing that day in the shop—the countryman with the massive red hands.

—Up to their kidneys, boys, he says, that's the way to make them squeal. The further in it goes the more they like the handle of your stomach.

Because of such unstylish utterances—hopelessly imprecise as they were—like any woman, Golly was by nature suspicious. It paid to be like that, her mother had counseled her, considering the numerous subtle hazards with which females had to contend. Right throughout, in spite of his flattering charms, she had always harbored certain reservations with regard to Pedro Gonzales. He was much too sweet and far too attentive not to have something to hide. It had taken only three visits to his room in the Siesta Motel for her to finally come to the conclusion that in all probability she had been wrong—and that, most likely, she was sleeping with the Miami Vampire.

He spoke Spanish to her all the time—especially when he was feeling under her nightdress.

—*Tú eres mas bonita que todas estrellas en el cielo.*

He asked her did she like it. Yes, she'd told him, very much. But most of the time she didn't even feel it. And when he eventually would "buck"—as she'd once heard her Patsy describe the act when he'd had a few jars—that he'd be prepared to do almost anything for her. That was when she'd said it, running her fingers through his thick black greasy boyish Cuban curls.

—This, then, is what I want you to do: Disfigure Blossom Foster.

Initially, unfortunately, he had demurred. Perhaps he hadn't expected her to be capable of persuading him as effectively as she did. But Golly, like most women, had learned not to expect very much of men—which was why, on account of the disfigurement meaning so much to her, she had come well prepared. Had been to Frederick's of Hollywood, in fact, whose adverts she had become aware of in *Picturegoer*'s back pages. She told him she'd let him lick her black waspie if he did it.

—Disfigure Blossom Foster, she repeated.

—I never see you like thees before, Golly, croaked Pedro, now you frighten me!

She told him she'd let him chew her ankles if he agreed.

—Disfigure Blossom Foster, she again whispered.

He couldn't believe it when she slapped him across the face.

—You'll do what I say—do you hear me, Norman?

Then she led him across the floor to the bed and gently took the handle of his stomach and placed it gently in her palm.

—And now you will receive the greatest prize of all. If only you will do what your Golly has just asked of you. What is it, Pedro?

—Disfigure Blossom Foster, her Cuban companion sheepishly replied.

—That's right, she said softly, before laying back and clamping his lower back with her legs.

—At last! she wept, at last I'll die happy!

As the little man groaned inside her then went soft.

* * *

To his credit, unlike Patsy, Pedro hadn't gone and made a great big unnecessary fuss about things. Or tried to get out of it after making his promise. Which her husband usually did, once he had released himself. But of course, in the case of the Cuban, there was the promise of further waspie-kissing on a nightly basis—for which he had, again sheepishly, professed a particular fondness.

—It would be ver' easy, you know, he now told her, to do what it is you ask on thees Blossom Foster. I theenk that maybe we do it with the brakes, yes? I sever the cable, then is no problem. What make car you know she drive?

—I don't know but I can find out, she had told Pedro.

And drifted to sleep like a child that night, slumbering happily on a soft cloud of sound—that of horrendously screeching brakes.

The next day was a lovely spring afternoon Sunday, and like a lot of people from the town, the Murrays decided to go for a walk. Everyone was in high spirits as they greeted Patsy and Golly, with the church bells ringing out and the shoots of the crocuses as they craned across their borders coyly offering the impression that they perhaps considered themselves the incarnations of some particularly gifted versifier.

There were cars parked here and there, and through lowered windows a delirious bleat was heard to deliver a scene-by-scene account of an important Gaelic football match which was proceeding. By all accounts—that is to say if the near hysteria of the commentator's observations was to be considered in any way indicative of proceedings—at this advanced stage, the equally matched teams were neck and neck. Golly froze as she spotted Blossom Foster.

—Dearest! exclaimed her neighbor, attired now in a ruffled

nylon blouse complete with brooch. How lovely to see you—and you, too, Patsy dear, of course!

She pecked the younger woman ever so lightly on the cheek. There then ensued a discussion on the recent spell of good weather. Subsequent to that they then attended to the subject of the forthcoming summer—and where both couples were likely to take their holidays.

—We're going to Miami, Blossom declared, yes that's Miami, Florida. We're jetting out next week. Do you know how much it costs? One hundred and sixteen guineas.

Once more Golly said that that was wonderful. Before blurting out:

—Will you be taking the car? What kind of car is it?

—No, we won't be taking the car, we never do. We're flying, you see. It costs one hundred and sixteen guineas—each. All in, of course.

—All in, replied Golly, somewhat dazedly. So you won't be taking the car then, you say?

—No dear, we won't be taking the car. We always rent a car when we get there.

—And what kind of car might that be? asked Golly.

—Goodness, dear you're so interested in automobiles all of a sudden. That's what they call them over there, you know.

—Automobiles?

—Yes, automobiles. As a matter of fact we'll be hiring a Pontiac. We like to hire a Pontiac, don't we, Bodley?

—Yes, dear. Chrome plated. Once in Miami we always rent a Pontiac.

—A great big pink chrome-plated Pontiac.

—Gleaming. A beauty.

—A Pontiac the color of Toytown Assorted! laughed Golly, unwittingly twisting her gloves.

As Patsy gripped her excitedly by the arm, affectionately and with a boyish innocence that made her feel so close to him:

—Jeekers tonight! Do you know what, if I'm not mistaken—I think that Down has this game in the bag!

The sea can be cruel and the sea can be cold and sometimes the sea can be snug as a glove. Especially if you're fortunate enough to be tucked up in bed beneath a nice warm candlewick counterpane with some heavy blankets and nice crisp clean sheets. Which Patsy Murray and his wife Golly were.

—You're listening to the BBC. And now, the shipping forecast.

Golly Murray tugged the bedclothes up to her neck. There go the pips, she said to herself, as big hairy men began hauling ropes in her mind. With massive breakers soaring in faraway places.

The time was now 12:01 A.M., with the shipping forecast almost concluding. Atlantic low 991, it continued, expected 130 miles west of Rockall, 1,011 by 0100 tomorrow. Area forecasts for the next twenty-four hours: Viking variable 3 or 4.

Golly loved the names—so cozykins and warm, like being wrapped in silk miles and miles from the horrible salty cold.

Cromarty Forth, Tyne Dogger 2 or 3, veering southeast 4 or 5. Occasionally rough in Cromarty and Dogger at first. Rain later. Moderate or good.

Her husband had been talking to her for some moments, she now realized. Yes, her spouse Patsy Murray lying beside her in the bed was asking her if she pleased would she mind adjusting her position "just a little." In order that he might maneuver the bolster. Which she did. She happily complied and the large pillow in question was duly adjusted.

As Patsy smiled and returned to his pools coupons—chewing on the end of his pencil as he did his best to calculate the first-division league results.

—I've never seen you in such good humor, he said to his wife, anyone looking at you would think it was you who had won the pools.

—No, darling, thought Golly to herself, smoothing out the glossy center pages of *Picturegoer,* depicting a city of mythical composition with modernist white facades in seafoam green with salmon-pink trims, architecture designed specifically to invoke feelings of the purest delight.

The BBC pips had once made the world seem giant, almost unnegotiable—but nothing about it now intimidated Golly Murray, as with a smile on her face she laid her head on the pillow, sighing luxuriously. The great thing about it all was that now she knew Pedro needed her. In a way it wasn't all that different from her husband—all big talk but in the end running around looking for his mama—sucking his thumb with those great big dependent bulbs of eyes.

When he came into the Fountainebleau bar the first thing she noticed was that he was extremely agitated and kept on looking behind him with his shoulders hunched, in the attitude of someone perceiving himself to be under surveillance. When he sat down beside her she saw that his forehead was heavily beaded with perspiration. But he was carrying the bag of tools, just like he'd promised.

—There's nothing to be worried about, she said to him, caressing his arm tenderly. Running her fingers through the whorls of his shiny curls. Feeling so proud of herself that she had done it—obtained the information that he'd requested.

—Ees where you say it would be, muy bonita. The Pontiac is parked in the lot of the hotel.

—My lovely baby, to do this for me.

—Every night and day I think of my Golly. And now that

you say you love me too there is nothing I will not do for you. *Tú eres muy bella.*

—After this we both disappear. Just you and me, Pedro and Golly.

—We take a boat to Key West and—we are gone!

—Now. Let's go, and put an end to my troubles once and for all.

—Blossom Foster—the things you tell me.

—What did you call her? What was that you said?

—*Puerco! Cochino!* That's what I said.

As a feeling of bliss overtook Golly Murray, gazing out across a city that looked like it belonged in outer space. To one of those programs, like Buck Rogers, that Boniface was fond of watching. In the humidity, there on that balcony where the two of them were now standing—it was ninety-six degrees—bewilderingly, Golly Murray found herself shivering.

But delight was the feeling she was experiencing on the way to the Fontainebleau Hotel to check up on her neighbors.

—Upon the allotted evening, she smiled mischievously.

As she made her way past the soaring finials, exaggerated parapets, and sculptural towers of this extraordinary place. Where exotic birds and tropical flora abounded, etched in stained glass on the windows or in bas relief on the facades of the buildings.

—*Amazing Stories*—Flash Gordon, Jules Verne, she found herself thinking—quite light-headed.

The interior of the hotel was chartreuse and forest green as she came through the revolving door.

Blossom, as might have been expected, was at the bar counter—doing all the talking. In her ruffled white blouse, dripping with jewelry, she was holding a long-stemmed glass in her hand—pretending to be amused by a joke of her husband's, tossing back her head and laughing. Her hair was piled up, blonde, on her head—as her husband shook his head in his loud Hawaiian-print shirt. Golly was tense as she waited for the call. Which she took in the lounge as Pedro, gasping, told her.

—It is done. Meet me in the Siesta Motel, and hurry!

Her heart was thumping loudly in her chest. As she took her wrap and raced outside, hailing a cab in the forecourt. Never in her life had she been so excited. Which made it all the more disappointing when she got back to the Siesta and discovered Pedro in a state of extreme agitation. Trembling violently with his face and hands still covered in oil.

—I theenk that maybe I have been seen. There was someone in the shadows when I lie under the car—O God!

In spite of herself, Golly Murray the barber's wife knew that she had no option—forcefully striking her lover across the face. As he fell, like Patsy, a baby, into her arms.

—No one saw you, Pedro. It's done. You have made your girl very happy tonight.

—Now we make love?

She didn't care—but she didn't mind either, as she stroked his forehead and gave him a smile.

—For you, Pedro Gonzales—anything!

As she took him by the handle of his stomach, leading him around the room like a puppy. Now she was exultant—now she could do anything.

—Kneel on the floor and beg like a puppy.

The Cuban complied.

—Ask me! she snapped.

—What ees I ask you my lovely Golly?

—Ask me can you bury it up to my kidneys.

—Bury what—I don' understand.

She smacked him again.

—Golly is the queen—don't you dare to ask her questions! She's a thousand times better than Madam Blossom Foster! Take that!

She knew he liked it—but of course pretended not to.

—Each leel boy he like his mama—even when she smack him, no? she found herself thinking.

As she slapped him again.

—Up to my kidneys. Implore me can you do it, implore me now to do it, with the handle of your stomach!

—Pliss can I do it in up to your kidneys?

As Golly fell backwards on the massive foam-rubber bed, making a V of her legs as she squealed:

—In you go to them kidneys, my lover!

As in her mind, two bloodied corpses waltzed almost poignantly on the small dance area of the Fontainebleau bar—with Blossom Foster looking hopelessly disfigured, as she leaned against her husband for consolation which he could not give her.

—Kidneys, fuck! Kidneys, fuck! Pedro Gonzales kept on repeating—until he snapped like elastic and then lay there, groaning.

—Mama.

As, Golly, abstractedly, twined his curls around her finger.

The BBC night tune, "Sail Away," was playing now. In a universe which cared only for the majesty of its own creation.

—Good night, said Patsy.

—Good night, replied his wife.

* * *

But the following day things did not go quite as planned. For a new, unanticipated bitterness once more overwhelmed Golly Murray. With the result that she almost forgot entirely the ecstasy which had been hers and Pedro's.

It had all begun while she'd been blackleading the kitchen range. Maybe, she considered, if she hadn't been so unlucky as to meet Blossom Foster directly after having been to the dentist's. With her wisdom tooth giving her unbearable pain.

What sort of a stupid idea had that been—asking Golly to another bridge session.

—In the middle of the day, for heaven's sake! hissed Golly. Her plans get stupider every time I meet her!

Just then—as she was finishing up—Golly heard the outside door close. It was Boniface, of course, arriving home from school. Listening with affection as she heard him skidding across the lino. Before bursting into the kitchen with a mighty yelp—tossing his schoolbag into the corner as always. But—to her dismay—on this occasion pushing right past her and flagrantly rejecting her affections, especially when she said:

—Give Babbie a kiss!

Embracing himself as he scrunched up his face, twisting his body as he hissed, ever so sourly:

—No want Dabby!

Which meant, of course, the boy wanted his father. And most likely, either, had no great desire to have another dessert spoon jabbed into his arm. As he ran upstairs and slammed his room door closed.

—I unnerstan', Golly Murray heard Pedro say, stroking the back of her hand as she poured out her troubles. But she knew that he didn't. How could he possibly? When, like Patsy, he was a man. A man who cared about nothing, only—kidneys.

—My husband would always understand, out of nowhere

she heard Blossom say—you see, Bodley Foster, he really is so sensitive.

—Is that so? said Golly. Well, we'll see very soon just how sensitive he is!

Blossom had been coming out of the hotel when she saw Golly. It had just been unfortunate that they met at that particular time—literally only minutes after Golly had been to the dentist. Her neighbor told her she had just been for a perm.

—What do you think? she cried, doing a little twirl.

Golly found herself on the precipice of hysterical utterance.

—I've been to the dentist's, you see the thing is I've just been to the dentist's! My wisdom tooth—it's *ugghh!*

—Do you know for years—I have had the exact same problem!

It seemed to Golly that Blossom Foster was probing the private and intimate spaces of her soul. And, against her will, like small hibernating animals, the words kept pressing from the darkness of Golly's mouth. As she said:

—O but your pain would be much worse than anything I could complain of. Why, mine is nothing, Blossom!

—Still, I'm sure when you get away on holiday you'll forget all about your wisdom-tooth troubles. So tell me, have you and Patsy made any plans yet?

—I don't know. I think there's talk of us going to the sea. Maybe Bundoran, in County Donegal.

—Bundoran in County Donegal, is it? Sure that in its own way is every bit as good as Miami! Well, lovey—honey—really must dash!

That was what had happened. That, essentially, was the wisdom-tooth incident. And now here she was—Golly standing cold and quivering in her very own kitchen. Motionless by the range with a single marrowfat pea in her hand. A marrowfat, of course, was a special kind of pea. Being of the type that her son liked to use whenever he was shooting at cereal boxes with his shooter.

The son who was now sobbing in the bedroom upstairs.

—Will you for the love of Christ stop it just for a minute! I'm your mother—I deserve more than this! she had snapped at him.

But deep in her heart she knew it wasn't her son's fault. Knew only too well whose fault it was.

Which was why she had gone against Pedro Gonzales's advice. When he had pleaded with her to follow the plan exactly as they had outlined it. What was wrong with her? he wanted to know. You can't go back there, he insisted. This could ruin everything, he pointed out. What was wrong with his Golly, he wanted to know—had she been drinking?

—It's none of your darn business! she had snapped, swinging her purse as she pushed the small man out of the way.

—You all make me sick, all of you—you and your damned kidneys! she had snapped.

It was the first time Golly Murray had sworn in her life. And did she care? No, because she only cared about one thing now.

As she mounted the embankment, making her way toward the freeway where the crumpled wreck of the Pontiac still lay, looking like an accordion and with the horn still blaring—the impact having taken place only moments before.

—Please! implored Pedro, but Golly didn't turn, didn't so much as pass Señor Kidney the time of day.

—It's over! she heard herself say. I'm going back to Patsy! But there's just one thing I got to do first.

* * *

As she pushed back the fine auburn curls of her hair and craned her neck forward—just in time to hear Blossom Foster. Releasing the softest and most plaintive of moans. Of something close to gratitude and pleasure, having just become aware that a familiar face—that of an actual neighbor!—had arrived on the scene to come to her assistance. Before, with mounting horror, as Golly's elongated shadow fell across the vehicle, she began to realize that assistance of that kind was not at all what was on her neighbor's mind.

For already Blossom's blouse had been torn open down the front, with the needle of her brooch glinting momentarily in the light, as Golly Murray's hands pressed vindictively into her neck—small as they were, possessing a quite unexpected, truly unearthly coldness.

It was to be some minutes before Blossom Foster realized the enormity of what had just taken place—and it was at that point she screamed. As Golly stumbled backwards, with warm crimson liquid now streaming erratically in small rivers from her lips, until she found herself positioned in the center of the freeway, with five lines of traffic perilously speeding past her. Her face in the moonlight showing a pallor and fixity truly terrifying as she flashed her incisors, wiping away a dribbling scarlet smear:

—See you on the shores of eternity, bitch!

It was 12:03 A.M.

Patsy, his wife noted, was frowning as he reached over to get his glass of water—but not at all anxiously.

—I just have this feeling Sheffield Wednesday might pull it out of the hat this weekend, he was saying, chewing on his pencil.

—Patsy dear, have you seen my *People's Friend* magazine? I could have sworn I left it on the sideboard.

—It's right over there, by the bed—where you left it, dear. But what happened to your other one—*Picturegoer*, is that what you call it?

—O, that's a silly old rag—I don't bother with that anymore, adding:

—O there it is! I really am such a silly—! as she turned back the covers and climbed into bed.

—A penny for your thoughts? asked the barber, smiling—marking an X as he chewed on his pencil.

As Golly replied, heaving as she turned the pages.

—All this talk about foreign holidays. There's times, you know, Patsy, when people get on my nerves.

—O now, foreign holidays. And all the places you can go to, here in our own little country.

—That's right, Patsy. Look, there's an advertisement here for Bundoran in County Donegal. Ten guineas, it says.

—Why, I'll go in and book it first thing in the morning!

Patsy leaned over and switched off the bedside lamp. As his wife, with the smallest of moans, thought one last time about Pedro Gonzales.

—*Tú eres muy hermosa,* she heard him repeat, thrusting inside her as she gently stroked his forehead. And mischievously whisper:

—What's that the Spanish for, pet—is it kidneys?

As her lover whimpered and shuddered as he bucked—with his handle going limp, for the last time, inside of her.

After which she left him to sleep like a baby, standing on the balcony of the Siesta Motel. Where now, as she'd somehow been expecting, on the stretch of white sand that reached out to the edge of the swaying blue ocean, she apprehended the image of the stumbling Blossom Foster, arrayed in what seemed as garments for the grave, with her arms raised up in pitiful mute appeal. With her hand tentatively hovering above the dark-stained ruffle of her torn nylon blouse, above her white bosom where her ickle nub had been. Staring as one bereft of sense.

—Please! she heard her plead, please give it back to me!

But the sound of the traffic coming from Ocean Drive drowned her out, and in the end she was faced with no choice but to turn and walk away. To haunt the boulevards of Florida forever, in the very place where Golly Murray, against the odds, had somehow found happiness.

As she remained there on the balcony, opening her small fist, revealing the shadowy circular outline of its contents. And which, in the moonlight, could easily have been taken for a marrowfat pea—one which a little boy might use with a cornflakes shooter.

But in texture Blossom's teat ("dugs," she had read, they called them in America) was fleshier and more pliable than a marrowfat—for all the world, in fact, like an areoled rubber button. As Golly Murray choked, closing her fingers over its captured mauve softness weeping:

—*Tú eres muy Boniface,* as the Florida moon's rays bathed the apartment buildings across the bay, systematically creating a palette of tropical pastels, washing them in faded pinks and the softest of greens and royal blues—until they seemed like a magical bag of Toytown Assorted.

That somehow, for no reason, had been shaken out of heaven.

I've Seen That Movie Too
VAL MCDERMID

I TRULY BELIEVED I'd never see her again. That she was gone for good. That the virus she'd planted in my bloodstream would be allowed to lie dormant forever. Which only goes to show how little I really understood about Cerys.

Everybody has an ugly secret. I don't care how righteous you are. Saint or sinner, there's something lurking in your past that looms over every good thing you do, that makes your toes curl in shame, that makes your stomach curdle at the thought of discovery. Don't try to pretend you're the exception. You're not. We all have our skeletons, and Cerys is mine.

The world as I know it falls into two groups. The ones who fall under Cerys's spell and the ones who are immune to the point of bafflement. Over the past three years, I've discovered there were a lot more in the former group than I'd ever suspected. The list of people she'd bewitched ranged from the daughter of a duke to a celebrity midget, from a prizewinning poet to a gay male member of parliament. It mortifies me how many of them I now know she was fucking during the months she was supposed to be my girlfriend. What's extraordinary is how many of them were convinced they were the special one.

For the members of the latter group, the word *even* is crucial to their insistent deconstruction of Cerys. "She isn't even beautiful." "She isn't even interesting." "She isn't even sexy." "She isn't even funny." "She isn't even blonde." But to those of us on the other side of the fence, she's all of those things. The only explanation that makes any sense is the notion of viral infection. The Oxford English Dictionary defines a computer virus as "a piece of code surreptitiously introduced into a system in order to corrupt it." In every sense of the word *corrupt*, that's Cerys.

The one good thing she ever did for me was to walk out of my life three years ago without a goodbye or a forwarding address. I don't think her motive was to destroy me; that would presume my reaction even entered her calculations. No, the suddenness of her departure and the thoroughness of her vanishing had been all about her need to get free and clear before the answers rolled in to the questions other people had started asking. But at the time, I didn't care about the reasons. I was just grateful for the chance to free myself. Deep down, I didn't mind the anguish or the self-loathing or the shame, because it's always easy to endure pain when you understand it's part of the healing process. Even then, I knew that somewhere down the line I would get past all the suffering and resume control over my heart and mind.

And I did. It took me well over a year to drag myself beyond what she'd done to me, but I managed it.

Yet now, in an instant, all that healing was stripped away and I felt as raw and captive as I had the day she'd left. Here, in the unlikely setting of the Finnish consul's Edinburgh residence, I could feel the gears stripping and the wheels coming off my reassembled life.

I shouldn't even have been there. I don't usually bother with the fancy receptions that attach themselves to the movie business like barnacles to a ship's hull. But the three Finnish producers who had become the Coen brothers of the European film industry had optioned a treatment from me, and my agent was adamant that I show my face at the consul's party in their honor at the Edinburgh Film Festival. So I'd turned up forty minutes late, figuring I'd have just enough time for a drink and the right hellos before the diplomats cleared their throats and signaled the party was over.

As soon as I crossed the threshold, I knew something was off-kilter. Cerys had always had that effect on me. Whenever I walked into a room where she was, my senses tripped into overdrive. Now my head swiveled from side to side, my eyes darting round, trying to figure out why I was instantly edgy. She saw me at the same moment I spotted her. She was talking to some guy in a suit and she didn't miss a beat when she caught sight of me. But her eyes widened, and that was enough for my stomach to crash like a severed lift cage.

I felt a ringing in my ears, stilling the loud mutter of conversation in the room. Before I could react, she'd excused herself and snaked through the throng to my side. "Alice," she said, the familiar voice a caress that made the hairs on my arms quiver.

I was determined not to be suckered back in. To put up a fight at least. "What the hell are you doing here?" I tried to make my voice harsh and almost succeeded.

Cerys reached out, circling my wrist with finger and thumb. The touch of her flesh was a band of burning ice. "We need to talk," she said, drawing me to her side and somehow maneuvering me back through the doorway I'd just entered.

"No," I said weakly. "No, we don't need to talk."

She turned to me then and smiled, the tip of her tongue running along the edge of her teeth. "Oh, Alice, you always cut straight to the chase, don't you?" She made a determined break for a staircase at the end of the hall. I couldn't free myself without drawing the wrong kind of attention from the other people milling round in the hallway. The last thing I wanted was for anyone to make a connection between me and Cerys. I'd kept my nose clean on that score and it had saved me from enough of the consequences of our association for me to want to keep it that way.

So I let her lead me up the broad, carpeted stairs without obvious protest. Somehow, she knew where she was going. She opened the second door on the right and pulled me into a small sitting room—a pair of armchairs, a chaise longue, and an antique writing desk with matching chair. She used my momentum to spin me round like a dancer, then closed the door briskly behind her, turning a key in the lock.

"To answer your question, I've been working with the Finnish film agency," she said. At once I understood her apparent familiarity with the layout of the Finnish consul's house. And that the chances were I wasn't the first person she'd been with behind that locked door.

I opened my mouth to protest but I was too late. Cerys took my face between her hands and covered my mouth with dozens of tiny kisses and flicks of the tongue. Her fingertips brushed the skin of my neck, slipping inside my open blouse and over my shoulders. The heat that flushed my skin was nothing to do with the Scottish summer weather. I despised myself even as desire surged through me, but I didn't even consider pushing her away. I knew I wouldn't be able to follow through and I'd only end up humiliating myself by begging for her later.

"This . . . is not . . . a good . . . idea . . ." The words came from my head while every other part of me was willing my mouth to shut the fuck up. Cerys knew this so she just smiled. Her hands moved under my skirt, the backs of her fingernails grazing the insides of my thighs.

"I've missed you," she murmured as her hand moved higher, meeting no resistance. I felt myself falling, the chaise longue behind me, the certainty of pain and trouble ahead.

Not love, not at first sight. I don't want to elevate it to something it wasn't. But it was something, no doubt of that. I'd emerged late one summer evening from Inverness rail station, hoping that someone from the Scottish Film Foundation would be there to drive me to the remote steading where I'd be spending the rest of the week. I'd been supposed to arrive with four other writers for a screenwriting master-class course that morning, but my flight had been canceled and it had taken the rest of the day to travel the length of the country from the West Country to the Highlands by train. I was not in the best of moods.

The woman leaning against the car in the courtyard caught my attention. Her languid pose: long legs crossed at the ankle, right arm folded across her stomach, hand cupping the left elbow, rollie dangling from the fingers of her left hand, a sliver of smoke twisting in the warm evening air, head at an angle, eyes on the middle distance, thick honey-blonde hair cut short . . . She made my breath catch in my throat. It was an image I suspected I would never forget. I feared I would keep on writing scenes for women in that precise pose for the rest of my career. I didn't even dare to hope she was waiting for me.

But she was. Cerys Black, Screenwriting Development Director for the Scottish Film Foundation. It was a fancy title, implying more than a department of one, but I soon learned that Cerys did everything from picking up late arrivals to pitching which projects should win the SFF's backing. That night, though, I wasn't interested in her job description. Only that I'd found myself in the company of a woman who made me dizzy for the first time in years. My grumpiness evaporated in less time than it took to stow my bags in the car boot.

She took me to a bistro by the river. "Everyone's eaten and you won't feel like cooking this late," she said. We ate pasta and drank red wine and talked. I've never been able to piece together the route of the conversation. I only remember that we talked about the women in our past. I now have an inkling of how severely Cerys edited her history, but at the time I had no reason to doubt her tale of a handful of youthful affairs and a single grand passion that had taken her to Hungary before it had finally died a couple of years before. It was the sort of conversation that is really an extended form of deniable flirtation and it kept us occupied until the waitress made it abundantly clear that Inverness had a midnight curfew and we were in danger of breaching it.

We drove out of the city along the side of the loch, the rounded humps of high mountains silhouetted against thin darkness shot with stars. We turned up a steep road that took us away from the mountains to a high valley surrounded by summits. We barely spoke but something was moving forward between us.

The cluster of low buildings that was our base for the week was in darkness when we arrived. Cerys led me to a cottage set to one side. "You're in here," she said. "Downstairs there's a computer room and library and upstairs there are two suites of rooms." We climbed the narrow stairs and Cerys dropped her voice. "Tom Hart's on the right and you're on the left."

She ushered me in and put my backpack by a table facing a pair of long windows. I swung my holdall onto a chair and turned to thank her, suddenly shy.

There was nothing shy about her response. She moved closer,

one hand on my hip, the other on my shoulder, and kissed me. Not the air kiss of the media world, not the prim kiss of a distant cousin, not the dry brush of lips friends share. This was the kind of kiss that burns boats and bridges in equal measure.

Time played its tricks and made it last forever and no time at all. When we finally stopped, Cerys looked as astonished as I felt. "I don't think snogging in an open doorway is the most sensible move," she said. "You should shut your door now."

I nodded, numb with disappointment.

Then she smiled, a crooked grin that lifted one side of her mouth higher than the other. "Which side of it would you like me to be on?"

If I could say that sex with Cerys was the most amazing experience of my life, it might make more sense of what happened between us. But that would be a lie. It was enthralling, it was adventurous, it was sometimes dark and edgy. But it never entirely fulfilled me. She always left me not just wanting more but feeling obscurely that somehow it was my fault that I hadn't found total satisfaction in her arms. So I was always eager for the next time, quick to persuade myself that the electricity between us meant the wattage of our sexual connection would rise even higher. I was addicted, no question about it.

I knew by the end of that master-class week that I loved her. I loved her body and her mind, her reticence and her boldness. We'd hadn't spent that much time together—she had other responsibilities, and by the third night, it was clear we both needed some sleep—but I was under her spell. I wanted to see her again, and soon. Her work tied her to Edinburgh, my life was at the other end of the country. But I couldn't see this as an obstacle. We could make it work. We would make it work.

Looking back, I can see all the cracks and gaps of lies and deception. But at the time, I had no reason to mistrust her. I believed in the meetings, the conferences, the working dinners, the trips to film festivals. I was just amazed and grateful that we managed to see each other one night most weeks. We spoke on the phone, though not as much as I craved; Cerys was only comfortable with the phone for professional purposes, she told me. And we made plans. I would sell my house by the sea in Devon and buy a flat in Edinburgh. Not with Cerys—that would have made her claustrophobic. After the disastrous end of her relationship with the Hungarian, she didn't ever want to live with someone else without her own bolt-hole. Given what she'd told me about their last months, I understood that. I'd have felt the same, I thought.

I was anxious about the move, though. Prices in Edinburgh were astronomical. I couldn't see how I was going to afford somewhere half decent. I'd tried to talk to Cerys about it, but she'd stopped my worries with kisses and deft movements of her strong, gentle hands.

And then one night she met me at the airport in the same languid stance. Only the cigarette was missing. As always, my heart seemed to contract in my chest. "I have the answer," she said after she'd kissed my mouth and buried her face in my hair.

"The answer to what?"

"How you can afford a flat."

"How?"

And over dinner, she told me. A legendary Scottish star had died a few months previously. The film foundation had just learned he'd left almost all of his many millions in a trust to benefit Scottish filmmakers. A trust that was to be administered by the SFF. "Instead of giving people piddling little grants of a few grand, we'll be able to fund proper development," Cerys said. "We'll essentially be putting money on the table like the serious players."

"That's fantastic news. But what's that got to do with me?"

The crooked smile and a dark sparkle in her eyes was the only answer I got at first. She sipped her wine and clinked her glass against mine. "You're going to be a star, sweetheart," she finally said.

It was breathtakingly simple but for someone as fundamentally law-abiding as me, unbelievably bad. We were going to set up a fictitious production company. Cerys had access to all the necessary letterheads to make it look as if they had backing from serious Hollywood players. I'd be the screenwriter on the project. We'd go to the SFF for the seed money and come away with a two-million-pound pot. The company would pay me a million via my agent, all aboveboard. And Cerys would siphon off the other million. And then the project would go belly-up because the Hollywood backers had pulled out. A shrug of the shoulders. It happens all the time in the movie business.

"It'll never work," I said. "How will we convince the SFF?"

Again the crooked smile. "Because you're Scottish by birth. Because I'm the person who makes the recommendations to the grant committee. And because you're going to write a brilliant treatment that will sound like it could plausibly be a Hollywood blockbuster."

It's a measure of how Cerys had captivated me that what worried me was not that we were about to embark upon a criminal fraud. What bothered me was whether I could write a good enough treatment to bluff our way past the grants committee.

It took me a month to come up with the idea and another six weeks to get the pitch and treatment in place. And of course Cerys was perfectly placed to help me knock it into shape. I called it *The Whole of the Moon* after the Waterboys track. The opening paragraph of the pitch had taken days to get right, but in the end I was happy with it. *Dominic O'Donnell is an*

IRA quartermaster who wants to retire from the front line in Belfast; Brigid Fitzgerald is a financial investigator from Seattle. When they meet, their lives change in ways neither of them could ever have imagined. The Whole of the Moon *is a romantic comedy thriller with a dark edge, strong on sense of place and underpinned by New Irish music.*

I'd have been terrified about pitching the grants committee if Cerys hadn't spent her lunch hour fucking me senseless in the hotel down the street from the SFF office. As it was, I was so dazed I waltzed through it as if a two-million-pound grant was my birthright. Not in an arrogant way, but in that "If Scotland wants to be taken seriously in the international arts community, we need to behave as if we are serious" sort of way.

And it worked. The grants committee was dizzy with its new powers of patronage and Cerys easily persuaded its members that this was the sort of flagship project they needed in order to give the SFF an international profile. The two million pounds was paid into the bank account of the company she'd set up in Panama, which was where we were allegedly going to be doing some of our location filming. My fee was with my agent in days. It took me all of two weeks to close the deal on a New Town flat with views over the Forth estuary to Fife.

Life wasn't quite as perfect as I'd expected. Cerys seemed to be out of town much more than before, and I barely saw more of her than I had when I was living at the other end of the country. And of course we had to keep our relationship under wraps to begin with. Edinburgh's a big city wrapped round a small village, and we didn't want the grants committee members to wonder whether they'd been stitched up. Or worse.

Three months after we'd been given the money, Cerys reported back to her boss that the production company had gone bust. She told me he'd taken it in his stride, and I believed that too.

And then a couple of weeks later, we walked into the breakfast room of a hotel in Newcastle and came face to face with the chairman of the grants committee and his wife. We tried to pretend we'd only just started seeing each other, but my lies were nowhere near as slick as Cerys's.

We were both quiet on the drive back to Edinburgh. I was glum and assumed she was too. A couple of days later, I realized her silence was not because she was worried but because she was planning furiously. She dropped me at my flat that night and went back to her place, where she packed the car with the few things she really cared about—clothes, DVDs, books, her Mac, and half a dozen paintings—and left. When I hadn't heard from her for three days, I borrowed the emergency key to her flat from her neighbor and let myself in. I knew as soon as I walked through the door that she was gone. The air was empty of her presence.

Sprawled on the chaise longue, I could smell her and taste her. If I'd been struck blind and deaf, my senses would still have recognized her. Having her back in my arms again drew me back under her command. I hated the terrible longing that possessed me but I didn't know how to make it stop. Before, only her absence had taken the edge off the craving. I thought I was cured but now I knew I was one of the backsliders. Just like those smokers who have given up for so long they think they can afford the risk of the occasional cigarette. And before they know it, they're back on a pack and a half a day. One fuck and I was no longer my own woman.

"Are you not taking a hell of a chance, coming back here?"

She pushed her sweat-damp hair out of her eyes. She'd let it grow and now it was like a shaggy helmet streaked a dozen different shades by the sun. Not what you'd call a disguise, but a difference. "If they had anything on me, I'd never have got another job in the industry. They can think what they like. It makes no odds without proof."

"So why did you run?"

She closed her eyes and ran her fingertips over my face, as if reminding herself of a tactile memory. "I couldn't be bothered answering the questions."

I felt a faint stirring of what might have been outrage if it had been allowed to take root. "You left me high and dry because you couldn't be bothered answering questions?"

She opened her eyes and sighed. "Alice, you know I hate to be pinned down."

"But you came back." I knew I was clutching at shadows, but apparently I couldn't prevent myself from going into pathetic mode.

Cerys shifted her weight to pin me down more completely, her thigh between my legs exerting a delicious pleasure. "I came back because of you."

I couldn't keep the joy and amazement from my face and voice. "You came back for me?"

A dry little laugh. "Not for you. Because of you."

"I don't understand."

"Because of what you've done. Because you owe me."

Now I was puzzled. "I owe you? You walked out on me, and I owe you?"

"I'm not talking metaphorically, Alice. I'm not talking about emotions. I'm talking about money."

It was a familiar Cerys roller coaster moment and it left me sour. "Money? You got your share. More than your share. You didn't have an agent taking fifteen percent off the top."

"I'm not talking about the grant money. I'm talking about the movie. You might have changed the title but I'm not stupid. As soon as I saw the advance publicity in the trade press, I knew what you'd done. You changed the name from *The Whole of the Moon* to *A Man Is In Love* and sold it to Hollywood for real."

"It's not a secret, Cerys. And it's my work to sell."

"It's work that wouldn't exist without me. You'd never have come up with the idea and developed it without me. According to my sources, you cleared another couple of million from the studio. The way I see it, that means you owe me at least another million."

I tried to tell myself she was joking, but I knew her better than that. "That's not how I see it."

"No, but if I can't persuade you to see it my way, the world is going to know how you got your first million. And how much of the work on that treatment was mine."

I managed a strangled laugh. "You can't drop me in it without dropping yourself in it," I protested, trying to shift my body away from hers but confounded by the arm of the chaise.

"I'll throw myself on their mercy. Tell them how I was so besotted by you that I did what you told me. It's what they'll want to hear because it lets them off the hook. Better to employ some woman led astray by her emotions than a crook, don't you think?"

Cerys telling lies would be far more convincing than me telling the truth. I knew that. And even as I listened to her duplicity, I knew I was still her prisoner. The thought of finding myself her enemy was intolerable. "I thought you cared about me. I can't believe you'd blackmail me."

"Blackmail is such an ugly word," she said, finally pushing herself on to her knees and moving away from me.

I shivered, disgust and desire mingling in an unholy alliance. "But an accurate one."

"I like to think of it as sharing. A down payment of fifty grand by the end of the week would be acceptable." She buttoned her shirt, picked her jeans and underwear off the floor, and slipped back into her public persona. "In cash."

"How am I supposed to explain that to my accountant? To my bank?"

She shrugged. "Your problem, Alice. You're good at solving problems. That's what makes your scripts work so well. Call me tomorrow and I'll let you know where to drop the money off."

I sat up. "No. If I'm handing over that kind of money, I want something in exchange. If you want the money, you have to meet me."

Cerys cocked her head, appraising me. It felt like a health and safety risk assessment. "Somewhere public," she said at last.

"No." I seldom managed any kind of assertiveness with her, but the understanding that had blossomed in the past few minutes made it necessary. "I want us to fuck one last time. Like the song says, for the good times."

I could see contempt in her face, but her voice betrayed none of it. She sounded warm and amused. "Why not? Shall I come to your flat?"

I'm not strong. Carrying a body down two flights of stairs and down the back lane to my garage would be beyond me. "I'll pick you up at your hotel. I've got a cabin in Perthshire, we can drive up there and have dinner. You can stay the night. One last night, Cerys, please. I've missed you so much."

A long, calculating pause. Then Cerys made the first

miscalculation I'd seen from her. "Why not?" she repeated. We arranged that we would meet in the car park near her hotel on Friday afternoon. "I might as well check out then," she said. "You need to have me at the airport by eleven on Saturday morning so I can make the Helsinki flight."

Perfect. "No problem," I lied, surprised at how easy it was. But then I'd had the best possible teacher.

That left me five days to make my plans. I arranged to withdraw the money from the bank because I wanted to reassure Cerys that she was still in the driving seat. I'd show it to her before we drove off to Perthshire, the magnet that would keep her on board.

Working out the details of murder was a lot harder. Once I'd made the decision, once I'd realized that I'd never be free of her demands or my desire while she was still alive, it wasn't hard to accept that murder was the only possible answer. Cerys had already transformed me from law-abiding citizen to successful criminal, after all.

Body disposal, the usual trip wire for killers in films, was the least of my worries. The Scottish highlands contain vast tracts of emptiness where small predatory animals feed on all sorts of carrion. Forestry tracks lead deep into isolated woodland where nobody sets foot from one year's end to the next. And of course Cerys had walked away from her life before—in Hungary and in Edinburgh that I knew of, which probably meant she'd also done it in other places, other times. Nobody would be too surprised if she did it again. I didn't imagine anyone would seriously go looking for her, especially since she would have checked out of her hotel under her own steam.

How to kill her was a lot harder to figure out. Poison or drugs would have been my weapons of choice. But in her shoes, I wouldn't eat a crumb or drink a drop I hadn't brought with me. I didn't think she would be suspicious of me—I thought she was confident in the power she had over me—but I didn't want to take any chances.

If movies have taught me anything, it's that blunt instruments, blades, and guns are too chancy. They're all capable of missing their targets, they all tend to leave forensic traces you can never erase, and they're all concrete pieces of evidence you have to dispose of. So they were all out of the question.

I thought of smothering her while she slept, but I wasn't convinced I could carry that through, not flesh to flesh and heart to heart. Strangling had the same problems, plus my fear that I wasn't strong enough to carry it through.

Murder, it turned out, was a lot easier in the movies.

I woke up on the Wednesday morning without an idea in my head. When I went through to the kitchen and turned on the light, a bulb popped, tripping the fuse in the main box. And a light went on inside my head.

Back when I bought my house in Devon, I didn't have much money. I'd only been able to afford the house because it was practically derelict and I learned enough of all the building trades to do the restoration and renovation myself. I can lay bricks, plaster walls, install plumbing, and do basic carpentry.

I also know how electricity works.

Cerys may be able to last overnight without eating and drinking. She won't be able to make it without going to the toilet. My cabin on the loch has been fitted out in retro style, with an old-fashioned high-level toilet cistern with a long chain that you have to yank hard to generate a flush. It turned out to be a simple task to replace the ceramic handle with a metal one and to wire the whole lot into the main supply. As her fist closes round the handle, two hundred and forty volts will course through her body, her hand will clench tighter, and her heart will freeze.

Part of my heart will also freeze. But I can live with that. And because nothing is ever wasted, I will find a way to make a script out of it. Such a pity Cerys won't be around to see that movie too.

The Story of the Stabbing

JOYCE CAROL OATES

FOUR YEARS OLD she'd begun to hear in fragments and patches like handfuls of torn clouds the story of the stabbing in Manhattan that was initially her mother's story.

That morning in March 1980 when Mrs. Karr drove to New York City alone. Took the New Jersey Turnpike to the Holland Tunnel exit, entered lower Manhattan and crossed Hudson and Greenwich Streets and at West Street turned north, her usual route when she visited an aunt who lived in a fortresslike building resembling a granite pueblo dwelling on West Twenty-seventh Street, but just below Fourteenth Street traffic began abruptly to slow—the right lane was blocked by construction—a din of air hammers assailed her ears—vehicles were moving in spasmodic jerks—Madeleine braked her 1974 Volvo narrowly avoiding rear-ending a van braking to a stop directly in front of her—a tin-colored vehicle with a corroded rear bumper and a New York license plate whose raised numerals and letters were just barely discernible through layers of dried mud like a palimpsest. Overhead were clouds like wadded tissues, a sepia glaze to the late-winter urban air and a stink of diesel exhaust and Madeleine Karr whose claim it was that she loved Manhattan felt now a distinct unease in stalled traffic amid a cacophony of horns, the masculine aggressiveness of horns, for several blocks she'd been aware of the tin-colored van jolting ahead of her on West Street, passing on the right, switching lanes, braking at the construction blockade but at once lurching forward as if the driver had carelessly—or deliberately—lifted his foot from the brake pedal and in so doing caused his right front fender to brush against a pedestrian in a windbreaker crossing West Street—crossing at the intersection though at a red light, since traffic was stalled—unwisely then in a fit of temper the pedestrian in the windbreaker struck the fender with the flat of his hand—he was a burly man of above average height—Madeleine heard him shouting but not the words, distinctly—might've been *Fuck you!* or even *Fuck you asshole!*—immediately then the van driver leapt out of the van and rushed at the pedestrian—Madeleine blinked in astonishment at this display of masculine contention—Madeleine was expecting to see the men fight together clumsily—aghast then to see the van driver wielding what appeared to be a knife with a considerable blade, maybe six—eight—inches long—so quickly this was happening, Madeleine's brain could not have identified *Knife!*—trapped behind the steering wheel of the Volvo like a child trapped in a nightmare Madeleine witnessed an event, an action, to which her dazzled brain could not readily have identified as *Stabbing! Murder!*—in a rage the man with the knife lashed at the now stunned pedestrian in the windbreaker, who hadn't time to turn away—striking the man on his uplifted arms, striking and tearing the sleeves of the windbreaker, swiping against the man's face, then in a wicked and seemingly practiced pendulum motion slashing the man's throat just below his jaw, right to left, left to right causing blood to spring instantaneously into the air—*A six-foot arc of blood at least* as Madeleine would describe it afterward, horrified—for never had Madeleine Karr witnessed anything so horrible—never would Madeleine Karr forget this savage attack in the unsparing clarity of a morning in late March—the spectacle of a living man *attacked, struck down, stabbed, throat slashed* before her eyes. The victim wore what appeared to be work clothes—work boots—he was at least a decade older than his assailant—late thirties, early forties—bareheaded, with steely-gray hair in a crew cut—only seconds before the attack the victim had been seething with indignation—he'd been empowered by rage—the sort of individual with whom, alone in the city in such circumstances on West Street just below Fourteenth Street, Madeleine Karr would never have dared to lock eyes. Yet now the burly man in the windbreaker was rendered harmless—stricken—sinking to his knees as his assailant leapt back from him—very quick, lithe on his feet—though not quick enough to avoid being splattered by his victim's blood. Making no attempt to hide the bloody knife he held—he seemed to be visibly brandishing the knife—the van driver ran back to his vehicle, deftly climbed inside and slammed shut the door and in virtually the same instant propelled the van forward head-on and lurching—with a squeal of tires against pavement—aiming the van into a narrow space between another vehicle and the torn-up roadway where construction workers in safety helmets were staring—knocking aside a sawhorse, a series of orange traffic cones scattering in the street and bouncing off other vehicles as in a luridly colorful and comic simulation of bowling pins scattered by an immense bowling ball; by this time the stricken man was kneeling on the pavement desperately pressing both hands—these were bare hands, big-knuckled, Madeleine could see from a distance of no more than twelve feet—against his ravaged throat in a gesture of childlike poignancy and futility as blood continued to spurt from him *Like water from a hose—horrible!*

As if paralyzed Madeleine stared at the stricken man now writhing on the pavement in a bright neon-red pool—still clutching desperately at his throat—amid a frantic din of horns—traffic backed up for blocks on northbound West Street as in a nightmare of mangled and thwarted movement like snarled film. Nothing so mattered to Madeleine as escaping from this nightmare—in a panic of thudding heart, clammy skin and dry mouth thinking not of the stricken man a short distance from the front bumper of the Volvo but of herself—yearning only to turn her car around—reverse her course on accursed West Street back to the Holland Tunnel—the Jersey Turnpike—and so to Princeton from which scarcely ninety minutes before Madeleine had left with such exhilaration, childish anticipation and defiance *Manhattan is so alive!—Princeton is so embalmed. Nothing ever feels real to me there, this life in disguise as a wife and a mother of no more durability than a figure in papier-mâché. I don't need any of you!*

So strangely Madeleine had seemed to be watching the spectacle a few yards away through a kind of tunnel—through the wrong end of a telescope—curiously drained of light and color; now she could see other people—fellow pedestrians approaching the fallen man—workmen from the construction site—on the run a police officer—and a second police officer.

Soon then there came a deafening siren—several sirens—emergency vehicles could come no closer than a side street peripheral to Madeleine's vision—Madeleine saw figures bent over the fallen man—a stretcher was lifted, carried away—nothing to see finally but a pool of something brightly red like old-fashioned Technicolor glistening on the pavement in cold March sunshine. *And the nightmare didn't end. The police questioned all the witnesses they could find. They came for me, they took me to the police precinct. For forty minutes they kept me. I had to beg them to let me use the women's room—I couldn't stop crying—I am not a hysterical person but I couldn't stop crying—of course I wanted to help the police but I couldn't seem to remember what anything had looked like—what the men had looked like—even the "skin color" of the man with the knife—even of the man who'd been stabbed. I told them that I thought the van driver had been dark-skinned—maybe—he was "young"—in his twenties possibly—or maybe older—but not much older—he was wearing a satin kind of jacket like a sports jacket like high school boys wear—I think that's what I saw—I couldn't remember the color of the jacket—maybe it was dark—dark purple?—a kind of shiny material—a cheap shiny material—maybe there was some sort of design on the back of the jacket—Oh I couldn't even remember the color of the van—it was as if my eyes had gone blind—the colors of things had drained from them—I'd seen everything through a tunnel—I thought that the van driver with the knife was dark-skinned but not "black" exactly—but not white—I mean not "Caucasian"—because his hair was—wasn't—his hair didn't seem to be—"Negroid hair"—if that is a way of describing it. And how tall he was, how heavy, the police were asking, I had no idea, I wasn't myself, I was very upset, trying to speak calmly and not hysterically, I have never been hysterical in my life. Because I wanted to help the police find the man with the knife. But I could not describe the van, either. I could not identify the van by its make or by the year. Of course I could not remember anything of the license plate—I wasn't sure that I'd even seen a license plate—or if I did, it was covered with dirt. The police kept asking me what the men had said to each other, what the pedestrian had said, they kept asking me to describe how he'd hit the fender of the van, and the van driver—the man with the knife—what had he said?—but I couldn't hear—my car windows were up, tight—I couldn't hear. They asked me how long the "altercation" had lasted before the pedestrian was stabbed and I said that the stabbing began right away—then I said maybe it had begun right away—I couldn't be sure—I couldn't be sure of anything—I was hesitant to give a statement—sign my name to a statement—it was as if part of my brain had been extinguished—trying to think of it now, I can't—not clearly—I was trying to explain—apologize—I told them that I was sorry I couldn't help them better, I hoped that other witnesses could help them better and finally they released me—they were disgusted with me, I think—I didn't blame them—I was feeling weak and sick but all I wanted to do was get back to Princeton, didn't even telephone anyone just returned to the Holland Tunnel thinking I would never use that tunnel again, never drive on West Street not ever again.*

In that late winter of 1980 when Rhonda was four years old the story of the stabbing began to be told in the Karr household on Broadmead Road, Princeton, New Jersey. Many times the story was told and retold but never in the presence of the Karrs' daughter, who was too young and too sensitive for such a terrifying and ugly story and what was worse, a story that seemed to be missing an ending. *Did the stabbed man die?—he must have died. Was the killer caught?—he must have been caught.* Rhonda could not ask because Rhonda was supposed not to know what had happened, or almost happened, to Mommy on that day in Manhattan when she'd driven in alone as Daddy did not like Mommy to do. Nothing is more evident to a child of even ordinary curiosity and canniness than a family secret, a "taboo" subject—and Rhonda was not an ordinary child. There she stood barefoot in her nightie in the hall outside her parents' bedroom where the door was shut against her daring to listen to her parents' lowered, urgent voices inside; silently she came up behind her distraught-sounding mother as Madeleine sat on the edge of a chair in the kitchen speaking on the phone as so frequently Madeleine spoke on the phone with her wide circle of friends. *The most horrible thing! A nightmare! It happened so quickly and there was nothing anyone could do and afterward . . .* Glancing around to see Rhonda in the doorway, startled and murmuring *Sorry! No more right now, my daughter is listening.*

Futile to inquire what Mommy was talking about, Rhonda knew. What had happened that was so upsetting and so ugly that when Rhonda pouted wanting to know she was told *Mommy wasn't hurt, Mommy is all right—that's all that matters.*

And *Not fit for the ears of a sweet little girl like you. No no!*

Very soon after Mrs. Karr began to tell the story of the stabbing on a Manhattan street, Mr. Karr began to tell the story too. Except in Mr. Karr's excitable voice the story of the stabbing was considerably altered for Rhonda's father was not faltering or hesitant like Rhonda's mother but a professor of American Studies at the University, a man for whom speech was a sort of instrument, or weapon, to be boldly and not meekly brandished; and so when Mr. Karr appropriated his wife's story it was in a zestful storytelling voice like a TV voice—in fact, Professor Gerald Karr was frequently seen on TV—PBS, Channel 13 in New York City—discussing political issues—bewhiskered, with glinting wire-rimmed glasses and a ruddy flushed face. *Crude racial justice! Counterlynching!*

Not the horror of the incident was emphasized, in Mr. Karr's telling, but the irony. For the victim, in Mr. Karr's version of the stabbing, was a *Caucasian male* and the delivery-van assailant was a *black male*—or, variously, a *person of color*. Rhonda seemed to know that *Caucasian* meant *white*, though she had no idea why; she had not heard her mother identify *Caucasian, person of color* in her accounts of the stabbing, for Mrs. Karr dwelt almost exclusively on her own feelings—her fear, her shock, her dismay and disgust—how eager she'd been to return home to Princeton—she'd said very little about either of the men as if she hadn't seen them really but only just the stabbing *It happened so fast—it was just so awful—that poor man bleeding like that!—and no one could help him. And the man with the knife just—drove away* . . . But Mr. Karr who was Rhonda's Daddy and an important professor at the University knew exactly what the story meant for the young black man with the knife—the young *person of color*—was clearly one of *an exploited and disenfranchised class of urban ghetto dwellers rising up against his oppressors crudely striking as he could, class vengeance, an instinctive "lynching," the white victim is collateral damage in the undeclared and unacknowledged but ongoing class war*. The fact that the delivery-van driver had stabbed—killed?—a pedestrian was unfortunate of course, Mr. Karr conceded—a tragedy of course—but who could blame the assailant who'd been provoked, challenged—hadn't the pedestrian struck his vehicle and threatened him—shouted obscenities at him—a good defense attorney could argue a case for self-defense—the van driver was protecting himself from imminent harm, as anyone in his situation might do. For there is such a phenomenon as *racial instinct, self-protectiveness. Kill that you will not be killed*.

As Mr. Karr was not nearly so hesitant as Mrs. Karr about interpreting the story of the stabbing, in ever more elaborate and persuasive theoretical variants with the passing of time, so Mr. Karr was not nearly so careful as Mrs. Karr about shielding their daughter from the story itself. Of course—Mr. Karr never told Rhonda the story of the stabbing, directly. Rhonda's Daddy would not have done such a thing for though Gerald Karr was what he called *ultraliberal* he did not truly believe—all the evidence of his intimate personal experience suggested otherwise!—that girls and women should not be protected from as much of life's ugliness as possible, and who was there to protect them but men?—fathers, husbands. Against his conviction that marriage is a bourgeois convention, ludicrous, unenforceable, yet Gerald Karr had entered into such a (legal, moral) relationship with a woman, and he meant to honor that vow. And he would honor that vow, in all the ways he could. So it was, Rhonda's father would not have told her the story of the stabbing and yet by degrees Rhonda came to absorb it for the story of the stabbing was told and retold by Mr. Karr at varying lengths depending upon Mr. Karr's mood and/or the mood of his listeners, who were likely to be university colleagues, or visiting colleagues from other universities. *Let me tell you—this incident that happened to Madeleine—like a fable out of Aesop.* Rhonda was sometimes a bit confused—her father's story of the stabbing shifted in minor ways—West Street became West Broadway, or West Houston—West Twelfth Street at Seventh Avenue—the late-winter season became midsummer—in Mr. Karr's descriptive words *the fetid heat of Manhattan in August.* In a later variant of the story which began to be told sometime after Rhonda's seventh birthday when her father seemed to be no longer living in the large stucco-and-timber house on Broadmead with Rhonda and her mother but elsewhere—for a while in a minimally furnished university-owned faculty residence overlooking Lake Carnegie, later a condominium on Canal Pointe Road, Princeton, still later a stone-and-timber Tudor house on a tree-lined street in Cambridge, Massachusetts—it happened that the story of the stabbing became totally appropriated by Mr. Karr as an experience he'd had himself and had witnessed with his own eyes from his vehicle—not the Volvo but the Toyota station wagon—stalled in traffic less than ten feet from the incident: The delivery van braking to a halt, the pedestrian who'd been crossing against the light—*Caucasian, male, arrogant, in a Burberry trench coat, carrying a briefcase—doomed*—had dared to strike a fender of the van, shout threats and obscenities at the driver and so out of the van the driver had leapt, as Mr. Karr observed with the eyes of a frontline war correspondent—*Dark-skinned young guy with dreadlocks like Medusa, must've been Rastafarian—swift and deadly as a panther*—the knife, the slashing of the pedestrian's throat—a ritual, a ritual killing—sacrifice—in Mr. Karr's version just a single powerful swipe of the knife and again as in a nightmare cinematic replay which Rhonda had seen countless times and had dreamt yet more times there erupted *the incredible six-foot jet of blood* which was at the very heart of the story—the revelation toward which all else led.

What other meaning was there? What other meaning was possible?

Rhonda's father shaking his head marveling *Like nothing you could imagine, nothing you'd ever forget. Jesus!*

That fetid-hot day in Manhattan. Rhonda had been with Daddy in the station wagon. He'd buckled her into the seat beside him for she was a big enough girl now to sit in the front seat and not in the silly baby seat in the back. And Daddy had braked the station wagon, and Daddy's arm had shot out to protect Rhonda from being thrown forward, and Daddy had protected

Rhonda from what was out there on the street, beyond the windshield. Daddy had said *Shut your eyes, Rhonda! Crouch down and hide your face darling* and so Rhonda had.

By the time Rhonda was ten years old and in fifth grade at Princeton Day School Madeleine Karr wasn't any longer quite so cautious about telling the story of the stabbing—or, more frequently, merely alluding to it, since the story of the stabbing had been told numerous times, and most acquaintances of the Karrs knew it, to a degree—within her daughter's presence. Nor did Madeleine recount it in her earlier breathless appalled voice but now more calmly, sadly *This awful thing that happened, that I witnessed, you know—the stabbing? In New York? The other day on the news there was something just like it, or almost . . .* Or *I still dream about it sometimes. My God! At least Rhonda wasn't with me.*

It seemed now that Madeleine's new friend Drexel Hay—"Drex"—was frequently in their house, and in their lives; soon then, when they were living with Drex in a new house on Winant Drive, on the other side of town, it began to seem to Rhonda that Drex who adored Madeleine had come to believe—almost—that he'd been in the car with her on that March morning; daring to interrupt Madeleine in a pleading voice *But wait, darling!—you've left out the part about . . .* or *Tell them how he looked at you through your windshield, the man with the knife*—or *Now tell them how you've never gone back—never drive into the city except with me. And I drive.*

Sometime around Christmas 1984 Rhonda's mother was at last divorced from Rhonda's father—it was said to be an *amicable parting* though Rhonda was not so sure of that—and then in May 1985 Rhonda's mother became Mrs. Hay—which made Rhonda giggle for *Mrs. Hay* was a comical name somehow. Strange to her, startling and disconcerting, how Drex himself began to tell the story of the stabbing to aghast listeners *This terrible thing happened to my wife a few years ago—before we'd met—*

In Drex's excited narration Madeleine had witnessed a street mugging—a savage senseless murder—a white male pedestrian attacked by a gang of black boys with switchblades—his throat so deeply slashed he'd nearly been decapitated. (In subsequent accounts of the stabbing, gradually it happened that the victim had in fact been decapitated.) The attack had taken place *in broad daylight in front of dozens of witnesses and no one intervened—somewhere downtown, below Houston*—unless *over by the river, in the meatpacking district*—or *by the entrance to the Holland Tunnel*—or (maybe) it had been *by the entrance to the Lincoln Tunnel, one of those wide ugly avenues like Eleventh? Twelfth?—not late but after dark*. The victim had tried to fight off his assailants—valiantly, foolishly—as Drex said *The kind of crazy thing I might do myself, if muggers tried to take my wallet from me*—but of course he hadn't a chance—he'd been outnumbered by his assailants—before Madeleine's horrified eyes he'd bled out on the street. *Dozens of witnesses and no one wanted to get involved—not even a license plate number or a description of the killers—just they were "black"—"carried knives"—Poor Madeleine was in such shock, these savages had gotten a good look at her through her windshield—she thought they were "high on drugs"—only a few yards from Madeleine my God if they hadn't been in a rush to escape they'd have killed her for sure—so she couldn't identify them—who the hell would've stopped them? Not the New York cops—they took their good time arriving.*

Drex spoke with assurance and authority and yet—Rhonda didn't think that the stabbing had happened quite like this. So confusing!—for it was so very hard to retain the facts of the story—if they were "facts"—from one time to the next. Each adult was so persuasive—hearing adults speak you couldn't resist nodding your head in agreement or in a wish to agree or to be liked or loved, for agreeing—and so—how was it possible to know what was *real*? Of all the stories of the stabbing Rhonda had heard it was Drex's account that was scariest—Rhonda shivered thinking of her mother being killed—trapped in her car and angry black boys smashing her car windows, dragging her out onto the street stab-stab-stabbing . . . Rhonda felt dazed and dizzy to think that if Mommy had been killed then Rhonda would never have a mother again.

And so Rhonda would not be Drex Hay's *sweet little stepdaughter* he had to speak sharply to, at times; Rhonda would not be living in the brick colonial on Winant Drive but somewhere else—she didn't want to think where.

Never would Rhonda have met elderly Mrs. Hay with the soft-wrinkled face and eager eyes who was Drex's mother and who came often to the house on Winant Drive with presents for Rhonda—crocheted sweater sets, hand-knit caps with tassels, fluffy-rabbit bedroom slippers which quickly became too small for Rhonda's growing feet. Rhonda was uneasy visiting Grandma Hay in her big old granite house on Hodge Road with its medicinal odors and sharp-barking little black pug Samson; especially Rhonda was uneasy if the elderly woman became excitable and disapproving as often she did when (for instance) the subject of the stabbing in Manhattan came up, as occasionally it did in conversation about other, related matters—urban life, the rising crime rate, deteriorating morals in the last decades of the twentieth century. By this time in all their lives of course everyone had heard the story of the stabbing many times in its many forms, the words had grown smooth like stones fondled by many hands.

Rhonda's stepfather Drex had only to run his hands through his thinning rust-colored hair and sigh loudly to signal a shift in the conversation *Remember that time Madeleine was almost murdered in New York City . . .* and Grandma Hay would shiver thrilled and appalled *New York is a cesspool, don't tell me it's been "cleaned up"—you can't clean up filth—those people are animals—you know who I mean—they are all on welfare—they are "crack babies"—society has no idea what to do with them and you dare not talk about it, some fool will call you "racist"—Oh you'd never catch* me *driving into the city in just a car by myself—even when I was younger—what it needs is for a strong mayor—to crack down on these animals—you would wish for God to swipe such animals away with his thumb—would that be a mercy!*

When Grandma Hay hugged her, Rhonda tried not to shudder crinkling her nose against the elderly woman's special odor. For Rhonda's mother warned *Don't offend your new "grandma"—just be a good, sweet girl.*

Mr. Karr was living now in Cambridge, Mass. for Mr. Karr was now a professor at Harvard. Rhonda didn't like her father's new house or her father's new young wife nor did Rhonda like Cambridge, Mass. anywhere near as much as Rhonda liked Princeton where she had friends at Princeton Day School and so she sulked and cried when she had to visit with Daddy though she loved Daddy and she liked—tried to like—Daddy's new young wife Brooke who squinted and smiled at Rhonda so hard it looked as if Brooke's face must hurt. Once, it could not have been more than the second or third time she'd met Brooke, Rhonda happened to overhear her father's new young wife telling friends who'd dropped by their house for drinks *This terrible thing that happened to my husband before we were married—on the street in New York City in broad daylight he witnessed a man stabbed to death—the man's throat was slashed, blood sprayed out like for six feet Gerald says it was the most amazing—horrible—thing he'd ever seen—he tried to stop the stabbing—he shouted out his car window—there was more than one of them—the attackers—Gerald never likes to identify them as* black—persons of color—*and the victim was a white man—I don't think the attackers were ever caught—Gerald was risking his life interfering—the way he describes it, it's like I was there—I dream of it sometimes—how close we came to never meeting, never falling in love and our entire lives changed like a miracle . . .*

You'd have thought that Mr. Karr would try to stop his silly young wife saying such things that weren't wrong entirely—but certainly weren't right—and Rhonda knew they weren't right—and Rhonda was a witness staring coldly at the chattering woman who was technically speaking her *stepmother* but Mr. Karr seemed scarcely to be listening in another part of the room pouring wine into long-stemmed crystal glasses for his guests and drinking with them savoring the precious red burgundy which appeared to be the center of interest on this occasion for Mr. Karr had been showing his guests the label on the wine bottle which must have been an impressive label judging from their reactions as the wine itself must have been exquisite for all marveled at it. Rhonda saw that her father's whiskers were bristly gray like metal filings, his face was ruddy and puffy about the eyes as if he'd just wakened from a nap—when "entertaining" in his home often Mr. Karr removed his glasses, as he had now—his stone-colored eyes looked strangely naked and lashless—still he exuded an air of well-being, a yeasty heat of satisfaction lifted from his skin. There on a nearby table was Gerald Karr's new book *Democracy in America Imperiled* and beside the book as if it had been casually tossed down was a copy of *The New York Review of Books* in which there was said to be—Rhonda had not seen it—a "highly positive" review of the book. And there, in another corner of the room, the beautiful blond silly young wife exclaiming with widened eyes to a circle of rapt listeners *Ohhh when I think of it my blood runs cold, how foolishly brave Gerald was—how close it was, the two of us would never meet and where would I be right now? This very moment, in all of the universe?*

Rhonda laughed. Rhonda's mouth was a sneer. Rhonda knew better than to draw attention to herself, however—though Daddy loved his *sweet little pretty girl* Daddy could be harsh and hurtful if Daddy was displeased with his *sweet little pretty girl* so Rhonda fixed for herself a very thick sandwich of Swedish rye crisp crackers and French goat cheese to devour in a corner of the room looking out onto a bleak rain-streaked street not wanting to think how Daddy knew, yes Daddy knew but did not care. That was the terrible fact about Daddy—he knew, and did not care. A nasty fat worm had burrowed up inside Daddy making him proud of silly Brooke speaking of him in such a tender voice, and so falsely; the *stepmother* who was so much younger and more beautiful than Rhonda's mother.

Here was the strangest thing: when Rhonda was living away from them all, and vastly relieved to be away, but homesick too especially for the drafty old house on Broadmead Road where she'd been a little girl and Mommy and Daddy had loved her so. When Rhonda was a freshman at Stanford hoping to major in molecular biology and she'd returned home for the first time since leaving home—for Thanksgiving—to the house on Winant Drive. And there was a family Thanksgiving a mile away at the Hodge Road house of elderly Mrs. Hay to which numerous people came of whom Rhonda knew only a few—and cared to know only a few—mainly Madeleine and Drex of course—there was the disconcerting appearance of Drex's brother Edgar from Chevy Chase, Maryland—identified as an *identical twin* though the men more resembled just brothers than twins. Edgar Hay was said to be a much wealthier man than Drex—his business was pharmaceuticals, in the D.C. area; Drex's business was something in *investments,* his office was on Route One, West Windsor. The Hay twin brothers were in their late sixties with similar chalky scalps visible through quills of wetted hair and bulbous noses tinged with red like perpetual embarrassment but Edgar was heavier than Drex by ten or fifteen pounds, Edgar's eyebrows were white-tufted like a satyr's in an old silly painting and maddeningly he laughed approaching Rhonda with extended arms—*Hel-lo! My sweet li'l stepniece happy Turkey-Day!*—brushing his lips dangerously close to Rhonda's startled mouth, a rubbery-damp sensation Rhonda thought like being kissed by a large squirmy worm. (*Call me Ed-gie* he whispered wetly in Rhonda's ear *That's what the pretty girls call me.)* And Madeleine who might have observed this chose to ignore it for Madeleine was already mildly drunk—long before dinner—and poor Drex—sunken-chested, sickly pale and thinner since his heart attack in August in high-altitude Aspen, Colorado, clearly in some way resentful of his "twin" brother—reduced to lame jokes and stammered asides in Edgar's presence. And there was Rhonda restless and miserable wishing she hadn't come back home for Thanksgiving—for she'd have to return again within just a few weeks, for Christmas—yet more dreading the long holiday break—wishing she had something useful to do in this house—she'd volunteered to help in the kitchen but Mrs. Hay's cook and servers clearly did not want her—she'd have liked to hide away somewhere and call her roommate Jessica in Portland, Oregon, but was fearful she might break down on the phone and give away more of her feelings for Jessica than Jessica had seemed to wish to receive from Rhonda just yet . . . And there was Rhonda avoiding the living room where Hay relatives were crowded together jovial and overloud—laughing, drinking and devouring appetizers—as bratty young children related to Rhonda purely through the accident of a marital connection whose names she made no attempt to recall ran giggling through a forest of adult legs. Quickly Rhonda shrank back before her mother sighted her, or the elderly white-haired woman who insisted that Rhonda call her "Grandma"—sulkily making her way along a hall, into the glassed-in room at the rear of the house where Mrs. Hay kept potted plants—orchids, African violets, ferns. Outside, the November air was suffused with moisture. The overcast sky looked like a tin ceiling. A few leaves remained on deciduous trees, scarlet bright, golden yellow, riffled by wind and falling and sucked away even as you stared. To Rhonda's dismay there was her stepfather's brother—Drex's twin—wormy-lipped Edgar—engaged in telling a story to a Hay relative, a middle-aged woman with a plump cat face to whom Drex had introduced Rhonda more than once but whose name Rhonda couldn't recall. Edgar was sprawled on a white wicker sofa with his stocky legs outspread, the woman in a lavender silk pantsuit was seated in a matching chair—both were drinking—to her disgust and dismay Rhonda couldn't help but overhear what was unmistakably some crude variant of the story of the stabbing of long ago—narrated in Edgar's voice that managed to suggest a lewd repugnance laced with bemusement, as the cat-faced woman blinked and stared open-mouthed as in a mimicry of exaggerated feminine concern *My brother's crazy wife she'd driven into Manhattan Christ knows why Maddie'd been some kind of hippie fem-ist my brother says those days she'd been married to one of the Commie profs at the university here and so, sure enough Maddie runs into trouble, this was before Giuliani cleaned up the city, just what you'd predict the stupid woman runs into something dangerous a gang of Nigra kids jumping a white man right out on the street—in fact it was Fifth Avenue down below the garment district—it was actual Fifth Avenue and it was daylight crazy "Made-line" she calls herself like some snooty dame in a movie came close to getting her throat cut—which was what happened to the poor bastard out on the street—in the paper it said he'd been decapitated, too—and the Nigra kids see our Made-line gawking at them through the windshield of her car you'd think the dumb-ass would've known to get the hell out or crouch down and hide at least*—as Rhonda drew nearer her young heart beating in indignation waiting for her stepfather's brother to take notice of her. It was like a clumsy TV scene! It was a scene improbable and distasteful yet a scene from which Rhonda did not mean to flee, just yet. For she'd come here, to Princeton. For she could have gone to her father's house in Cambridge, Mass.—of course she'd been invited, Brooke herself had called to invite her, with such forced enthusiasm, such cheery family feeling, Rhonda had felt a stab of pure loneliness, dread. *There is no one who loves me or wants me. If I cut my throat on the street who would care. Or bleed out in a bathtub or in the shower with the hot water running . . .*

So she'd had a vision of her life, Rhonda thought. Or maybe it was a vision of life itself.

Not that Rhonda would ever cut her throat—of course! Never. That was a vow.

Not trying to disguise her disgust for what she'd heard in the doorway and for Edgar Hay sprawling fatuous drunk. The ridiculous multicourse Thanksgiving dinner hadn't yet been brought to the dining room table, scarcely five thirty P.M. and already Edgar Hay was drunk. Rhonda stood just inside the doorway waiting for Edgar's stabbing story to come to an end. For maybe this would be the end?—maybe the story of the stabbing would never again be told, in Rhonda's hearing? Rhonda would confront Edgar Hay who'd then gleefully report back to Drex and Madeleine how rude their daughter was—how unattractive, how *ungracious*—for Rhonda was staring, unsmiling—bravely she approached the wormy-lipped old man keeping her voice cool, calm, disdainful *Okay then—what happened to the stabbed man? Did he die? Do you know for a fact he died? And what happened to the killer—the killers—the killer with the knife—was anyone ever caught? Was anyone ever punished, is anyone in prison right now?* And Edgar Hay—"Ed-gie"—looked at Rhonda crinkling his pink-flushed face in a lewd wink *How the hell would I know, sweetheart? I wasn't there.*

The Beheading
FRANCINE PROSE

AS A CHILD, I was fascinated by decapitation. Not what we think of now: grainy terrorist videos, or Hong Kong sword-fight films, or serial killers with trophies grinning in the freezer. And not by every beheading, but only certain ones. The virgin martyrs left me cold, as did John the Baptist, though the volume of *The Lives of the Saints* on our otherwise sparse suburban bookshelf featured an illustration of a luscious Salome with the Baptist's head on a platter. Marie Antoinette held me for a while, but finally what drew me were the legal executions with which kings got rid of their wives.

I was obsessed with the history of the court of King Henry VIII. I read through the school and library books and asked my parents for more. It was how I learned about sex—that is, something beyond the basics. What other reason could there have been for a man to tire of one woman and divorce her if he could, kill her if he couldn't or when the divorces got to be too much trouble? Why else would he keep marrying his dead wife's ladies-in-waiting, and what charges convinced a judge to execute them so cruelly? Had the women really fallen in love with those handsome young nobles? This was nothing I could have learned at home, where my religious parents stayed lukewarmly married until they died, months apart. Like only children everywhere, I got a partial education: isolated, by turns removed, and unhealthily attentive.

I used to imagine the moment when the head is severed from the body. What *were* head and body, one without the other? Where did the person go? Was there such a thing as a soul, and where did it reside? I became a child expert on the mind-body problem. I used to imagine what it was like to order your wife's head chopped off, or to be married to a man who had done that to his wife. I imagined being the executioner's child, and the odd mood in the house at night when Dad came home from his job. I imagined being a courtier, being formally presented to the new queen and everyone trying their hardest to ignore what had happened to the last one.

I should say that I was good in school, I had friends, I played sports. Beheading was only part of what I thought about in my spare time.

I was eleven or maybe twelve when I began to have a recurring dream. It began with me knocking on a door, always the same door, which was opened by a man, always the same kind, friendly, handsome man, who led me to the same room in which there was a chopping block, an ax, and a pyramid made from the heads of children. And I always understood that I was about to join them.

The dream returned fairly often. Each time I woke up screaming. Worried, my parents took me to the family doctor. He said, Sure, I'd been an easy kid, but—winking at my parents—the next few years might be bumpy. He advised us to fasten our seat belts.

Around this time a new couple moved onto our block. The

wife was having a baby. I learned this from my parents, who met them before I did. I also learned, without anyone saying so, that this young couple was thrilling; everyone wanted to be their friends. There had been competition about who would invite them for dinner first, and, lucky for once, my parents won.

My mother cooked for days, tested family favorites, green beans with fried onion rings, along with elegant experiments, beets halved and stuffed with dollops of lightly bleeding egg salad. Multicolored liquor bottles lined up on the sideboard, though my father never drank more than a few beers on weekends.

Two by two, the guests arrived, filling the house with the exotic aromas of gardenia and tobacco. My mother had begged me to dress up and help, and it was easier to agree. I was bringing out a bucket of ice when the new couple arrived.

The wife was tall and graceful, with a column of smoky blonde hair twisting up the back of her proud head. Probably it was the first time that anyone in that crowd had seen a pregnant woman in black. This alone sent a tremor through the already charged, bright room.

Her husband followed, guiding her elbow. He smiled at everyone at once and somehow made everyone think that his smile was intended for each of them, alone. I recognized him from my dreams. I watched him from the kitchen.

How hard it is to remember a dream, even the morning after—and how exponentially trickier when decades have elapsed. I have said he was the man in my dream, but the truth is I can't exactly remember the man who opened the door in my nightmares, nor can I precisely recall the man who walked into my parents' house. Did he really look like the man, or did he just give me a similar feeling?

Fortunately, I was a sensible kid. I knew such things didn't happen. You didn't dream about people, then meet them. I watched as coats were shed, introductions made, hands shaken, kisses exchanged. The strangers kissed our neighbors, they kissed my mom and dad.

Finally my parents brought the new couple into the kitchen. The pretty wife shook my hand. Then her husband turned my way and shone his blinding light on me. Never had a grown person smiled at me like that—a movie-star smile, friendly enough, but intimate and suggestive. A smile like the rosy heat lamps that kept food warm at our neighborhood diner.

Who knew what his smile conveyed? I was sure that I did. Did it mean he was glad to meet me? It meant that he knew me and knew that I knew. He knew that I had seen the ax, the chopping block, the heads.

I screamed, the scream I'd practiced to wake myself from the dream. I dropped the ice bucket and the cubes crashed and skittered across the floor so violently that everyone scrambled as if I'd broken a glass.

Perhaps my mother recognized the scream. Without a word she scooped me up and led me off to my room. She felt my head and a few minutes later returned with an ice pack, made from the ice I had dropped, which she pressed to my forehead until I fell asleep.

By morning, I had recovered. At breakfast my parents seemed to feel that their party had been a success. Apparently their new friend had been gracious about my behavior. He said he'd never gotten that reaction from a kid before, maybe he'd better work on it, now that he was about to have one.

As it happened, their new friends did not become their new friends. Maybe because their child was born, impeding their social life, but the heartfelt promises of returned invitations were never kept. Maybe it was my fault. My parents didn't blame me, they never asked what happened. They seemed fractionally more disappointed, though by such a small fraction, how could it have been measured?

Not long afterward, my father was transferred to a distant office. Our home dissolved and recrystallized in another house, another suburb. The bad dreams stopped, as did my fascination with beheading and with the wives of King Henry VIII.

Since then, whenever I read or heard a story about a killer of children, I found myself searching for evidence accusing my parents' former neighbor. But of course there was none. Where did my suspicion come from? What evidence did I have? A child had had a bad dream. A man had done nothing wrong. But whenever I think back on that time, I reach a different conclusion.

I think, He got away with it. I think, They never caught him.

Celebration

ABRAHAM RODRIGUEZ JR.

Celebrate good times
Come on
—Kool and the Gang

AN OFFICE CROWD, partying it up somewhere near the West End. Bodies packed on the dance floor, bopping up and down. Drinks spilling, bottles clinking. Loosened ties and rolled-up sleeves on saggy white shirts. The office girls were whoop-whooping themselves beyond silliness. The mindless giggle attack when Benny from accounting started doing the robot, and Jenny countered with a frantic funky chicken. It was a small, garish hall, mirrored walls, gold columns that ringed a glimmery scuffed dance floor.

The DJ was in a booth opposite the dance floor, bopping to his rig. He played the usual assortment of disco hits, eighties synth pop, and some hip-hop of dubious quality, stuff one could find on any office party CD, the kind that includes such anthems to office bonding as Sister Sledge's "We Are Family." After that came the inevitable Kool & the Gang song, "Celebration." Loud and pounding, whoops and screams, it flowed out along that sullen, marble hallway outside the hall. It hit M in the face like a sharp uppercut to the jaw. (He was calling himself M now, because of what Myron said.) It half blinded him, made his stomach burn. It set off the colors, strange flashes of red, of yellow, of black. The red especially—he headed back toward the bank of elevators frantic fast, pulling the hood over his head. The pounding, the sick feel, was it the music, pounding a burning hole through his brain? Was it his fists punching at the elevator buttons senselessly, flashing red, blink blink, no elevator in sight, the song would not stop. He turned swift. Stairs!? There must be stairs, some way off this ride, fast.

He hurried down the marble hall, which looked like a relic from some fifties movie. The elevator bank led nowhere, there was a barred window, there was a locked door. He went back the only way he could, and that meant going past the racket, the madhouse, the pulsating sick sound. There was a cluster of people over by the entrance to that man-made hell, that inferno of bodies and spandex skin, but he was sure no one had looked at him, and why would they? They weren't even turned toward him, in their glittery dresses and pressed pants and shiny shoes. Someone was smoking a cigarette, a cigarette, he would just KILL for a cigarette, the red flash, the yellow, the black, he pressed his temples, he went straight right past, and people like that, dressed like that, in the throes of double martinis, would not waste a glance at some sneakered low-class going by in his hoodie. Maybe he had a delivery! Maybe someone ordered a pizza. Candygram? M rounded the corner. A dead end, another barred window, and a door, a door, there was a fucking door and it had to be the stairs because it was getting very hard to see and he went through the door fast and it wasn't the stairs, no stairs, it was a fucking men's room and he slammed the door hard and hard again, it killed the music when he slammed it felt good to slam it slam it again just some sound beating in his head FLASH the bright fluorescents FLASH the mirrors over the pair of basins FLASH the tiled wall, all of it blasting brightness at him. The door, the door, he slam slam SLAMMED it again and again and it was almost blotting out the noise and maybe if he could keep that up he could beat the noise because Myron said the best way to blot out the noise is with another noise, adding cryptically that this was the solution and paradoxically (he used that word), also sometimes the problem

and that made M laugh in midslam, it was possible he was doing it he was going to beat this because they weren't going to get him. And that's when the guy came out of one of the stalls, looking mad as hell and somehow puffed up with all the authority his three-piece suits gave him.

"Hey! What the hell are you doing?"

It was a color thing, and a sound thing. Both at once: Now it was two marbles clacking together, clacking together hard, over and over again. It was wood breaking all sharp and crack, it was chicken bones splitting. It was the guy's skull splitting, cracking against the wall over and over. Whimpering cries. Mad bursts of air, gurgled gasps. A body crumples down crash against the toilet and sets it off to flush. Fresh water bursting spin with that muffled, crash thump.

At the last breath . . . the song changed.

He was not calling himself M anymore. He was O now. Myron said it was good to use letters, just letters. It throws the waves off. Counts to change what you call yourself, even while just telling a story on the inside, because these people, they have machines. They're inside your brain and every time you talk to yourself in there, they pick up on it. They zero in and send you things. That's why calling yourself something different in your head throws them off. The machine, it can't find you so fast. Of course, O hadn't asked Myron why he was always a Myron, or what he called himself inside his head. It didn't occur to him to ask ball-breaking questions like that, because Myron had all the answers. O liked that, he needed that. Myron came along at the perfect moment, seemed to lift the gray fog with just a few words. Everything he said had double meanings spinning on a wild axis, and though O hadn't told him about the red yellow black attack, or about the things Joanna was doing to him, Myron said a few words and right from the beginning started to connect all the dots.

It started and ended with Joanna, his white-girl dream. Myron made him realize. You come across people in life and you interact with them and all of a sudden it feels like they were planted there on purpose, a setup to put you on a certain path. He had that feeling those first moments with Joanna, feeling himself slowly falling, morphing into someone else. He was a stranger obeying commands, another person growing inside him doing things and he didn't know why, these voices . . . they all belonged to Joanna, coaxing, teasing, laughing with pleasure when he gurgled in pain. It wasn't until Myron that he started to really think about what she was doing to him. Myron, another "chance" meeting, or was that all on purpose, again a setup?

Joanna was a nice white girl from a small town in Texas. She moved to New York, studied marketing at NYU. She had blonde-reddish hair and green eyes. O met her at a tiki bar on the West Side the night he was supposed to meet his friend Nero there, who never actually showed up. He met Joanna there while he stood at the bar, having a red cocktail. She was magically drawn to his cocktail and almost swiped it and he told her the bargirl had made it especially for him and there was only one per night and she picked the people especially and Joanna didn't believe him and so he called the bargirl over and tried to get a red cocktail for her but the bargirl said no dice, only one per night, so he got her a mojito instead and the mojito made her talk about how much she loves Mexico and how she had been there and how she loves the music and he said he's not Mexican he's Puerto Rican and she freaked out and said she LOVES Puerto Rico and how she was in San Juan last summer and how much she loves the music and the people and he admitted that she had probably been to the island more times than he ever had, and she said ohhhh that doesn't matter because Puerto Ricans from New York are sexier which created a fast, warm pulse between them. And her eyes stared at his lips as if she would touch them.

"I'm Joanna," she said, pronouncing it *Jo-awna.* They spent hours snuggled in the small lounge by the dance floor. The smell of her wrapped itself around him like a drug, the closer together they came on those pink cushions. Those first kisses. How she bit on his lips, teasingly, at first—then, the sudden, sharp sting of her teeth.

"Yah," he said, involuntarily.

"I have to warn you," she said. "I'm a nymphomaniac."

He laughed, but she was looking him seriously in the eyes.

"I don't know a single guy that doesn't dream of hearing that," he said.

"But it's true. I send men running into the night, screaming. They never come back." She gave him another biting kiss.

"Uhhhhhhhh," he said, involuntarily. Vaguely tasting blood.

"I can be very demanding," she said.

She drove a black Ford Escort that slinked along streets like a shiny cockroach. Her apartment was a modest three-room on Ninety-second Street. (He only ever really saw the bedroom.) The going there was a red blur through yellow flashes of passing street lamps, the black-hole night that turned into morning as first light blued the windows.

He was naked. She was wearing black stockings. It started with kisses and snuggle words. Then she began biting him. These weren't tickly nibbles but deep bites that set off manic tremors of pain. She would suck on his neck and dig her teeth in and grind them. She sucked his cock with such a voracious desperation that he was soon swirling in mad delirium, up, down, all direction lost. She sat on his face and smothered him with her pussy until he was faded to black, the lingering yellow-red when he came to and realized he was alone on the bed. That his hands were spread out and tied to the bedposts. And then it was

that song. The one she started it all with, the one she started

blaring from the living room, getting louder, boomier still. She came back, sliding her body over him. And his cock is a stiff stick and moves as if no longer under his control. Her pussy is a sudden, flaming breath. He was sinking, twitching his way back to the surface, just that song, just that song,

and then she started scratching him. Not just soft strokes with the tips of her nails, but grinding in her fingers deep into his sides, his chest, his ass. The tendrils of pain burned all through him. Her deep laugh shook her body and resonated in his cock. She paused for a moment, there on top of him, just looking down on him and the crisscross designs of the fresh scratches she had made on his chest and stomach. She leaned a little to the side and picked up the thin, green knitting needle. Her eyes were different, a different face from any he had seen before. Some feeling like that. He strained against the bonds.

"Joanna," he said.

"Are you going to beg? I would like you to beg."

"Yeah, no kidding. Joanna, what's the knitting needle for?"

She smiled, but her eyes looked different. (Again that feeling.) Oh shit.

He strained.

"I already told you," she said, picking up a small remote. "I like to scratch." She pressed a button on the remote vigorously. The music got louder and louder. That same song, that same fucking song.

"Sorry about the music," she said. "It's just the walls are pretty thin here. I don't want the neighbors to hear the screaming."

"Joanna, Joanna, please . . ."

A slow smile. It pleased her to hear him say her name.

"I would like you to beg," she said. "Are you going to beg for me?" And she teased the tip of the knitting needle with her finger.

The first time (deep breath). He didn't mean to, he didn't mean to. Be taken so far. The woman scared him, she was possessed with some mad, demon spirit. She could see things in him. She had a certain smile for when it hurt the most and he cringed he squirmed he twitched—he had to keep the slamming sound going, see? He had to drown out that other sound, nothing would stop it until that slow, last breath, clean water cascading down rocks in a Japanese garden, the nagging question why, why, and that was like asking why does she hurt you? and why does she like to see blood? The two flowed together, it was all one sea. He shouldn't see her, he should stop. He said that after the first time, he said it again and again for three months of fuck dates that came and went in her bedroom and that one time in the hotel on Fifty-seventh Street because "if I'm going to kill you, I'm not going to do it at home," and she even wore a wig and joked about how the guy in reception won't recognize her when she leaves as a brunette. (She didn't get to kill him that time.) Or that Friday night, and how she kept him there until Sunday, a nonstop fuck attack that left him paralyzed and senseless, tied to the bed for a large part of the day while she went shopping with friends. When she came back, that song came on, that fucking song . . . felt drugged and falling and he hadn't eaten and his chest was sticky with blood from where she was carving her name. Appeared at the door in nothing but her black shiny tights, just leaning against the jamb, looking at him, looking at him lying there . . . no more, no more please, no more weekends ever again . . .

"You're still here," she said softly, warm breath against him shiver. "Don't you know, the more you come back, the more I'll hurt you?"

Was she laughing, was she crying? Was that him making that sound? She was twisting the needle . . . she was twisting him deeper . . . no, he said, he said it again, he wouldn't go back to her. And every time, he found himself calling her again and again and again, as if under some hypnotic spell he couldn't break. They didn't date and they didn't hold hands or cuddle in the park, they just met and fucked or whatever you call what she was doing to him, carving her name meticulously across his chest (the sound of plastic irritated him anywhere he heard it, she said she didn't want to get blood on her sheets) and it made him feel somehow sick and not like a person so he started appearing at her jobs. She had two of them. She always seemed pleasantly surprised to see him mostly, but if he came upstairs to see her like at that place on the West End she would be too busy to see him for long and would tell him she'd call him. And maybe she would, maybe not. And the next day he would show up at her other job, that small copy shop on Prince Street. "Good baby," she said, finishing the last *a* on JOANNA carved deep across his chest, a jagged bloodied wound that stung him with daily pain no matter how he moved. Then she just stopped calling him. And he wouldn't go to the West End anymore, he was still trying to figure out how she worked that, how she made that yellow red black happen, how the day after she called him.

"I want to see you so bad," she said. "I almost can't stand it."

He was lying in bed, in the darkened room, his hands in a bowl of ice.

"I can't see you tonight," he said. "My hands are messed up."

That night when she straddled him she asked him if he was a very bad boy last night, driving the knitting needle through his calf as she rode his squirmy twitchings

a scream and a scream and bloodstains on the mirror. And he was standing across the street, like always, waiting but he kept appearing at the copy shop, the whole morning until noon, when she would appear on her way to her car. And she might say a few words to him, she always said she would call him. And he would take that home with him like a blessing from the pope. And all the time he was going there, standing across the street from the copy shop, he wasn't aware that someone had seen him and been watching him. He had maybe seen the guy before, shaggy-haired, bearded, lying there in a side alley beside an Italian deli that made the block reek of fresh salami.

"Hey," he said, gaps in his teeth visible when he spoke, "what's her name."

O (who wasn't O yet, not consciously) looked at the copy shop across the street, then at the bum lying there by the green Dumpster.

"It's not like I'm asking you your name," he said. "What's her name?"

O felt a strange chill.

"How do you know it's about a her?"

Myron smiled, looking over at the copy shop.

"You just look like one of the chosen. Winner of the yellow drink. They use women, you know. Send them out to hook people to the machine. Sick, crazy women. Some guys, they think they meet women. But it's the woman who meets them."

O had that strange feeling, almost like when he was with Joanna. He wanted to get away and at the same time wanted more.

"Do you get the feeling you're losing control of yourself since you met her? That day in, day out, you can't stop thinking about her or the things she does to you? That something inside drives you to do insane, mindless things?"

O almost nodded. His lips moved. Nothing came out. A weird electric pulse.

"Some people think that's love. Am I right? Do you think that's love, what she does to you? Think about that one real hard."

"I don't know what to call it," O said, his head feeling light.

"It's a psyop. A mental manipulation. You've been picked up by an agent."

"An agent?"

Something inside O buckled. It made him immediately think of cops, of that moment he saw the video on his TV a long time ago, was it a long time ago? A video clip of a guy in a hood, going down a stairwell. It made him throw out his TV set.

"That's right." Myron leaned back against the Dumpster, his

lips pursed with disgust. "That copy shop right there is a front for a domestic CIA operation."

"A what?"

"A front. A holding station for CIA operatives who run operations on civilians."

O laughed, maybe it was relief, maybe it was just funny, a good way to take that shine off those creepy words, those words that resonated with him still. A fucking relief that the guy was nuts, right?

"Hear voices? They want you to hear one voice, but they haven't perfected the machine, so you hear a lot of them. Have to filter it out. Like radio static."

"Yeah right," O said. "Maybe you get too much sun here. Can I give you a buck, so you can go get yourself a sandwich?"

Myron looked at him, eyes glimmering with knowing, knowing something, and O saw something else: compassion, some kindness that seemed to come from above, and this touch of sadness as he looked over at the copy shop.

"Her name was Mira," he said, "pronounced *meer-ah*. She was from Vermont. She picked me up in a bar because I had a red drink. Isn't that funny?"

O felt a sick tremor in his stomach, an electric pang. "Mine was red," he wanted to say, he wanted to say, he said nothing.

"A lot of that is blurry. She did things to me, awful things. A year ago, that was me, standing here like you. Watching her come and go. Until that one day when she was gone."

"Gone?"

"Gone. Poof. Transferred to another shop in Chicago."

Again that moment, just when things were starting to chime, then comes a line that makes O think the guy is fucking with him. He peeled off a buck.

"Look, man, you're starting to waste my time, okay?"

Myron took the dollar.

"Right, right. Don't let me disturb you from just standing there. You can't help it. You're driven. Stuff is happening and you don't know why. Right? And it all started when you met her, didn't it? Didn't it?"

O couldn't stand there anymore. He left, even though he hadn't seen Joanna, he went straight to the subway with Myron's words ringing in his head and this strange feeling that he was being monitored would not go away and for some reason he fought off the urge to call her. And the next day he fought off the urge to go down there at all or even to call her, but the morning after that he showed up bright and early and when he got there he almost felt like he was looking for this guy and when he didn't see him, he felt relief and disappointment at the same time that he could see Joanna inside the copy shop behind some machines, and he got a scared feeling standing there, and then the voice came from inside the alley.

"Just when I thought you were getting the message," Myron said with disgust.

"What message is that," O said, lighting a cigarette and looking over at the copy shop.

"To get away. To just run as far and as fast as you can," he said, "before you do something bad."

A red heat crept up O's back.

"Bad like what, bad like what." O felt like he was falling into a trance.

"Something you can't control. It comes on you like an attack. It's all colors and sounds. You can't control your hands. They'll do stuff while you watch. You know what I'm saying?"

Myron had gotten up from his spot, had edged closer. O was sweating, blinking fast, frantic puffs. He tossed the cigarette.

"Oh ho," Myron said, noticing O was wearing gloves on his hands. "I see you've been punching the walls lately."

It didn't occur to O anymore to act like he didn't know what the guy was talking about. It was too painfully obvious that Myron was on to something, though his rocky road to truth and enlightenment was dotted with detours.

"Not walls," O said pensively. "Not walls."

O peeled off a bill.

"Get yourself something," he said.

Myron looked at the bill a moment but didn't take it.

"I won't take the dollar," he said, "but I'll take a sandwich. And a carbonated beverage."

O looked into Myron's bottomless eyes.

He's thinking no time like the present to make a change, any change is good, but how many times has he moved this year already? The idea of being in one place for a long time terrifies him, even waiting for the subway, standing at the bus stop. Can't hide his face enough. Avert the eyes, look away, hood on, baseball cap low over the eyes. Anything with official documents, credit cards, ATMs, any kind of official transaction . . . because then they can find you, find you easier, every transaction leaves a trace and maybe even a video trail. YES he is ESPECIALLY upset about surveillance cameras and these shits are everywhere, can't even have a smoke outside the hotel regulation distance: two hundred feet from the door WITHOUT being taped. He's getting better at thinking that way all the time, being aware . . . no, the best thing he did, really, to quit his job when he did. Sure, he misses his old friend, Nero, who used to take him out on the town, the principal reason he met Joanna. (These days, because of Myron, he tends to see everything in terms of connections, the one thing that leads to the other.) This just mentioning her name like this is enough to send him careening back into the past, to play the old game of trying to make sense of what had happened to him, some process that started when she came into his life. Now he fights it, because Myron says the most important thing to do is chop up the story forever in your brain in parts, and label those parts any way you want so you can remember them. But don't go into the past so much. Fight the urge for flashback. And so he fights the urge, battles to stay in the present. The right now. The minute you step into *was*, you're lost. To stay in the present: the new apartment. Located on a tree-lined stretch of Dawson Street, an apartment in a private house, top floor, creaky boards, ancient wood smell to the stairs, rooms small and mostly empty. He buys a bed, he buys a sofa. He gets a TV and a DVD player and then decides to stop spending money because he doesn't have a job right now and is living off savings. And it may be a little tight for a while, there is NO WAY he's going back to live with his mother. (And maybe it's a good thing he doesn't have a job now, right now, time to figure this out.) Again this somehow feels like he's slipping into past and he doesn't want that so he decides instead to stay in the present and head downtown to see if he can find Myron and that usually is easy because Myron is usually always camped out somewhere across the street from the copy shop on Lafayette Street, which is where he met Myron because he went to the shop looking for Joanna (and that brings us back to doe, doe, doe, doe). And no matter how much he tries to stay present by thinking of images of sitting in the subway, black tunnel walls speeding by in the windows, he can't stop it. Maybe it was Myron's fault why it happened. Maybe it was Myron that led him to do that, to be in that particular place right at the moment when the sound came, and the red, the yellow, the black. But it couldn't be Myron. Myron knew the truth. Myron was a voice, a guiding light. He couldn't doubt him, he shouldn't. The moment you showed doubt, it would be over. It was the same with the Great Pumpkin. It was easy—Myron only said he should forget this Joanna woman fast and go find another one because nothing takes a screw out of the wall like another screw. And he shouldn't be tailing her and he shouldn't be showing up at her jobs, he shouldn't even try talking to her. And Myron said that to him with great certainty even though M hadn't told him anything about her at all. (He was calling himself M now because Myron said it was good to only use letters in your brain when you think of yourself, never mention your name or even think it, because the machines can pick that up and hone in on you.) Now M wanted to go downtown and tell him what was really happening.

He hadn't told Myron about the red the yellow the black, but somehow he got the feeling from the things Myron said that he already knew about that. It had to be true what he was saying, so when he said go find another screw, M went out that night to a spot near the Bruckner Expressway, all the way up Southern Boulevard. There was an old warehouse there that had been converted into a disco, and all kinds of business was possible all along that street. The girls walked up and down the block. They dotted the block where the disco was, walking amongst the small clusters of people milling around, either because they came out of the disco or they were going in or they came out for a smoke or to buy drugs or to get some air, spandex asses and shiny minidresses reflecting the lights that started to blind him, this thing with the eyes is how it started last time. And the noise and the sound, the beat pounding into his brain like a mad, merciless hammer. Turned, not to walk on the block where the disco was, turned away and the noise was still hurting him. Brittle and weak, less people now or he just couldn't see them, colors and he just wanted to get away from the sound. Felt like he was on the edge of a cliff and the wind would knock him down. And then it happened, that sharp hot jab of a sharp blade sliding across his ribs, the sharp edge leaving a trail of red that she rubbed with her hands, the caked salt sending jolts of stinging pain through him. (Blot out the sound. Blot out . . . he pulled the hood up over his head.)

"No Joanna," he pleaded, "please don't."

that song. The one she started it all with, the one she started

And he spun around right at the moment when she came out of the alley, she came out of there or she was in there and he didn't know why she was there or why she came out at him when he was trying to just pass fast and get away, he wanted to get away but something held him there, she was saying something to him and the flashes were making it hard to see and her dress was red and her dress was yellow and her legs were black fishnet stockings and he said get away from me please, and she said I'm not going to hurt you, and she laughed and why was she laughing? and he told her to make it stop and she laughed and said honey I can't make it

stop

and he pulled her and pushed her all at once, or they fell or he was falling, and nothing could stop it slamming the door slamming the door and it was so fast but the harder he slammed the smaller the sound got and the colors got better. He could see her face disintegrating as if caught behind the motion of his fist in a strobe. Blood splash, teeth, crackling bones on a witch doctor's necklace, a pulpy squishy mass twitching and bucking and squealing sounds that ended with the thunder boom of her body collapsing against the metal Dumpster, the way she fell all broken doll. No movement, no breath. Suddenly, no sound. Or a different sound, but that one, special sound, no longer.

The street exhaled.

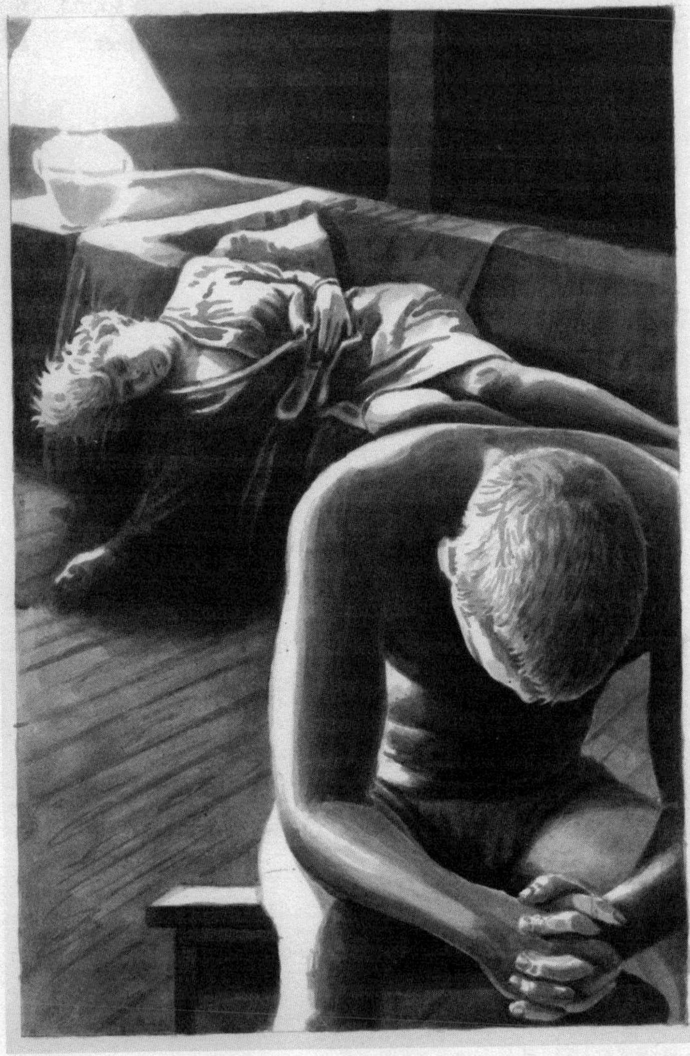

Daybreak

S.J. ROZAN

ON YOUR KNEES!"

The savage's words roared down with hopeless finality, recalling the thunder of the boulders that rolled from the breached walls of her father's city to lie mute and useless on the plain. Even now, after all these weeks in the barbarian kingdom, she comprehended little of what was said to her. But this phrase she understood, and understood as well the pain and penalty for disobedience. She knelt.

He gazed, grinning, at her ivory skin and huge dark eyes. Her hair rippled like blue-black silk, glinting even in the sickly fluorescent light. Her pink nipples stood from her breasts, hardened not by desire, he knew, but dread. Her fear inflamed him; and even more, her pride. He waited until he could barely stand it, so he could watch the beads of cold sweat form on her brow as she bent motionless before him. Then he barked the command. Flinching, she raised her slender hands, and slowly, the way he liked it, she worked his zipper down. He marveled at her movements, her control, steeling herself even against her own trembling. He could make her weep in pain—he had—but not from terror, or despair, though he knew she felt both, felt them more powerfully every day. He'd never known a girl like this. He wondered how long it would take, what it would take, to break her.

When first her father sent her into barbarian lands she had been frightened, but proud to go. A bride as tribute to the conqueror was an ancient tradition in wars across the land and across the ages. Her father had chosen her of all her sisters. That alone proclaimed her value. She set her chin high and determined he would not have reason to regret his decision. The savage would find her an obedient, industrious, and honorable wife. She would behave exactly as she would have if married to a prince of the people.

She was good, he gave her that: supple fingers, a tireless tongue. She'd discovered early what pleased him and when, though sometimes, just for the fun of it, he'd smack her for doing something he'd ordered her to do the day before. Most of the girls he bought were stupid, they whined and cried and weren't worth the trouble. Some of them, when it dawned on them what their mommies and daddies had sold them into, they went nuts, batshit nuts. Even though his trafficker knew what he wanted, even though he paid top dollar, he often got losers. He had to admit that made a kind of sense. What parents would sell a girl they could turn out themselves, who could work the streets of home and keep the money coming? He could use whatever he got, no question, but some of them didn't last long. But this one was something special. Of course, once he broke her pride, she'd be like the others and the magic would be gone. The thrill he got from the spark of hate in her eyes, the anger she suppressed like her own shivering: He'd miss that, once he extinguished it.

The barbarian, as always, used her in degrading, painful ways, beating her once he was too spent to respond to her touch. At the beginning, the horror of the hours with him had filled her mind completely, other thoughts staggering and unable to breathe under the weight. Now harsh experience had taught her what to expect. Now, while with him, she was able to remove part of herself, a precious, untouched part, from this blank-walled room and his heavy, sweating flesh. As he panted and groaned, she returned to the city of her childhood, to the perfumed rooms, the delicate silk-string music and the cool breeze wafting through the shaded walkways of the palace garden.

He rolled away finally and lay on his back breathing hard. She scuttled to the far side of the bed, knowing better than to touch him at this point. Eventually he heaved a satisfied sigh, and sat. That was her signal and she rose fast, stifling a groan, standing straight only with effort. He recalled punching her; maybe he'd broken a rib. He didn't care about that but he was annoyed when he saw he must have socked her in the jaw, too: Her lip was broken and bleeding. Damn. He liked their faces perfect.

Pressing away awareness of the new pain in her side, she crossed to the table and brought him the glass bottle as she had learned to do. Sometimes he forced her to drink from it also, which could be both blessing and curse. She disliked the taste of the gold liquid and she hated the path it scorched from her lips through her chest; but a few swallows could ease the agony, both in her body and in her heart.

He slugged back some whiskey, waving her off the bed, making her stand so he could survey her pale skin. He played his private game of measuring the fading of the yellow-green bruises and guessing where the purple ones would be blooming. A swollen crimson line glowed on her side already. Damn, that rib might actually be broken. She stood, biting her lip, trying to control her breathing, and once more he had to admire her: He didn't know if he could have taken what she took, day after day. But what choice did she have? Bought by his trafficker on the streets of some filthy city half a world away, smuggled through places she'd never heard of by a route she didn't know, she had no reality here, she didn't exist. No one missed her, no one was searching. She couldn't escape from this locked basement room with its single window high in the wall. She wouldn't try: The trafficker had made clear to her—graphically clear—what would happen to her father and young sisters back home if she did. No, locked in this room, her only hope was to please him, marking time, waiting and hoping for a future that would never come. He'd kill her in the end, like all the others. He could kill her now, this very minute, if he wanted; that thought made him laugh and then laugh harder as he saw her scared eyes widen.

She crushed down a shiver as she stood, fire burning her side, fear stabbing her heart when she heard his laugh. She tried to show him nothing, holding herself perfectly still, her back straight, her chin lifted and her hands quiet as she'd been taught at the court of her father.

He considered killing her, and he considered screwing her again. "Nah," he said in English, knowing she couldn't understand, "I'm through for the day. That okay with you? You want more?" He watched her struggle with herself, understanding she'd been asked a question, not sure whether her response should be a nod or a headshake, knowing the wrong choice would bring a kick, a blow. Finally, she nodded. He cackled. "Nope, you bitch, you're lying." He slapped her, but not hard enough to knock her over, though she staggered before she stood straight again. He thought about clocking her another one, but the hell with it. Boy, she'd really drained him. He marked the whiskey label, stood and pulled on his clothes. When she'd first arrived he used to take the bottle with him. Now he marked the level and left it because she'd learned that whiskey dulled the pain. He knew it would sit on the table all day calling to her and she wouldn't dare take a drink.

She remained standing straight and still after the barbarian left. Often he threw the door open suddenly, having not really gone away at all; or, after many hours, he returned. If he found her lying down, on the bed or even the floor, he would beat her again. He was a cruel man, her barbarian husband, subtle and pitiless. But once dark had fallen, he would not return. Then she was permitted to move, to eat the food he'd left her—its aroma filled the room and made her light-headed, but she didn't dare taste it yet—to attend to her other bodily functions, and to sleep. So she stood and she waited for dark, watching through the high window the light changing on the pink flowers of the cherry tree. In the gardens of her father's palace, the cherries must also be in bloom.

He chuckled to himself as he climbed the basement stairs, recalling her bewildered horror those first days as the rules of her new life became clear to her. She'd had trouble comprehending that she wasn't allowed to eat, to piss, to curl into a ball under the blankets and weep boo-hoo until after the sun went down.

She did catch on, though, and after the first week he never found the food touched or the bed warm, no carpet impressions on her silken skin, no matter how long he'd made her stand. Once it was dark, he left her alone: Fair's fair, after all. And he had a life to live. Openings, benefits, and parties to go to. He couldn't give her all his attention. It wouldn't be right.

Finally the sky behind the cherry blossoms turned a deep cobalt, the color of her father's formal robes. She forced herself to wait unmoving until the first star appeared, though the barbarian rarely returned this late. Once she saw the pinpoint gleam through the branches, she breathed deeply, and stretched very slowly, wincing at the new fire in her side. She moved carefully to the sink, where she washed in hot water, cleansing herself of the barbarian's touch and his smell. Only then did she pull the blanket from the bed, wrap her naked body in it, and, cross-legged on the floor, begin to eat.

As he dressed for dinner he reflected on the problem he'd been putting off. The trafficker would be back soon, in fact should have been here a few days ago. He'd be bringing half a dozen girls to choose from. He wasn't nearly done with this one yet. But the trafficker was following instructions and would want to be paid. He purely hated the idea of paying for something he wasn't going to use.

Having eaten—heavy, unaccustomed food, which she nevertheless forced herself to devour completely as she thought back to the delicate rice and fish of her childhood—she climbed into the bed and lay on her back, staring at the cherry tree now gray against the black sky. The light in the room where she was kept never went out, but was never bright. Weak and dull, it left shadows in the corners. In the palace, sunlight streamed through the windows, and along the roofed walkways cool shade enveloped her as, with her sisters, she ran and laughed. In the perpetual twilight in which she lived now, she thought of those days, and slept.

Well, he'd made his decision. He'd like to have kept this one longer. She got him seriously worked up; and he very much wanted to find her breaking point, a challenge he'd never been faced with before. But novelty had always been a turn-on for him, too, and there was the fact that whatever was coming in he was going to have to pay for anyway. He had an odd feeling, also, that the memory of this one might be even more exciting when he had another in front of him than the reality of her was now. Too bad, a bit of a waste: But tomorrow, she would go.

The new pain in her side woke her, again and again. Breathing grew agonizing as the night went on. The injury throbbed when she lay still and stabbed her when she moved. The thought of her barbarian husband's weight crushing her, of the rhythmic pounding of his grunting pleasure—of his smile when he saw the hot and swollen wound—was terrifying. She understood: It was, finally, unbearable.

He canceled meetings, made sure his schedule was clear most of the day. He'd take as long as he wanted with her, since it was the last time; and then there'd be the messy part. He'd gotten it down to a routine: knees on her chest, thumbs on her neck, press, release, let her gasp and cough and think she was going to live; press, release, again, until finally, no release (except for him, usually, at that moment), then the shovel, the orchard; but it still always took longer than he expected.

She awoke at daybreak, as she always had in her father's palace. Although she couldn't hear it, birds would be calling in the cherry trees, creatures stirring in the undergrowth, new life starting on a new day. The thought cheered her as she washed, allowing herself to wish, just briefly, for a cup of the fragrant tea with which she used to begin the morning. Then she prepared the bed and went to the door. She would be standing when he came in.

He finished a leisurely breakfast, trying to remember where he'd gotten this coffee, because it was damn good. He collected a few things he hadn't used with her yet, because it usually took a girl a couple of days to recover from them before she was any good again. But she wasn't going to have to recover, was she?

The sun had not fully risen when she took her post. He had never arrived this early. But she did not want to be surprised by him.

He unlocked the upper door, closed it behind him, and trotted down the stairs, humming. He almost pocketed the key, then decided to make her hold it in her hand the whole time. He'd done that to others before. It nearly drove them mad.

She stood, awaiting him. It might be hours; but it might be this next minute. Pain and fear had taught her well over these last weeks. The new fire in her side was a distraction, but she crushed any thought of it. She could stand, motionless, for a very long time.

Now the basement hallway, now the lower door. He turned the key and stopped for a moment, savoring the delicious knowledge that she'd be standing naked, facing the door, waiting as she had been, he knew, for hours. He tasted her fear as she heard the click of the lock and he could barely stand the thrill.

She heard the key turn in the lock. She drew a slow, deep breath to calm her heart. He didn't enter immediately. This was his way sometimes, to increase her fright; but he never waited long.

He swung the door open.

She wasn't there.

She wasn't standing and the curled form under the blankets flooded him with fury. Seeing nothing but that mound, and in it her disobedience, her defiance, her pride and hate, he charged blindly toward it. He howled, reaching clawlike for the bed. He'd tear her apart.

As he bent to the bed she stepped from behind the door, arms raised. She swung with all her power, crashing the bottle onto the back of his head. It broke in a shower of glass and gold liquid. He staggered but did not fall, and turned to her, eyes wild. Wielding the shattered remains of the bottle like a dagger, she sliced it once across his throat, and again the other way, and again a third time, because she wanted to be sure.

The hate in her eyes was a raging inferno; the sight of it made him shake with desire. The moist heat of his own blood cascading down his chest was the most glorious sensation he'd ever known. He stirred and swelled and died erect.

She pushed the barbarian's body to the floor and felt through the tangled blankets for the key. He'd had it in his hand and she picked it from the bed, glad she would not have to search his clothing, to touch him again. She went to the sink and, one last time, washed the reek of the barbarian from her skin. Pulling the blue blanket from the bed, wrapping it around herself like a robe, she walked calmly through the door and up the stairs. The barbarian had been destroyed. Now she could return to her father's kingdom.

"Whoa!" The coroner's man stopped at the door. "Someone made a mess outta him, huh?"

"We were about to close in, too," the detective said glumly. "Wish we'd been faster."

"Why? Someone sorry he's dead?"

"The opposite. Dead's too good. Look at this place."

The coroner's man did, taking in the wall-hung chains, the leather whip, the high, barred window. "What's the story?"

"Bastard was buying girls."

"Buying?"

The detective shrugged. "Illegals, from overseas. Sold by Mom and Dad to feed the rest of the family. We took up a trafficker a few days ago, that's who gave him up. Girls thought they'd hit the jackpot, that they were coming here as mail-order brides."

"Jesus."

"There was any justice," the detective said, "this bastard would be spending the rest of a long, long life with bastards bigger, meaner, and with nothing to lose."

"So who got to him?"

"No idea." The detective heard a patrolman call him from above. He said, "You don't need me, right?"

The coroner's man snapped on his gloves. "Nope. Go ahead."

The patrolman met the detective at the top of the stairs. By his ashen face the detective understood they'd found their killer.

He knew what had happened even before the patrolman led him to the bruised and naked body hanging by a blanket noose from a branch of the blossoming cherry tree.

Her father's garden was as beautiful as in her memory. Her sisters laughed and ran to her, the youngest carrying a robe of cobalt silk. She wrapped herself in it and, together, to the strains of silk-string music, they walked through the brilliant sunlight to the cool shadowed walkway that led to the gates of the palace.

Ben & Andrea & Evelyn & Ben
JONATHAN SANTLOFER

Friday

BEN DRAPES HIS sport jacket across his lap. His shirt is sticking to him, the train hot and airless, cigarette smoke, including his own, making it hard to breathe. He's switched trains at Jamaica and the older train, which is cramped and has no air conditioning, sits on the tracks for ten minutes, Ben thinking about his walk to AndiAnn where he will spend his day with the dress designer and pattern makers, cutters and sewers, his job to make sure everything is on schedule and ready to be shipped to retailers while Morty deals with the buyers; Morty, who wears three-hundred-dollar suits and a gold pinky ring and calls the buyers *darling* and everyone else *bastard* and lives in the Forest Hills apartment he used to share with Andrea's dead mother, which is three times the size of the split-level he bought for his favorite daughter. Ben liked their Greenwich Village walk-up even with the dining room serving as a room for their kid, but how could he refuse Andrea the "better life" her father offered even if it meant commuting an hour each way and living in a house he only gets to use on weekends?

He runs a hand through his thick, dark hair, just starting to gray at the temples. There is a woman sitting across from him, his age, maybe a year or two younger, thirty-one or -two, knees almost touching his, hair up in a French knot, stockings on her legs. He pictures clips and snaps as he watches her drag red-lacquered fingernails along her collarbone then play with a gold crucifix between the V of her breasts, a wedding ring on her finger. She lifts her eyes from her newspaper—headline: ANDREA DORIA SINKS OFF NANTUCKET—and they exchange a look. He crushes his cigarette into the tiny ashtray and when the train hurtles underground and everything goes black he leans forward, slides his hand up her leg and into her panties and hears her gasp over the sound of rattling train tracks and she opens her legs a bit wider. When the lights flash on, the woman drops the newspaper into her lap and Ben slips his hand out and as the train pulls into the station they exchange one last look before she gets up, adjusts her skirt, and disappears into the crowd.

Outside, Ben can't remember how he got here. He brings his hand to his nose, presses fingertips against nostrils, proof of what just happened. He moves with the throng of commuters up Seventh Avenue, the air hot and thick.

The Neiman Marcus buyer, a hard fortysomething blonde from Dallas, is in the showroom when he gets there, Morty saying, "Darling this, darling that—" He nods at Ben, who is fifteen minutes late, and Ben doesn't bother to say the train sat at the Jamaica station with engine trouble and no air conditioning because Morty won't care.

The in-house model pivots for the Neiman Marcus buyer. Ben knows she will do this two dozen times in two dozen outfits. She disappears behind a screen to change but Ben does not hang around even though the showroom is deliciously frigid, the air conditioner cranked up to high.

In the back, Ben guesses it's close to ninety. He nods at the young women bent over sewing machines making samples, two older ones hand sewing sequins and beads. He arranges his jacket onto his chair, his desk tucked into the back corner where a fan whirls hot dirty air in through an alley window. He loosens his tie, makes a call to order fabric—the new polyesters that are becoming *the* thing—then goes to see Max, the patternmaker, who has stripped down to his sweat-stained tee, and from there to see Artie, the fag dress designer, who Ben likes because he's nasty and funny and hates Morty almost as much as he does. He spends longer than necessary discussing hemlines and cruise wear, about which he cares nothing, because Artie has the only air-conditioned office.

At lunchtime he eats a tuna on rye at his desk and Andrea calls to say she has invited the neighbors for a barbecue.

"Why?" he asks.

"Why not?" she says.

Ben can think of a dozen reasons but says nothing and it's not just the fact that he has been sweating all morning and would prefer not to sweat over a barbecue.

"I bought steaks," she says.

Ben hangs up and then, like a movie on an endless loop, makes more calls, confers with Max and Artie, checks the beadwork on a cocktail dress, and is back on the train sniffing at his fingertips, the smell of the woman with the French knot and gold crucifix still there, or is it the tuna he had for lunch?

Ben slathers A-1 onto the steaks. He's had no time to change or shower, his shirt sticking to him, a corny apron that Stevie by way of Andrea got him for Father's Day tied around his waist: DAD, KING OF THE GRILL.

"Is that one of the new gas kind?" Jerry asks.

"Gift from my father-in-law," says Ben. He looks at the grill, the outdoor furniture, the house—everything a gift from Morty. He sniffs at his fingers but all he can smell is the A-1 sauce.

"I'm sick of accounting," says Jerry, who spends the next ten minutes complaining about his job.

Ben nods to show he's listening, but behind his aviators he stares at his neighbor's wife, Evelyn, who is wearing short shorts and a blouse tied under her breasts. She is just a few feet away on a plastic lounge chair talking to Andrea, a whiskey sour sweating in her hand, Andrea beside her in a white Peter Pan–collar blouse from AndiAnn with matching Capri pants, loose rather than formfitting. Ironic, he thinks, that the boss's daughter is such a bad advertisement for her father's clothing line.

"I like your hair," Andrea says to Evelyn.

"I couldn't take it long anymore, not in summer, in this heat." Evelyn runs a hand through her short black curls. "Jerry hates it, says it makes me look like a man."

Andrea plays with her ponytail, takes in Evelyn's breasts swelling at the top of her blouse, her curvy hips. "I think it's very . . . Italian, very . . . Gina Lollobrigida."

"I'm thinking about quitting," says Jerry, shrugging his shoulders, a high school football hero ten years later, short-sleeved plaid shirt showing off muscled arms gone soft, snub-nosed face starting to bloat, crew cut trained with Butch wax. He finishes the beer, his third. "I wanted to be a ranger."

"A what?" Ben pokes at the steaks with tongs.

"A forest ranger, you know, in a national park, like in Colorado or Oregon. I even took the test."

Ben thinks about the dark-haired I. Magnin buyer from Portland, Oregon, who stays at the Pennsylvania Hotel only a block away from AndiAnn when she comes to town twice a year and how he fucks her during his lunch hour and how she screams so loud he tells her to keep it down or his father-in-law might hear and she laughs then screams louder. "Did you pass?" he asks.

"Yeah, I passed. But there's no money in it and Evelyn says no way she's living out in the middle of nowhere."

"I never said that," says Evelyn.

"What do you call *this*?" says Ben.

"You don't like it here?" Jerry asks.

"It's fine," says Ben.

"Better than living in the city with all those animals," says Jerry.

"I like the city," says Ben, thinking they should have stayed in the Village or bought a house in Hewlett or Levittown, where there are other Jews.

"Where are you from?" Jerry asks.

"Brooklyn," says Ben.

"Never been," says Jerry.

"I'm from Forest Hills," says Andrea. "Where are you from, Evelyn?"

"Outside of Boston, Somerville."

"*Slum*-erville," says Jerry.

"Jerry's from Yonkers, *so* fancy," says Evelyn.

"Jerry's from *Yaaan-kaaas*," says Andrea, aping her.

"Oh, that's perfect," says Jerry, smirking. "She really nailed you, huh, Ev?"

"Sorry," says Andrea. "I've always been good at accents and voices."

"Hey, Ben," says Jerry. "I go to a shooting range out in Hauppauge. Want to come sometime?"

"You have a gun?" Andrea asks.

"Two," says Jerry. "What about you, Ben?"

"Do I have a gun?"

"No, your job? What do you do?"

"Oh. *Schmatas*," says Ben.

"What's *that*?" asks Jerry.

"You know, women's wear—dresses, blouses, slacks."

"You must be surrounded by fags," says Jerry.

"*Jerry*," says Evelyn.

"It's a living," says Ben, eyes on Evelyn's crotch, trying to figure out if she's wearing panties.

"A *good* living," says Andrea. "Ben has a terrific job. He should thank his lucky stars, production manager for Daddy's company, AndiAnn. It's named for me and my sister, but I haven't been called Andi since I was ten."

"You must get a lot of free clothes," says Evelyn.

"Yes," Andrea taps her blouse and pants. "You should come up to AndiAnn with me sometime."

"Evelyn's already got way too many—what was that word, Ben?" Jerry asks.

"*Schmatas*."

"*Schmatas*," says Jerry, and laughs.

"So, Ben, you wanted to be an architect?" Evelyn asks.

"Where'd you hear that?" asks Ben.

"From your wife," says Evelyn.

Ben glares at Andrea.

Andrea leans closer to Evelyn. "Are you wearing Tabu?"

"Ambush," says Evelyn.

"I used to wear Tabu but I became allergic." Andrea fiddles with the transistor radio, stops at Gogi Grant, "The Wayward Wind," and sings along.

"You have a nice voice," says Evelyn.

"I'm just a good mimic," says Andrea.

Jerry follows Ben to the picnic table, chugging another beer.

"Rare, medium, and charred," says Ben, setting the dish of meat onto the table; blood sloshes over the side.

"Careful!" says Andrea.

"You should thank your *lucky stars* I didn't get any blood on *you,*" says Ben.

Andrea takes a deep breath, arranging containers of potato salad and coleslaw on the table. "These are better than I can make so why pretend I made them, right?"

"Where did you get them?" asks Evelyn.

"Mandel's, over in Plainview?"

"The Jewish place?" Jerry asks.

"The deli," says Andrea. She forces a smile, goes into the house, comes out with a pitcher of lemonade, hard icy chunks still floating in the water.

Ben opens more beers, hands one to Jerry.

"What about me?" Evelyn asks.

"You want a beer?" Ben asks.

"In a glass. With lots of ice."

"With *ice*?" Jerry makes a face.

"What's it to you?" says Evelyn.

Andrea pours dressing over iceberg lettuce. "Is Thousand Island okay with everyone?"

"My office is testing that new oral polio vaccine," says Jerry.

"It's not a vaccine if it's oral," says Evelyn.

The sky is slate gray, no stars, no moon.

Andrea serves dessert, ambrosia. "From Mand—the deli," she says.

"But better than you could make?" asks Ben.

"I have a Sara Lee in the freezer that I meant to bring over," says Evelyn. "You know, that new cheesecake? Shall I get it?"

"None for me," says Ben.

Everyone ignores the marshmallow fruit salad. Evelyn lights up a Cigarillo.

"Can I have one?" Andrea asks.

"Since when do you smoke?" Ben asks.

"Since now." Andrea plucks one of the small cigars out of the box, places it carefully between her lips; Evelyn lights it for her.

"You don't have to inhale," says Evelyn. "You can just use it as a prop."

"Is that what you do?" Andrea asks.

"No," says Evelyn. "I inhale."

Andrea drags on the Cigarillo, strains not to cough.

"You're crazy," says Ben.

. . . sixteen hundred and sixty people were rescued and survived, but forty-six people died as a consequence of the collision off Nantucket . . .

"Please turn that off," says Andrea. She pictures people jumping off a ship that bears her name, drowning in black water. She snatches the transistor, finds another station, the Platters, sings along: "Oh-oh-oh—yes, I'm the great pre-te-en-der—"

Evelyn smacks her leg. "I'm getting bitten."

"Let's go inside," says Andrea. "I want to show you the house. Just leave everything here."

Ben plants himself behind the knotty pine bar, shakes a packet of whiskey sour mix into the blender, adds the liquor, flips the switch, runs it longer than necessary so he doesn't have to chat with Jerry while the girls are upstairs.

"I considered the Cape Cod, like yours," Andrea is saying to Evelyn as they come into the den, "but I like the idea of going from level to level."

"We've got levels," says Jerry.

"But not the *split*-level," says Evelyn.

"It was the most expensive of the three models," says Ben, "but that's what Andrea wanted, and what Andrea wants, Andrea gets."

"Evelyn's an artist," says Andrea. "And she's doing a painting of me."

"It's just a beginning," says Evelyn.

"But I'm going to keep posing," says Andrea.

"When did this happen?" Ben asks.

"This morning," says Andrea.

"Evelyn's a regular da Vinci," says Jerry, his meaty hand squeezing Evelyn's thigh. "How come you never painted me, Ev?"

"Because you never asked," says Evelyn.

"Where's your kid?" Jerry asks.

"Sleepaway camp," says Andrea. "For six weeks."

"Isn't he young to go away for so long?" Evelyn asks.

"He's seven," says Andrea. "Same age when I first went. Everyone I know went to camp."

"Really?" says Evelyn. "Not me. Did you go to camp, Ben?"

"Ben's parents couldn't afford to send him," says Andrea.

"We were destitute," says Ben.

"Really?" Evelyn asks.

"No," says Ben.

"Oh, it's Elvis," says Andrea, turning up the volume on the radio. "Dance with me, Ben."

"In this heat?"

"I'll dance with you," says Evelyn. She kicks off her sandals, twirls Andrea around while she swivels her hips, bare feet disappearing into deep pile carpet.

"We could be on *Bandstand*," says Andrea, laughing.

Jerry rolls his beer bottle across his forehead. "You have an attic fan you can turn on?"

"It's on," says Ben.

"I'm dizzy," says Andrea.

"Sit down," says Evelyn. "It's the heat."

Andrea flops onto the love seat. "The room is spinning."

"Get some ice for her forehead," says Evelyn.

"I'm fine," says Andrea.

"You look pale," says Ben. "Why don't you go to bed. I'll clean up."

"I'll help," says Evelyn.

"Oh, I couldn't," says Andrea.

"Don't be silly," says Evelyn. "It's my pleasure."

Outside, the chirping of crickets adds an electric buzz to the still air.

Ben scrapes plates. "What do you think you're doing?" he asks.

"Helping you clean up," says Evelyn.

"You know what I mean. What are you doing *here*?"

"She asked. What was I supposed to say?"

"How about *no*?" Ben drops a dish; it clatters onto the slate patio but doesn't break. "Melmac," he says. "And you're *painting* her?"

"It just happened." Evelyn collects empty glasses and beer bottles. "You never told me you were from Brooklyn."

"You never told me you were from *Slum*-erville."

"Fuck you," says Evelyn, tossing the container of ambrosia into a trash bag.

Ben pulls her to him. "I've had a hard-on for you all night."

"Cut it out," says Evelyn. "She could see us."

Ben tugs her toward the house, gets her against the brick wall, unzips, presses into her. "I can't wait till Wednesday."

"Then go fuck your wife!" Evelyn dashes toward the fence, disappears. A minute later the light in her kitchen goes on. She stands in the window, opens her blouse, unhooks her bra.

Ben grips his cock; a few strokes and it's over.

The light goes out.

"You're still awake."

"My head is pounding," says Andrea.

"Too much booze—and that cigar. What was that about?"

"I felt like trying one."

"It looked ridiculous."

"Even when Evelyn smoked one?"

Ben takes off his shirt, squashes it into the hamper.

"You should do some exercise," says Andrea.

"Like what?" Ben pats his belly.

"Something other than *bowling.*"

"I like bowling."

"I know," says Andrea. "How about tennis?"

"Oh, sure. I'll play at the Brookville Country Club where they don't allow Jews." Ben turns around to take off his pants, worried he's still hard. He tugs on pajama bottoms. "Let's not make that a habit, okay, having them over."

"Did you think Jerry's comment was anti-Semitic?

"You mean about the *Jew* deli?" Ben gets into bed, aims the

Lazy Bones remote at the TV. "We should have bought in Plainview or Hewlett."

"Daddy said Jericho was a better value."

"You like being the only Jews in the neighborhood?"

"Evelyn seems nice."

Ben stares at the television.

"Do we have to have that on?" Andrea asks.

"I thought you liked *Gunsmoke*," he says.

"It's *your* favorite, not mine, and it's a rerun. I saw it on Wednesday, when you were out, *bowling*."

Ben switches the station, *The Tonight Show,* Jack Paar making small talk with Zsa Zsa Gabor.

"Do you think I should cut my hair?"

"No."

"You didn't like Evelyn's hair?"

"No."

"Do you love me, Ben?"

"What a thing to ask. Of course." He leans over, kisses her forehead.

"I never had anyone paint me before. It's exciting."

"I think it's stupid." Ben presses the remote, but nothing happens. He shakes it, violently.

"You're going to break that and Daddy just bought it."

Ben shakes it again.

"Why is it stupid?"

"Wasting your day posing for a painting isn't stupid?"

"I thought you liked art?"

"When did I say that?"

"When we met. When you wanted to be an architect."

"I don't remember," says Ben.

"If the painting turns out well will you buy it for me?"

"Has Evelyn *asked* you to buy it?"

"Of course not. But if I like it I'm going to, and if you don't buy it for me Daddy will."

Wednesday

Ben leaves his bowling team before the last game. A headache, he says, the excuse Evelyn recommended when she called him at AndiAnn suggesting they meet earlier, that she couldn't wait to see him.

It takes him ten minutes to drive his turquoise-and-white Ford Fairlane from Bowl-o-Rama to the Howard Johnson on Jericho Turnpike, the whole time picturing Evelyn showing off her tits in her kitchen window.

The motel is separate from the restaurant, a one-story strip of rooms that Ben knows well. Before Evelyn there was Babs, who worked at Bowl-o-Rama, fresh out of Holy Family High School over in Carle Place. He parks the Fairlane near the trash bins so it's half hidden.

The room is dark but he can smell her perfume, Ambush, and just make her out sitting on a chair against the back wall, smoking a Cigarillo. He starts to unzip his pants before he even says hello.

"Wait," she says.

"What's wrong?"

"We have to talk."

"Why?"

"I've been painting Andrea for days," she says in a hoarse whisper. "And I'm getting to know her."

"Yeah," says Ben. "It's all she talks about—*Evelyn this, Evelyn that.* I think she's got a crush on you!"

"She's sweet."

"Sweet, my ass! She's a spoiled brat! Daddy's little girl."

"Is that so bad?"

"If you're married to her, yeah."

"So why don't you divorce her?"

"Because she's my meal ticket, remember? And I don't want to lose my kid. I thought I was clear, that you understood. Hey, I didn't come here to talk about Andrea." Ben kicks off his loafers, takes a step forward.

"Wait."

"Now what?"

"Take off your shirt," she whispers. "And your pants."

"Now you're talking." Ben laughs, strips. He's already hard.

She switches on the lamp, her face cast in harsh light, brows penciled black, lips dark red.

"Jesus—" he says. "What the—"

"Good imitation, huh? The voice, the accent. I nailed it, just like Jerry said."

"How—"

"You didn't think I knew? Please, I've known for years."

"It's only been a month."

"I'm talking about *all* of them, all the women. The smell of them on you. Do you think I couldn't tell? Do you really think I'm allergic to perfume? I gave it up so I could smell *theirs*—so I could smell *them*!" She crushes the Cigarillo into an ashtray, stands, cocks her hip.

Ben tries to think what to say, what's expected of him. "I'll end it."

"No, *I* will."

"Where the hell did you get *that*?"

"I asked Evelyn to show me Jerry's guns this morning—after I finished posing—and I took it when she wasn't looking."

"And what—you're going to *kill* me?" Ben forces a laugh.

"No, *Evelyn* is. I made sure the motel clerk got a good look at me, at *Evelyn*—from a distance of course—and I'm sure he recognized me—*Evelyn*, that is." Andrea tugs off the short black wig. "Though I hate to do this to Evelyn. I really think we could have been friends."

"This is crazy, Andrea. I love you."

"I thought I was your *meal ticket*?"

"I was kidding. I knew it was you."

"Is that why you said I was a spoiled brat?"

"I'll make it up to you."

Andrea steadies the gun with both hands.

"What is it you want, a divorce?"

"I discussed that with Daddy and he said no."

"You discussed this with your father?"

"Of course."

"And what did *Daddy* say?"

"That your AndiAnn life insurance policy is a million dollars."

"Come on, Andrea. This isn't you."

"You're right. I'm *Evelyn.*" Andrea switches the television on, flips the dial. "Oh, look, your favorite show, *Gunsmoke.*"

"Evelyn is going to be here any minute."

"Of course she is," says Andrea. "Just after I shoot you. I'll leave the gun behind for her."

"And what makes you think she'll pick it up?"

"Oh, Ben, she doesn't have to. Evelyn's prints are already on it. I made sure she held the gun, and my gloves won't leave any prints."

"There's no way you'll get away with this, Andrea. Evelyn will deny it."

"Of course she will. But isn't that always the way? A lovers' quarrel, that's how I see it. She thought she was the only one, then found out about all your other women."

"And what about you?"

"Me? Oh, Daddy will say I was in Forest Hills with him all night." Andrea turns up the volume on the television, Marshall Dillon and his posse on horseback firing their rifles at escaping outlaws.

"Andrea, please—" Ben shouts over the blare of the television. "We can talk about this. I'll change, I'll—"

"I've gotta go," says Andrea. She fires the gun, watches as a stunned Ben presses a hand to a red leak that has exploded in his chest, then another in his stomach. "Daddy's waiting."

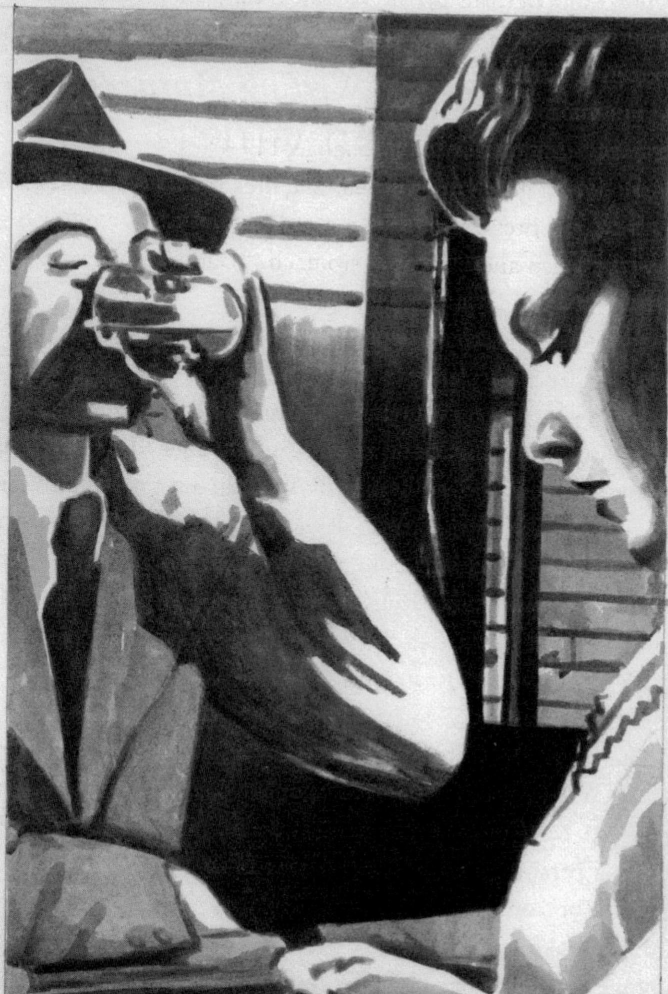

The Creative Writing Murders

EDMUND WHITE

I NEVER GO anywhere without my iPod, which is usually rattling my teeth and every bone in my face. Today I'm listening to great rage-filled yelps by Vivaldi, a soprano biting off words over rapid, stormy, descending passages played by massed violins. The whole thing's called "In Furore Lustissimae Irae," which I couldn't translate, though I did two years of high school Latin in Catholic school two decades ago and of course I speak Spanish. "In a fury of lusty—*very* lusty—anger?" Could it possibly mean that?

That captures my mood exactly. The two days a week I come out to Wilford College make me feel invisible and usually depressed. My undergrads seem profoundly incurious about me as a person, though a few of the senior boys check out my breasts, but only covertly, never brazenly. The boys and girls are all hooking up with each other, even if no one ever *courts* anyone else. That must be why they drink so much. Their only seduction method is to fall in a big sodden pile every Saturday and thrash around until they pair off, *in furore lustissimae irae*.

Otherwise the students are all obsessed by their homework

and their infernal activities, because everyone here is expected to fence or row and work in a community literacy project and write editorials about Africa or Asia for the Will, as they call the weekly student paper. Everyone is busy and most of them seem wracked by obsessive-compulsive disorders. Nancy wrote a story about a kid who counts all the letters of all the words *spoken* in her presence.

web woof sing the song crazy brats prats rats kill them little fuckers oh baby you know you likah freaks

The poor crazed kid's brain was just one quiet adding machine. When I asked on a sudden whim, "How many other people in this room do this? Count letters?" four of the twelve students in the workshop raised their hands. Oh, yeah, and Kim, seeing the others, at last timidly raised her hand, too.

I didn't say anything. Since I'm the only Hispanic woman in the department my elderly white colleagues all prize me as if I were the last extant panda in a North American zoo. They would probably like me just as much if I were neurotic and resentful or frequently absent or if I insisted on organizing three-day Chicano festivals, but I'm not like that, which makes them even more grateful. I'm cheerful and prompt and I've got a book that Copper Canyon has promised to publish if I can just finish two more stories.

I went to Emory and then I was a Stegner Fellow at Stanford. There was a missing year somewhere in there when things got a bit hairy, but hey, we're all artists, right, and sort of crazy. I had a leggy blonde roommate who moved out and created a scandal (I had to quiet her down). But otherwise my profile is impeccable and everyone here, I'm sure, is thrilled to have a polite, hardworking minority instructor on the staff. I organize the entire reading series, I introduce most of the speakers, arrange for their limos to bring them out from the city, pay them their lavish speaker's fee, and escort them to dinner in one or another of the dire ethnic restaurants in the vicinity. I can't help laughing when I think someone (Bert?) actually made the mistake of inviting Jhumpa Lahiri to the local Indian slop shop, Curry in a Hurry. I'm sure she's

you fuckers so you think you can oh yeah pretty girl get you in those garters fuckin fruit

told everyone on the East Coast that Wilford treated her to the most insulting repast of her life.

I can smile my way through tangled departmental politics, through constant student demands on my time, through the two-hour commute in a dirty, smelly train, through the tedious readings in a nearly empty hall that resembles a hot, murky, sleep-inducing aquarium, a tank where no one has changed the water in a year. It even *smells* like stagnant chlorine buildup. I just smile my way through dutiful perusals of six student stories a week that almost always repel the attention with Teflon efficiency—I can smile my way through all this because my real emotions, furious and frustrated, are being enunciated for me by Vivaldi. My iPod is like a neck gland that collects all the venom in the body. If I'm close to snapping I just listen to Cecilia Bartoli stuttering and shrieking her way through Vivaldi's *Opera Proibita*. That does the trick.

Of course I don't know why I bother to be cheerful and hard-working (strangely enough, the student evaluations never mention my cheer). They pay me only $32,500 a year and after all the deductions for taxes and the health plan and social security I take home just seventeen hundred dollars a month. My rent is seven hundred dollars a month and my train tickets are $120 and I'm still paying off that old credit card debt to the tune of two hundred a month. My poor mother is just barely squeaking by on her nurse's aid salary; it's a miracle she can stuff a ten-dollar bill in an envelope every month or two and send it to me with one of those stupid kitten cards she likes. Of course she does own her house in El Paso, which I'll inherit someday and sell for a hundred grand, big whoopty-doo. Sometimes I hate my colleagues, such spoiled brats. My mother always wants to tell me stories about her Mexican neighbors but I never let her.

My boss, an enormously fat dyed-blonde elderly gay man who writes genuinely depraved novels about drugged, homeless queers, is a tricky one. Bert. His books (at least the one I dipped into until, slightly nauseated, I had to put it down) might make you think he's a wild thing but in fact he's prissy and pedantic and a real stickler for the rules. Like most old queers he wants a woman to be a "lady," and I lay it on thick—if I didn't restrain myself I might even bob a curtsy.

You'll look a lady my pretty with this thing up your ass and filthy old fucker why the hell are you shitting shitty, pretty

You can just see he thinks he's adorable and avuncular, his cataract-clouded eyes looking feebly out from over his half-moon glasses, but in fact he's cagey, an accomplished meddler, a born traitor. He doesn't have a "partner," but occasionally he'll bring a twenty-year-old studly beauty to a campus function just to wow everyone—though I'm the only one who can see right away that it's just a hustler, uneducated, uninterested, and flipping out his cell phone every minute to message his next customer. Strictly eye candy. Of course I'm the only person at Wilford from the ghetto . . .

The tenured faculty teaching writing at Wilford is dim and ancient and "famous." I always hang those quotes around their "fame" since no average person has ever heard of them despite their membership in the American Academy and their Guggenheims and National Endowment fellowships. They all have prestigious publishers like Knopf and FSG but they only lay one slim volume once a decade and it usually hatches right on top of the remainder pile.

I'm not better. In the last three years I've grunted out maybe five pages, two of which I've torn up and the other three I've rewritten fifty times. Of course I tell Crafty Bert the Boss that at last I'm in the home stretch and that it's Chicano all the way. I know he wants me to succeed since he's too lazy to seek out another minority woman, but he can't keep me after next year if I don't have a book, at least one scheduled for publication. Unless he made an exception. Unless he went to the president. Gave me the Woolcraft Award for distinguished classroom performance. But he'd never do that for me, a mere woman, only for a cute junior guy. Maybe if I really did write stories about Chicanos, but for me that Mexi stuff has about as much flavor as week-old tacos. I prefer my stories about clean athletic blonde women.

I have a little office without a window I share with two other adjuncts, neither of them a threat. One is Corbin, a young, handsome, but thickening white boy from Kentucky who writes poems (he's published a grand total of nine in various little magazines over the last seven years) and sings in a garage band. The resident playwright, Edgar, seems to have a crush on little Corbin; he's always hanging around during Corbin's office hours and smiling foolishly and raking his long white beard with his pale fingers and talking about Bob Dylan, as if that proves his interest in pop culture.

The other adjunct in my office is Adam, a balding Englishman (two novels) whose father owned a London tabloid. He's loaded but keeps his hand in to get the medical benefits for his wife and three children. He lives in Wilmington, a horrendous commute. He flits in and out for his one class a week and gets good student evaluations for some reason. No one dislikes him but then again no one ever exactly *remembers* him—and anyway both my officemates are too white and male to be tenured.

It seems everyone at Wilford has family money except me. There's Emily, a gaunt seventy-five-year-old poetess from the Philadelphia Main Line who won a Pulitzer in 1977 for her collected poems, *Elements*, fiendishly complicated forms like sestinas and double rondeaux about water and air and fire. Although she says she's a socialist, her father strip-mined coal in Appalachia (which she never, ever mentions). That's where her money comes from. She's anorexic and proud of it; we once had lunch and she said with a reproachful look, "We'll each have three lettuce leaves." It's true I've been getting fatter and fatter, what with my midnight Ambien eating sprees.

Edgar, our prize-winning playwright with the hearing aid, created a stir in the sixties with a verse drama about Abraham and Isaac set in modern Scranton. He's a closeted gay and derides what he calls Bert's "flamboyance." He has that billy-goat white beard and red-rimmed eyes and a portly partner who puts up store-bought cherries every fall in two-hundred-proof eau-de-vie and hands out the jars two months later as alcoholic Christmas presents. I think Edgar's lover played Isaac in the unsuccessful 1975 revival. Edgar's the one who hovers over Corby and talks about Dylan and snaps his fingers, as translucent as church tapers.

Our staff is so old that in a general department meeting they voted down screenwriting as too radical for such an august institution (forgetting that Wilford was just a girls' finishing school, good only for a laugh until 1972 when it went coed and got serious). The one holdover from that period is a snowy-haired New England gentleman, Alfred, who used to teach the girls to appreciate Keats and now teaches something called "life writing" in which the students are encouraged to tell all about their amateurish sex routs and predictably dysfunctional families. Alfred tells them all they're courageous and then at faculty lunches regales us with their confessions. He has a stageworthy way of slapping his knee and "guffawing," which is strangely different from a laugh. He's famous for his lovely manners, which means he always holds your hand in both of his, looks you deeply in the eye, and says, "We must get together very, very soon." I always want to snap back, "We're together right now. What was it you wanted to talk about?"

The first murder didn't surprise me. Or rather it seemed so unreal I scarcely reacted except to whisper, "Oh my God, it's happened," which I immediately regretted.

I was in my Boro Park apartment, which I share with two other women. Neither of them was there—it was a Tuesday at noon and so disgracefully late to be awakening that I sang scales before answering to chase the sleep out of my voice. I suppose I was a little perky by the time I picked up. (I must be the last person who doesn't have a mobile—or what's it called? A "cell" phone?) The phone almost never rings. I don't have that many local friends and those I do e-mail me. I suppose we've all decided it's more polite than telephoning.

So I was half expecting a pollster or bill collector when I heard from Edgar, the closeted playwright, that our boss, Bert, had been hanged while wearing a girdle and makeup.

"What?" I shrieked, longing for a cigarette though I no longer smoke. "What did you just say?"

Edgar seemed to resent my alarm. I suppose he must have called me last, since I was the only one, he must have figured, who'd make a "fuss." "This is hard on all of us, Manuela, as you can imagine." He was clearly registering a reproach.

"But did you say Bert was hanged?"

"Yes," Edgar sighed, then added, as if I was a bit stupid, "He's dead."

I decided to behave more coldly—like an Anglo. "Murdered?" I asked, neither too callous nor too crisp, I hoped.

He hesitated, almost as if my question were a bit vulgar. "It's not clear." He swallowed. "You know there's something called autoerotic strangulation?"

I couldn't believe this was old ofay Edgar talking. "You mean like when the dude gets hard—"

"Yes," he said, cutting me off.

"I read about that in *Naked Lunch,*" I said. My literary reference checkmated him.

That night I had another call, this time from Alfred, the life-writing prof. Maybe because of his experiences with salacious collegiate confession, he went into a whole lot of detail. He went on and on, letting himself enjoy the lurid stories until he'd catch himself and remember to be solemn. "After all," he'd say, more to himself than to me, "we *are* talking about the death of a colleague."

"Do you think he was murdered?"

"I don't." I could hear the loud dry snap of ice being twisted out of a plastic tray. "I think . . ." first audible sip, "I think he just got a little carried away. After all, as Edgar points out, he was pretty much *in your face*, as the kids say."

"So you think he was getting off on his garters and girdle and his bra and really getting into his groove and then—"

"There was also," Alfred added with a sense of theater, "the issue of electrodes."

"Electrodes!" I brayed, afraid I'd laugh. "What for? What on earth for?" I was afraid I could guess.

No one will stop me my pretty you done shit on me I told you web and I told you web and woof move hoof

When I got impatient and started to make conversational moves toward wrapping things up, Alfred said almost punitively, "There's going to be an investigation tomorrow. They want us all here by ten. In our offices."

"But it's not one of my usual days," I objected. Then I realized I was sounding silly. "The police?"

"I'm not sure if it's the state police or the FBI or school authorities. I was just told by Wilma—" the new department secretary, an extremely attractive off-hours basketball player who, sadly, is a lesbian—"to be in my office at ten. She asked me to call you." Wilma has a short reddish-blonde haircut.

"So we're all suspects?" I asked.

"I imagine. Yes. We would be, wouldn't we?"

It turned out next day that Bert, the victim, our boss, wasn't quite the fag we'd imagined. He'd had not one but two ménages with women, with two children by each woman, neither of them his wife. It's too much to go into, but he'd been hired in the eighties precisely because he was gay and the then-president had heard at a dinner party in New York about Queer Studies and that there was a homosexual alumnus willing to put up five million to hire Bert Hawkins, whose novel, *Sad Gays*, he'd read as a lonely teenager. It had helped him to "come out," as queers say, as if we were supposed to see their sinking into depravity as—well, no matter.

The only problem is that about the time Bert came on board at Wilford he'd inconveniently *stopped* being gay and taken up with a woman *and*, two years later, a second, concurrent woman. Of course he had to hide his heterosexual households; that's why he hired all those bored hustlers for faculty samba parties; one of his two wives found them in the Philadelphia Yellow Pages shamelessly listed under Escorts.

I'll shove your quatrains filthy stinking holes both of them

Since it was a question of a possible interstate crime, the FBI interrogated each one of us. I told them right away that I thought it was one of the hustlers, that I was sure it was murder, not autostrangulation or anything fun like that. I said that another suspect, in my opinion, was Corbin, my officemate. One of his nine poems, I pointed out, was about transvestism with an undercurrent of hysteria and that his collection, if he ever finished it, was going to be called *Dressing Up*.

When the investigator asked me where I'd been at the time of the death (he obviously didn't want to commit himself to saying murder or suicide), I said I'd been in Boro Park eating tuna out of a can and watching reruns of *Friends* with one of my two roommates. She had her own reasons to confirm the story.

The whole thing upset me so much that I invited Wilma out to lunch to the one honest place in town that had good ol' burgers and wasn't ethnic. She put an arm around my waist as we left the building, out of a shared sense of sisterhood in the face of our departmental shock rather than any dykey funny business. By the end of the meal, during which she'd recounted three of her affairs (all involving the Upper Peninsula of Michigan and sordid pickup trucks), her abandoned phys-ed career (bad knees), and a few laughs at the expense of our colleagues ("Not one of them understands the blackboard function on our PCs!"), we were ready to face the rather sour music emanating from our building. Even without my iPod I could hear the deafening strains of Cecilia Bartoli. "In furore lustissimae irae," she was shrieking, so loud I couldn't hear Wilma, who'd become entirely too cozy, though I could see by her pretty wet teeth and shaking diaphragm that she was laughing.

The rich gay donor, I learned, was outraged that *his* professor, Ol' Bert, had been not only straight but bigamous! He was demanding a refund from the school, if you can imagine such a thing, and the current president, an astrophysicist by trade, was definitely not up to speed.

The FBI let it be known that they were carefully and scientifically

goddamn rich bitch you think your shitty little porn fuck take that in the crapper I'll make you a porn you won't forget too bad your fuckin' memory is leaking out of one end while your shit dribbles out the

accumulating the evidence and soon they'd have a definitive answer to many questions.

Edgar, the deaf closeted playwright, was named acting interim chair of creative writing. His protégé Corbin was suddenly much in evidence. There was talk of extending his contract, and his garage band was asked to perform during the annual talent night on campus. They were called Ill Met by Starlight.

Edgar pretended that he disliked "administration" of any sort but he demanded (and got) course relief; starting next fall he'd be down from four courses a year to just one. As for his duties as chair, he threw them all at Wilma, who seldom leaves the office before ten at night. He couldn't do anything. Poor Wilma had to crank out everything: budgets, teaching schedules, room assignments, year-end summaries of departmental activities and achievements, lists of students selected to write "creative theses" (sixty pages of doggerel or three or four lame, confused stories warmed over from sophomore or junior year), lists of students awarded prizes or given summer traveling fellowships (so they can go back to Shaker Heights or Indian Hill and track down their shallow, expensive "roots"—dyed blonde, no doubt).

The second murder was of Corbin. In *our* office, of all places, the one Corbin and I share with the strangely elusive Adam. I received a call from our resident poetess Emily. I'd almost never heard her voice before and I was astonished she knew how to work a phone. "Hello, Manuela?"

"Yes?"

"This is Emily. Emily from school?"

"Yes," I laughed warmly. " I know which—"

She interrupted in her tiny voice: "It seems Corbin has been killed."

"So they got him too," I said—the words just shot out of me.

"Yes?" Emily asked in her tentative nearly inaudible voice. At last she concluded, "Yes."

"How was it . . . done?" I asked. "And when?" I didn't want to lament too much in a tacky Latino way, but then again I feared I might be underdoing it.

"I don't know if I can—I have to get off . . ."

The instrument went dead. After a few moments I called Edgar on his mobile. I explained to him that Emily had hung up on me.

"That's our girl," Edgar said. "There will be a double sestina by noon tomorrow with only *red* as one of the six end words to suggest the whole bloody massacre."

He explained that Corbin had been found this morning castrated, his face smeared with mascara and his rectum wedged wide open by an orange traffic cone. One of his transvestite poems was pinned to his chest, directly into the flesh.

"This must be especially horrible for you, Edgar," I said.

"Why do you—well, yes. It is. I've had a—well, I've had a sort of breakdown. I don't think I can really go on. I think Don and I—" Don was his partner, the one who puts up cherries in booze—"are going to go somewhere. I've canceled my classes. I can't—" and here he began to sob.

When he finally pulled himself together he said he was going to hang up and call back. Before he could, I received a second call from Emily. With no prologue she announced, "The worst thing is that the FBI is going to commandeer our students' computers and read their *stories*. And ours, too. Our stories and our *poems*!"

"That's not the worst thing," I said in gentle reproach.

"No," she murmured.

"The worst thing," I prated on, "is that poor Corbin was castrated and reamed with an orange—" But Emily had hung up a second time.

No sooner had I replaced the receiver than it rang again.

Edgar: "I was wondering if you'd be willing to fill in as chair for the rest of the semester."

Me: "Me?"

Edgar: "It's only five weeks more. I know it would be . . . strange since you're not tenured but, remember, as soon as that book is finished—"

Me: "You mean my collection, *Border People*?" I'd just made up the name a second ago.

Edgar (momentarily delighted): "Oh, is that the title? Is it about—"

Me: "Mexicans. Mexican-Americans."

Edgar: "The committee will be very heartened by this news. How far away . . . ?"

Me: "I have just one new story to write, 'Big River Wall.' "

Edgar: "Big . . . oh! Rio Grande. And the wall is very—"

I knew he wanted to say "topical" but he contented himself with "relevant."

Me: "Yes."

Edgar: "Do you think you'd be willing to run the department?"

I knew that he was too lazy ever to take up the reins again once I'd replaced him and that no one on the permanent staff—Emily? Arthur?—would ever step forward.

Me: "I might be willing to consider it if someone would nominate me for the Woolcraft Award. With something like that backing me up, I might have the necessary *heft* to direct a program as distinguished as ours."

Edgar hinted that this award for best teacher was already in the works and that, come June, I might be happily surprised. I asked if there might not be course relief and a salary override if my directorship "dribbled on." He said, in his best mimsy-woolsy academic manner, "This too may come to pass."

I immediately called my mother and interviewed her long distance for two hours about all the worst excesses of American immigration officials against what in my mind I called "wetbacks." My mother was thrilled to help me. I knew I'd need this material for a last long story, "Big River Wall," the capstone to

Border People. I'd have to rework lots of the earlier stories, changing blonde gym teachers into suffering Chicanos. Of course it would be the expected indictment of whites.

A week later, Edgar and Don were on a Mediterranean cruise on the *Napoleon Bonaparte* and I'd moved into Bert's office. Wilma helped me make it cozy. We had Bert's sicko homo books boxed and put into storage, his rotting green carpet replaced by a tasteful new beige one, and his gloomy Shakespeare prints stored to make room for my newly bought Mexican Day of the Dead dolls, which my mother had just FedExed. I'd never liked Mexi kitsch but I'd decided to play up the wetback connection till the day I got tenure—then out it would all go.

Wilma and I had lunch every day. She thought she had me in her pocket as her new boss and took advantage of the situation by drinking two margaritas in my so-called honor. I was alarmed by her effrontery. I was trying hard to work on my stories but I couldn't concentrate, and bits of unassigned dialogue or monologue kept slipping in, grotesque and inappropriate to say the least.

One day, after Wilma had come back to my office with me and was sprawling provocatively and a bit tipsily on the daybed, she said, "I guess you hate men as much as I do." She even had the nerve to let one hand dawdle between her legs; fortunately she was wearing slacks.

"Hate men? Why do you say that?"

"Well," she said, "don't we see a certain . . . oh, forget it."

"A certain what?" I prompted.

"A certain pattern in the . . . events of the—forget it."

"Yes," I said, standing up. "I think we should forget it." I held the door open for her. She took it badly and waltzed out impertinently, saying, "I've got more on you than you—forget it."

filthy bitch forget everything if your memory spills out of your dirty little mouth and cunt bitch or bloodies your mouth

We didn't speak for three days (two of those were weekend days), but then on Monday she said she'd like to have lunch. I said I couldn't do lunch but that I'd be willing to have a late dinner with her in my office. I tried all afternoon to work on my stories, but a loud disturbing voice began to dictate what I should do next, and it had nothing to do with the Rio Grande. In fact the language seemed to be Italian—and the voice was Cecilia's, something about lust and anger.

A NOTE ON THE EDITORS

S.J. Rozan, a native New Yorker, is the author of twelve novels. Her work has won the Edgar, Shamus, Anthony, Nero, and Macavity awards for Best Novel and the Edgar for Best Short Story. *Bronx Noir*, a short-story collection S.J. edited, was given the NAIBA Notable Book of the Year award. She's served on the national boards of Mystery Writers of America and Sisters in Crime, and is ex-president of the Private Eye Writers of America. In January 2003 she was an invited speaker at the Annual Meeting of the World Economic Forum in Davos, Switzerland. The 2005 Left Coast Crime convention in El Paso, Texas, made her its Guest of Honor. A former architect in a practice that focused on police stations, firehouses, and zoos, S.J. Rozan lives in lower Manhattan.

Jonathan Santlofer is the author of five novels as well as a highly respected artist whose work has been written about and reviewed in the *New York Times*, *Art in America*, *Artforum*, and *Arts*, and appears in many public, private, and corporate collections. He serves on the board of Yaddo, one of the oldest artist communities in the country. Santlofer lives and works in New York City.

A NOTE ON THE ILLUSTRATIONS

All of the drawings have been created with black India ink and silver pigment built up in thin washes and made specifically for this anthology. Some are based on film noir, others invented. None were made to illustrate specific stories, but rather to echo the mood and tone of the collection.

—JS